About the author

Born in Liverpool, though brought up in East Lancashire, Meg J. Parry spent many childhood holidays in Lytham St Anne's.

After working for a major bank for fourteen years in Lancashire and London, she spent many years entertaining and doing musical therapy with Alzheimer's and dementia patients, alongside presenting local history tours and managing a theatre on the south coast.

Resident in Malta since 2007, she teaches English as a foreign language. The author plays the organ in a local church; she has written for the theatre, and has published books on theatre history and a novel.

ROSES OF LACE

Meg J. Parry

ROSES OF LACE

Vanguard Press

VANGUARD PAPERBACK

© Copyright 2021
Meg J. Parry

A CIP catalogue record for this title is
available from the British Library.

ISBN 978-1-80016-062-0

Vanguard Press is an imprint of
Pegasus Elliot MacKenzie Publishers Ltd.
www.pegasuspublishers.com

First Published in 2021

Vanguard Press
Sheraton House Castle Park
Cambridge England

Printed & Bound in Great Britain

Dedication

For Yvonne-Marie, with love and gratitude

Acknowledgements

The author wishes to acknowledge the support and encouragement of her family, who have tolerated and facilitated the hundreds of hours spent working on this book. Also, Doug and Diane, at the Cumbria Hotel, St Anne's, for their kindness, and without whom this book might never have been started.

On a practical front, the author would like to express her deep appreciation of the efficient and helpful team at Pegasus Elliot Mackenzie Publishers Ltd, especially Vicky Gorry, production coordinator, and Suzanne Mulvey, who first read the text and believed in its potential.

Finally, a special thank you to Cheryl Bilocca, whose lovely inspired artwork enhances the appearance of the book.

PART ONE

The sense of taste is not activated in some male butterflies, whereas a female can detect both attractive and toxic traits of plants.

ONE

"How many times, Mr Silverman, do I have to remind you that without his authority I cannot discuss your client's loan terms with you? If he really does want to save his home, I suggest he stops ignoring correspondence and talks to me himself." Laurel sighed loudly as the lawyer made another pitch.

"I've been very patient and far too helpful, Mr Silverman. And by the end of this week, it may be out of my hands. Now, I have other work to get on with. Good morning." Laurel Ashworth, manager of the South Kensington branch, slammed the receiver into the body of the phone. "Insufferable little man!"

She grabbed her cigarettes and marched down the short passageway from her office, past the staff toilets, to the back door. There was a small yard at the rear, surrounded by a high wall, with razor wire atop it. Laurel had successfully fought the bank's premises people for its retention; and since her friend Maddie had stopped, a part-timer and Laurel were the only smokers in the office.

The 2019 spring rain and sunshine had produced abundant weeds in the scruffy yard. The mildly deranged loner who rented the flat above often dropped takeaway wrappers from his window and, occasionally, his underwear if he had been drying it on the window ledge. Neither was particularly edifying; and reminder messages went unheeded. The jovial Colonel Sanders had obviously enticed his business from McDonalds and the local Chinese, the chicken bones mercifully less pungent than an unfinished 'Number 27' in a foil tray.

"Are you okay, Laurel?" Maddie asked. Before Laurel could respond with anything more than a weary look, Maddie had answered her own question: "Not. Whatever's wrong, hon? You didn't seem yourself when you arrived."

The branch manager wafted the smoke away from her friend's face, knowing there was nothing that ex-smokers hated more than second-hand fumes.

"I got up with a splitting headache; and that idiot solicitor has just made it worse." A pause. After twenty years of friendship, Maddie knew Laurel too well.

"And?"

"I don't know, Maddie," Laurel sighed, rasping the sole of her shoe on the concrete. "I'm fed up with this job, with London, with being single, with everything."

Maddie put her arm around Laurel's waist. Being six inches shorter, it was more comfortable than around her shoulders. "You don't look good. Why don't you go home? I'll see Mr Eddleston for you later." Maddie smiled.

"I bet you will. And after work too," Laurel joked. A very handsome guy of about fifty, Mr Eddleston was refinancing as a result of a recent divorce settlement. "Seriously? Would you mind?"

"Of course not."

"One look at those flirty eyes, Maddie, and he'll be putty in your hands."

"I wish," the shorter woman giggled.

A few moments later, having thrown her odds and ends into her bag, Laurel stood by the door, scanning the office. The desk, the bank computer, the folder of reports, statistics and those infernal targets; the frosted glass window, the slightly threadbare carpet, the dented filing cabinet. Stale. Same. Enough. That was it: enough.

Enough of the memos from the smug git who, years ago, had aggressively sold, and had leaned on others to sell, dodgy insurance policies; since then, the bank had repaid billions to the customers who had been coerced into taking them out. Despite the corporate chagrin, the weasel-like individual had later managed to ingratiate himself with senior management, who had, ironically, appointed him Head of Compliance.

"Compliance, my arse," Laurel muttered, as she slung her black Michael Kors Voyager bag over her shoulder and glanced down at her name badge. She unpinned it and pulled open the shallow top drawer on her desk, where she laid the tag to rest with an air of finality. At the age of forty-eight, had Laurel Ashworth, in the compass of a few moments, decided to walk out on twenty-seven years in the bank?

Striding to the underground station, her mood was one of indignant determination. Yet, there was a feeling in the pit of her stomach: a nervous, sickening, empty feeling that she could not define. Instinct told her that she was walking away, and that she would probably not return.

While normally and naturally cautious, her life had been determined, to an alarming extent, by the occasional quixotic decision. So long and so often following the predictable path, she would suddenly veer off at an acute angle. Maddie, by contrast, was always impulsive, unpredictable, living life on the edge. Laurel's few seismic shifts had erupted from the feeling of being hidebound for too long; like a butterfly confined within its chrysalis for months, one day waking to a new reality, struggling free, extending its wings, darting off in a random direction.

As she rode westwards, she reflected on her past. The decision to move to London, more than twenty years ago, had been one of those defining moments. She had liked it, loved it, at first. She had arrived in high summer and had spent several evenings watching open-air drama in Holland Park; she had filled weekends with walks by the Thames or in the Downs.

Laurel had grown up in Lancashire, where her father had died almost three years ago. Since then, she had found a visceral desire to maintain the memories and the umbilical links with familiar safe places: her home town and where she had holidayed as a young child, with her parents. The places, the memories; a bolt hole? Somewhere away from here, where she would have time to think; away from London, away from the bank.

Once back at her flat, Laurel opened her laptop to book a train ticket. There was no point simply turning up at Euston; using Virgin Trains was almost as complicated and process-ridden as flying. It was a wonder you did not have to take your passport and check in two hours before you travelled, then submit to a full body scan. Bloody Branson! The days of going to a station and buying a ticket to anywhere in the country, with the fare calculated at x per mile, had gone.

There were no direct trains from London to Blackpool any longer; she would have to change at Preston. There were two trains every hour, leaving Euston only about fifteen minutes apart, one slightly cheaper than the other. She had just clicked BUY when she suddenly realised that her chosen train took an hour longer. Oh, whatever. Whether it was 12.30 or 12.47, she would still be there by late afternoon, relaxing, far away from here.

Her screen recommended the VT app, so that the ticket could be sent to her phone. *Stuff downloading Branson's app, Laurel; collect it from the machine at Euston.* The transaction was done, paid. As she slipped her card back into her wallet, the bank emblem seemed strangely unfamiliar. Had she distanced herself from all that in a matter of minutes? Or had she just taken the first practical step of a journey she had already been making subconsciously?

She lit a cigarette and lounged on her sofa. Never having smoked addictively, she had started again a few months earlier, after going two years without. She had made no conscious decision to quit; she had merely finished one packet and not bothered to buy any more. But she enjoyed the taste; she found the aroma comforting. Her maternal grandmother, who died when Laurel was only five and a half, had smoked. Nan had doted on the child, often caring for her while Laurel's mother was busy or unwell.

The decision to start smoking again had been equally random. Arriving at Rhodes airport for a winter break, she had noticed a cigarette vending machine, of the kind banned by the nanny state in Britain. She had fed it gleefully; then, sitting in the late afternoon sun, had drawn luxuriously on a Dunhill. It had been easy to obtain a light, for the social stigma of smoking seemed to have passed Greece by. At least for now.

Laurel smoked between six and eight a day, half of those in the evenings, and more when she was not working, having time on her hands. She checked the packet: two left. She grabbed an unopened packet that lay on the table and threw it into her bag.

Of course, after a few days Laurel would have to face the music and tie up the loose ends. But she was determined, more determined than she had been for a long time. This was it. That was that. Over.

She kept a weekend bag permanently packed; a few quick additions would suffice. So, she set about dealing with other practicalities. She scribbled a note to Mrs H in flat 2, an elderly lady who always liked to know if Laurel was going to be away for a few days. In retirement, she had assumed the role of a Neighbourhood Watch; and she could probably have recited a far more accurate list of the bank manager's visitors over the years than Laurel herself.

Rather than tramping back to the underground station, Laurel called a private cab firm, whose business account she had poached from Barclays. She knew most of the drivers well. Fifteen minutes. She checked that her lunchbox, containing the salad prepared several hours earlier, was still in her tote bag, in case the on-train catering staff failed to show up, as had happened on her last journey north with Virgin Trains. Finally, she phoned Maddie at the bank.

"Maddie, I've just got to get away for a few days. I'll phone in sick tomorrow and let Regional Office know. Any real emergencies, you can phone me, but nobody else calls, OK? Tell them I've got... I don't know. Lie for me, Maddie. You're brilliant at being spontaneous. I'll text you this evening."

"Are you sure you're okay? Where are you going, honey?" Maddie asked, deeply concerned.

"The Fylde coast — St Anne's, Lytham, even Blackpool. I've only booked a train ticket. I just need to clear my head, get some proper fresh air; reconnect with things that are more important than banking. I'll find a B&B; it shouldn't be difficult at this time of the year."

Laurel quickly shed her business attire, throwing her bank neckerchief into the bin, and then scattered handfuls of clothes across her bed. Being slim, with good legs, she liked tight leggings for slobbing around in; she loved tights and stockings, especially ones with lacy tops — hot pants in summer. Not being a fan of trousers, she never wore them to work, preferring the traditional skirt. She owned skirts of all lengths and oodles of dresses.

Returning from the bathroom, Laurel tossed the small case onto her bed and selected some underwear and a couple of tops, which she folded and laid neatly inside the bag, before squeezing in a pair of ballerinas. She slipped into a new floral print top and a long navy skirt, whose alluring split ventured well up her toned thigh. *You've got legs, Laurel; flaunt them.*

Her face was not unattractive either, she acknowledged, glancing at herself in the dressing table mirror. In no way was she vain, however, being under no illusions about her ordinariness: she would have preferred a shorter, cuter nose. She was attractive, all the same; and by combining moderate eating and regular exercise — jogging in the nearby Acton Park — she had remained trim.

Laurel reached for the sober plum-coloured lipstick she had applied a few hours earlier, but had second thoughts. Instead, she picked up a tube of lip gloss in a much bolder, brighter red. She painted her lips confidently and smiled at herself. This was not a day to be timid and demure. Having brushed her shoulder-length, wavy chestnut hair, which had darkened from auburn in her early twenties, she dropped the hairbrush into her bag.

She turned her eyes back to the old dressing table. It had been her mother's, and Laurel had brought it from Lancashire shortly after moving into the flat. Her mother had died suddenly several years before that, and her father had not wanted it. A piece of her northern childhood in her London home. Now, today, at the age of forty-eight, she was heading back, though there would be no parental arms to welcome her. The last trip north had been for her father's funeral.

A car horn sounded. Three beeps. That would be her taxi. She swung the case off the bed, took two strides, then paused. Knickers! She tugged at one of the drawer handles, and pulled out a pair of olive-green satin French knickers, part of a set that an old flame had bought her. The camisole top was buried somewhere in the depths of her collection, but the pants were her favourite. Not wanting to keep the driver waiting any longer, she stuffed them into the pocket of her jacket.

With the note to the woman in flat 2 between her teeth, Laurel bundled herself, her case and her handbag out of her apartment, pulling the door firmly closed. The Yale lock clicked. Instinctively, she felt for her keys. Wrong pocket. Knickers again!

The lover who had given them to her had not lasted long, like most of her relationships. *Most? Who are you kidding, Laurel? All.* She was a butterfly, flitting from flower to flower, drawing deeply on the nectar, from stamen or stigma, before realising the nectar was poison; or before a gust of wind blew her off balance, rending flower head and butterfly asunder. On other occasions, her presence had proved too much for the delicate bloom, which had snapped beneath her.

In the case of the lingerie donor, it had been her own fault, uncertain whether she wanted to settle down with the man and his passion for Wagner operas and German military helmets. He'd been wholly committed to both the relationship and the bedroom action, and he was a genuinely nice guy. However, the more he had pressed his suit, the more claustrophobic she had felt. In spite of that, she could never explain her feelings on that rainy Sunday afternoon, nor why she had told him that it could not go on. She had tried to let him down gently, but the parting had been difficult. He had reasoned with her, pleaded with her and, finally, in a maelstrom of frustration, screamed at her, "You keep saying what you don't want. What is it that you DO want?"

Now, years later, Laurel was still unable to offer a rational answer. She dragged her small case through the entrance hallway, slipped the note under Mrs H's door, and glanced back towards her own. The gilt number 1, the perpetual 'one', the eternal single, glared back at her accusingly. *What is it that you DO want, Laurel?*

TWO

The taxi ride to Euston was largely uneventful. The Filipino driver, who was quiet and about forty, evidently had a passion for Queen's Park Rangers. There was a photo of him with a player in a blue and white hooped jersey, whom Laurel, not sufficiently into football, could not name. Clearly a family man and a Catholic, the driver had a photo of himself with three children; it was carefully framed by a set of rosary beads.

"Are those your children?" Laurel asked casually, if only to break the rather awkward silence. He recited their names and ages, before adding that they were his 'life.' "They're cute," Laurel said.

"Thank you," the driver said, smiling. "Their mother, she die last year. Cancer." He crossed himself.

"Oh, I'm so sorry," the shocked passenger replied.

"She is with God," he assured himself. Laurel kept silent. She was not religious, though she had grown up in a Catholic family.

"My sister, she help me with the children. She don't get married. She want to be a nun."

"Me too," Laurel replied. The driver looked startled. "Oh, I mean I'm not married," she said, laughing. *Heaven forbid, Laurel! Taking holy orders with your sexual CV!* "I don't think I could be a nun."

Slightly unnerved by the turn of the conversation, she plunged her hand into her jacket pocket. She loved those olive-green French knickers. They were finished off at the legs with a generous band of lace that joined at the crotch, creating a sensual delight whenever she moved in them. The pattern of the lace was roses, fully opened roses, ready to receive the attention of a lover: ready to serve that lover.

In the days after the break-up, Laurel had often traced her fingers over the lace flowers. In her more morose moments, she had seen the lace roses as a metaphor for her relationships: fanciful representations that made her feel feminine for a while, but lacked true scent and touch; they lacked the most earthy and visceral qualities of real love.

Her finger sensuously fondled the lace in her pocket, rekindling the memory of the first time she had delighted her lover with his own present. She had allowed his hands to roam, pressing and drawing the satin over her firm buttocks, and then swirling over her smooth mound. Her flower had opened and surrendered to the insistent drone, yielding her nectar, dewing the lace roses. Reliving those moments in the months afterwards, her moroseness replaced by heightened sensuality, she had worn them; and her own fingers had transported her to a similar ecstasy.

"You okay, lady?" the driver asked, as he slowed on the approach to Euston Station.

"Oh, yes. Sorry, I was miles away."

An ocean of lost humanity flooded the station concourse, gawping at the destination boards. About eight minutes before the scheduled departure time, the gates to the platform were finally opened; and the pressing, nudging and increasingly seething mob was allowed to proceed down the ramp towards the train. 'Curse bloody Branson,' Laurel thought, as her legs and hips were clattered by bags and cases during the erratic stampede of human cattle. It was like Ryanair on rails.

Rail privatisation had been puffed to the public as giving travellers more choice; however, when Virgin had taken over the East Coast Main Line franchise as well, it had secured a monopoly of rail travel from London to Scotland. Some choice for the passenger: getting screwed via Crewe or porked via York.

Having finally found a window seat without a 'Reserved' docket, Laurel settled herself down for the journey. As the last passengers scrambled and stumbled to their seats, she closed her eyes and began to formulate a to do list. First of all, she would book a B&B, which she could do from the train. She would also, at some point during the week, pay a visit to Blackburn, where people owed her several thousand pounds.

She owned two terraced houses in a suburb to the west of the town, in which she had invested most of the money left by her father. Better than most people, she knew that there was little point sticking it in a bank account to earn nothing. A percentage of the rent was kept by her letting agents, who reacted quickly if there was any problem: in one house the central heating boiler had been condemned twelve months before the previous tenant, a Lithuanian, had left. Don't Lithuanians ever wash?

No, the problem she had started experiencing with the letting agents was their dilatory forwarding of rent money. On one property, there were arrears of eight months; on the other, she had received very little for eighteen months. The repeated promises to 'look into it' had become laughable; and Laurel had recently written, threatening action in the County Court. Perhaps she would surprise them by walking into their office and refusing to leave until they paid up.

She thought of her dear father, how he had declined in his last two or three years! She had cried seeing him hobble across the garden that had once been his pride and joy, but which had become too much for him to deal with. She closed her eyes again and, lulled by the smooth ride, dreamily remembered the far-off family holidays on the Fylde coast.

Crumbs! The coast! Find a bed for tonight before falling asleep, Laurel! She grabbed her phone from her bag. A few years earlier, she had stayed in a B&B just off the seafront, about ten minutes' walk from the main square. It had been clean and reasonably priced. What on earth was it called? Of course! The Cumbria. She found the phone number and dialled.

"A single room? Thirty pounds a night, including breakfast. How many nights do you want it for?"

Silence. *OMG, Laurel! You haven't even thought this through, like you're on the run from some heinous crime.*

"Erm, five — five for now. I'm not exactly sure how long..."

"What time are you expecting to arrive? Just to make sure that someone's in."

Laurel looked at her watch and did a quick calculation. "Probably around five — say between five and six. Is that okay?"

"That's fine. Look forward to seeing you later."

The man sounded nice, a hint of Scouse in his voice; but so had a lot of people on the Fylde coast, where she had spent so much of her childhood. There had probably been grey days and rainy days, dark days and glum days, but she could not recall any. Unpleasant events had been edited out of her memory. And here she was, speeding back to the place where she had been so happy.

Frequently, after another botched relationship, she had wished that she could go back to some point in her childhood and do it all again: press rewind and record over the last thirty-odd years. But would she get it right a second time, or get it even more wrong?

Laurel finished her salad and wiped her mouth gently. After stops at Coventry and Birmingham International, the train meandered slowly through built-up areas until it descended into the cavernous gloom of

New Street. It pulled into a platform alongside a train with Welsh words painted on it.

"Trefor! I must let Trefor know!" Laurel spoke her thoughts aloud.

Trefor Rhys, the manager of a neighbouring branch of the bank, had been widowed only a month or so earlier. His wife had been ill for a long time, but had suffered complications after a ground breaking operation that might have improved her quality of life. As he had remarked, "Why do the medics say 'complications'? To cover their own incompetence?" There was nothing complicated about death: one day she was here; the next she wasn't. Laurel had supported both Trefor and Carolyn, finally just Trefor, through it all.

Hi, Trefor. How are you? I'm on a train heading north for a few days. Just had to get away. Fed up. Told Maddie, my MA, to call you if she has a major prob. But she shouldn't have — she knows what she's doing. Will let u know more midweek.

Trefor was a nice, sensitive man, though they could never be a match. Great as a friend, not as a lover. He just didn't do it for her, probably on account of being quite short, no more than five foot five. But he had always been generous with his help and advice, especially in her first months as a branch manager. They usually met up before regional meetings, entered the room together, sat together and backed each other up.

Laurel, Sorry I haven't written properly to thank you for all the support and everything you did to help with the funeral. Feel bad I haven't seen you since, but as you know, I'm only just back to work.

Don't be silly, Tref. No more than a friend would do. And you've always been a great help to me. So long as you're OK.

Much better. That week away after Carolyn's funeral was a great idea of yours. And I met a couple of guys from Scotland, so we walked together. You were right; that coastline is amazing.

Laurel had arranged the catering for the wake. The guests gone, she and Trefor had been draining the last bottle of wine, when Laurel suggested a hiking holiday along the Amalfi Coast, something she had undertaken three years earlier. Besides the stunning scenery, the highlight had been Emilio, a tall, refined, softly-spoken man from Puglia; an absolute gentleman by day, but a voracious lover on both nights they had spent together.

The memories caused Laurel to wriggle in her seat as the train slowed into Sandwell & Dudley, hardly the most prepossessing place on the rail network. Was this thing going to stop at every nondescript station between

Birmingham and Preston? For a moment, Laurel wished she was flying to Naples; but Emilio, who had been on a trial separation from his wife three years ago, was now dutifully back at home.

Will be in touch later in the week. BFN.

Beyond Crewe, the train put on some speed, but it was doubtful whether she would arrive in Preston in time to catch the Blackpool South train. She didn't. The next one was nearly an hour later. There was a Blackpool North train due in, though; and she knew they were faster and stopped at fewer places. Perhaps it would catch the other up at Kirkham, where the lines to the two Blackpool termini diverged. She would run across the platform there, shrieking like a silly schoolgirl if she had to.

Having willed the train to greater speed, Laurel was horrified to see the rear of the Blackpool South train disappearing around the left curve as she stepped onto the Kirkham down platform. She glanced up at the monitor: fifty-five minutes to wait. However, with the spring sun shining and a copse of trees in vigorous young green beyond the track, it was not the most unpleasant place to sit.

Even better, she was glad to see the sign 'Unisex Toilet' on a nearby building of terracotta and cream-coloured bricks. Laurel had walked halfway up the ramp to its door when she noticed a tatty handwritten message taped to the frosted glass: 'Out of Order'. Typical.

The platform was otherwise deserted, quiet enough for her to crouch down and pee behind the small building. There was no one about. Glancing around a second time, however, she realised that the station lamps were the type that doubled as CCTV cameras. It would be just her luck to get filmed and shamed on *Filthy Rotten Scoundrels*. She could hear the irritatingly self-righteous presenter snarling triumphantly at the camera: "And worst of all, the person spending a penny turns out to be a bank manager on the run from her job. Unbelievable!"

"Is there a pub nearby?" Laurel asked the rather chubby ticket clerk in the station building.

Shaking his head, he replied, "There's a vending machine if you want a drink."

"I need a toilet and I've got ages to wait. And that one on the platform…"

"Aye, I know," he nodded sympathetically. "They keep vandalising it. The nearest pub is the Stanley Arms. Turn right out of here, then first left. It should be open by now. It'll only take you about three minutes."

"Thanks."

"Leave your case here if you want. I'm open till six."

"Really? That's so kind."

"Just drop it there. I'll bring it inside. If you're back by twenty to, you'll be okay."

What a nice man! How different from the usual surly jobsworths in London, who would have called the

Bomb Squad if she'd asked to leave a bag somewhere for ten seconds. People in this part of the country were generally nicer and friendlier, though.

The late afternoon was sunny, not summery warm, but pleasant. There was a bounce in her step as she walked with the jubilant gait of a convict in the first moments after release. The sound of her shoes on the pavement, the birdsong in nearby trees, the playful laughter of children in a garden all announced 'Freedom'.

The Stanley Arms stood on a street corner. Curious, she peeped down the side road and discovered, with childlike delight, that it led into the Fox's biscuit factory. She returned to the pub door, where a sign promised, 'A warm welcome in this friendly local.' *Sure. Don't they all?*

Laurel entered a light, spacious saloon, momentarily the focus of attention for the three customers already in there. She approached the extensive bar, three-sided, with its row of hand pumps for real ales, from behind which a tall, grey-haired, strong-looking man smiled. Fancying something with a bit of edge, she ordered a gin and tonic.

"Single, or double?" The landlord beamed with aspiration.

"Go on, you've won me." Laurel smiled. Why not? No clients to see this afternoon. She could already feel the stress of work and London ebbing away. "I'll have a double."

The large saloon was clean and tastefully decorated in light grey and white, with framed photographs of bygone Blackpool. Several small blackboards on the walls and above the bar advertised some of the dishes available.

"Ice and lemon, love?"

"Lime, if you have any," she replied, taking a note from her wallet. "I just fancy something bitter."

Nodding in the direction of the man sitting furthest from Laurel, the host grinned. "Something bitter, eh? You want to get to know Joey there. He never stops moaning." The other drinkers sniggered as Joey the malcontent shook his head ruefully.

"Do you mind if I use your loo first?" Laurel asked, the pressure in her bladder becoming intense.

"Go ahead, love. In the corner over there." The landlord indicated with his head as he placed her drink on the bar counter. Picking up the ten-pound note, he watched the stranger walk across the room and disappear into the Ladies. So did the other three, to whom he nodded approvingly.

"Your clientele's looking up, James," grinned Bitter Joey, sardonically adding, "At last." The four men chuckled.

Having grown up in Lancashire, Laurel was not in the least offended by the term 'love'. She was neither patronised nor unnerved by it. Market stall holders used it to men, women and children alike, without some politically correct harridan suggesting the language was inappropriate.

When she returned from the clean and well-maintained toilets, the four men were focused on a televised snooker match. At the end of the frame, the landlord turned to Laurel, who had perched herself on a bar stool. "Are you local, or just visiting?" Laurel explained her appearance in the pub. "Aye, it's been shut for months that toilet on the platform."

The snooker session over, he switched channel to the BBC News. For a few moments, Laurel eyed the screen warily, lest it should announce that a runaway bank manager was being searched for. *Don't be daft, Laurel. Relax and drink up.*

The train was an old two-coach type, known affectionately as a 'nodding donkey.' Busy, though not overcrowded, it bounced its jolly way towards leafy Lytham. Glimpses of Laurel's childhood flashed by: the cricket ground, Lowther Gardens; the neat brick-built terraces of Fairhaven facing the famous Royal St Anne's golf links. Near St Anne's station, some of the houses looked somewhat seedier.

With about a dozen others, Laurel stepped off the train, through the swinging wooden gate and across the forecourt. At first, she ignored the taxis waiting in the wide turn, but she then thought of the distance to the B&B and of the time. She headed back, smiling as she read 'Whiteside Taxis'. Older generations of cars had parked and waited for customers there when she was a child, and probably long before that. An old family firm; a link with her family past.

A pleasant man in his sixties, the driver chatted cheerily as they motored towards the promenade. Turning left, he pointed out the pier, the ornamental gardens and the cinema; Laurel responded politely, though she had known the seafront all her life. A minute later, they turned off and pulled up outside a well-kept three-storey house that bore the sign 'Cumbria Hotel'.

Doug, a friendly, cheerful man, showed her up to her room at the rear of the first floor. Bright, clean and airy, the room was decorated in blue and white, with a seaside theme. It had an adequate private bathroom, an ample wardrobe and a chest of drawers, on top of which rested a kettle and the tea and coffee making stuff. Above, on the wall, was a television.

"Please make sure you switch off at the wall," added the proprietor, after pointing out the binder of useful information. "Oh, what time do you want breakfast? It will suit me better if you leave it till eight — unless you have to be out early." Laurel assured him that eight o'clock would be fine. She had never been one for long lie-ins, but as she was trying to de-stress, there was no point in getting up at the crack of dawn.

"Just ring the bell if you need anything and enjoy your stay with us," he said, handing her the keys.

Laurel considered having a shower, if only to rinse away the contamination of Virgin Trains; but not intending to go anywhere posh, she settled for a quick wash and a change of top. Then, facing the mirror, she pulled up a long handkerchief skirt, taupe in colour, embellished with panels of lace in the same shade, with its own soft faux-leather belt. Her fingertips stroked the lacy stylised butterfly sewn onto the skirt at the top of her thigh. Perfect: the gipsy boho look chimed sweetly with the unrestraint that she desired. She swung her hips, making the pointed folds sway and dance around her lower legs.

She hung up her jacket, her navy skirt and the one dress she had brought; the smaller stuff could wait. She re-touched her make-up, darkening the natural shadow on her eyes, before brushing her hair. The sun was still shining through the bathroom window; but being the end of April, it was likely to turn chilly before nightfall. She grabbed her long cardigan, threw her bag over her shoulder and headed towards town, determined to make the most of a bright evening on the Fylde coast.

The menus of a couple of restaurants near the main thoroughfare tempted her; but Laurel decided that it was too nice an evening to sit indoors at a table for one. It had to be al fresco. Tesco, opposite, was advertising MEAL DEAL. A chicken sandwich, a flapjack and some juice would suffice.

Laurel walked over the crossroads, past the Lord Derby pub, and up to the pier. Keeping to its right, she trudged onto the hard, flat sand, retracing steps she had taken countless times in her childhood. Defying the safety notice, she walked between the Victorian iron supports; after one hundred and thirty years, was there any serious likelihood of it collapsing on her head? Freedom meant Freedom. *Heavens, Laurel! You sound like the beleaguered Prime Minister, with her increasingly desperate 'Brexit means Brexit' mantra.*

Clear of the structure, Laurel ploughed her way through the softer dry sand, towards the slope of squared stones buttressing the promenade. A younger woman was sitting alone, reading. Laurel sat a respectable distance away, gazing into the distance, where the Ribble estuary met the open sea. If the waves had ever threatened the promenade, it must have been many years ago.

While she was enjoying her 'freedom meal', Laurel observed the dog walkers, couples, families and lone strollers crossing the hard sand. She twisted the cap off the plastic bottle; the apple juice burst vitally on her palate. The evening air and its breeze thrilled her, as did the openness, the space and the freedom. Intoxicating.

It was only seven thirty; there was easily another hour of daylight left. *Pity to waste it, Laurel, and not to celebrate a momentous day with a drink — a proper one.* Knowing that there were few pubs in St Anne's, she walked back to the Lord Derby.

A small cluster of businessmen stood joking at one end of the bar; lone drinkers and couples were imbibing in the dark recesses of the lounge. Laurel carried her large glass of Shiraz outside, where several people were sitting in ones and twos at the picnic tables.

At five foot eight, Laurel had legs that were long enough to climb easily over the seat. She sat facing the pier, now closed for the night. The spicy, peppery wine tingled like sour sherbet; after enjoying the sensual pleasure in her mouth, she swallowed. Scarcely had the wine coursed down her throat, leaving a satisfying warmth in its wake, when Laurel felt a heady sensation: it was liberation.

She lit a cigarette, inhaling deeply and contentedly. She savoured the situation, sipping her wine, as the daylight slowly yielded to night. Lamps came on here and there; most of the outdoor drinkers gradually drifted away. She had just lit a second smoke when the pub door opened; a smartly dressed man, one of the group at the bar, emerged.

Laurel studied him discreetly as he stood on the steps. He was quite good-looking, early fifties, clearly a professional. From a pocket in his quality suit, he produced a packet of cigarettes. After lighting up, his eyes scanned the garden area, halting on Laurel.

"I'm glad to see I'm not the only one. I'm beginning to feel like a social outcast these days."

"Me too," she said, nodding. "We aren't so wicked, are we?"

Her body language invited the man to approach. Laurel observed his clothing in more detail. Mildly eccentric? He was wearing a silk cravat that matched the handkerchief in his breast pocket. He had several gold rings, two with large semi-precious stones; his hands made very expressive and somewhat effeminate gestures. Probably gay, she thought, a little deflated.

While smoking, they chatted in a way that made Laurel feel at ease. Very well spoken, he told her that he was a solicitor, the senior partner in a small practice close to the square. Laurel joked that perhaps their meeting was fortuitous, explaining her problem with the letting agents. From his wallet, the man presented a business card: BERTRAM SIMMONDS, LLB.

"Give me a call if you need help. The first half hour is free anyway." He beamed. "I'd better get back to my partner. He'll be wondering if I've turned and escaped with a woman." Laurel smiled and thanked him. So, her gaydar was functioning correctly. Pity, though.

Laurel stared at her nearly empty glass. She was considering whether to have another drink when her phone bleeped. A message from Maddie.

R U OK?

Perfect.

Found someone already?

Not that perfect — unless you count a gay solicitor, LOL.

So, by the law of averages, the next 15 won't be! Take care, hon.

Typical Maddie. Laurel sent a love heart.

She did love Maddie, though not in that way. There had never been anything romantic or sexual between them. Maddie had been the best friend Laurel could have wished for. Years ago, shortly after they had met, Maddie had saved Laurel from herself; and she had defended Laurel in times of unfair and vicious criticism. In return, Laurel had supported Maddie through the ups and downs — mostly downs — of her crazy love life. Naturally impulsive, Maddie tended to jump into a relationship with both feet, only later pausing to wonder if the water was safe.

Laurel picked up her phone again, remembering she had left Maddie to see the very eligible, newly divorced Mr Eddleston.

BTW, Mr E?

A cinch. Signed his son up too. Just inherited 50k!

As dishy as his dad?

Nah. Spotty and bashful. Blushed every time I spoke to him. Prob traumatised him for life!

Laurel relived fond childhood memories, strolling past the lifeboat memorial statue and through the ornamental gardens, where, in the velvety dusk, she stood atop a little hump-backed bridge. She had run around here often when she was a child, under the little waterfall, trotting or skipping the winding course of the paths.

There, on the bridge paved with pebbles, she reeled for a moment, as the reality of the closing day caught up with her. *So, you're here — here on this little bridge where you first stood more than forty years ago. Here, more than two hundred miles from your flat, your job, from where you ought to be. You're here: betwixt day and night; betwixt light and dark, heaven and hell; betwixt the past and the future.*

Her future! What had she done? And what was she going to do now?

THREE

Laurel Ashworth blinked, her eyes shocked by daylight. "Ten to six," she mumbled. "What the hell…?"

The room faced roughly east; and the curtains were not closed, so tired had she been the previous evening. No wonder the sun had woken her! She gazed at the ceiling. Should she get up and make a cup of coffee? Or just roll over and shut her eyes, in the hope of another hour's sleep? Pondering, she watched the orange glow broaden across the ceiling.

Laurel rubbed her eyes and walked gently to the chest of drawers. She made some coffee in a mug that matched the duvet cover. She clocked her face in the mirror; it was a six o'clock face. She stuck out her tongue at it. After brushing her hair, she sat on the edge of her bed, drenched in golden sunlight, luxuriating in the knowledge that she was far away from the crowded commute, from work, from pests like Silverman; with a whole day ahead of her.

Finishing her coffee, she decided to start her new adventure as she meant to go on, with a run along the shore. In black workout pants and a long T-shirt, she had just pulled some ankle socks from her case when she froze in disbelief.

"Bugger!" Her trainers were at home, where she had dropped them after her Sunday run in Acton Park. She could hardly run in the three-inch heels she had worn the previous day, nor in her ballerinas. Her only other footwear was a nice pair of thong sandals, in dark brown leather, which she had bought just before the wonderfully warm Easter weekend. "Bloody great!" she sighed, lifting the sandals from the case, whose contents were now reduced to a top, a T-shirt, underwear and a bag of tights and stockings.

Laurel schlepped across the main road and into a car park, where she loosened up and did some stretching. The early morning air was keen and clean, with just a hint of seaside saltiness, the waters of the estuary being a fair distance out. She inhaled it almost greedily. Having warmed up, she jogged lightly along a path between the low dunes, and onto the beach. The sandals would have to come off; she would run barefoot on the firmer sand.

She glanced around for a place where she could leave her sandals. One or two dog walkers were about. She chose a spot that she would easily recognise later, a little hollow in the dune, about two metres from the path. 'Should be safe there,' she thought, stashing them where they were partly hidden by the grass.

Beyond the soft, dry sand, she reached the harder surface. It was surprisingly cold on the soles of her bare feet, but invigorating. She ran towards the pier, keeping a steady pace, the freshly oxygenated blood pumping vitally through her limbs, her body warming and thrusting forward into the yielding air.

Turning near the pier, whose furthermost legs were being licked by the sea, she retraced her strides, now facing the rising sun. Through the trickle of sweat from her forehead, she discerned the silhouette of another runner, a female form, coming towards her. They nodded a greeting as they passed each other.

She continued past the car park, reminding herself where she had secreted her sandals, and over what seemed to be more muddy silt than sand, almost to the boundary wall of Fairhaven Lake, before heading back to her starting point. Flagging by now, she slackened her pace to a trot and scanned the hollows of the dunes for her shoes. Recognising a dip in the grassy mound, she approached; there was nothing. *You're kidding!* She kicked at the grass, partly in frustration, partly in the forlorn hope that the vegetation was playing a trick on her.

About a hundred yards away, near the end of the promenade, a man was throwing a ball to a dog, which dutifully gave chase and returned it. Squinting through her perspiration, Laurel could see something in the man's hand, something dark. There was nobody else close enough. It had to be him. *Just your luck, Laurel, a bloody shoe fetishist!*

She broke into a trot again, then lengthened her stride. The nearer she got to the man, the more certain she became. Suddenly, the dog noticed her approach

44

and put itself between the two humans, sensing danger to its owner. Laurel skirted wider and ran past him, before turning abruptly. She stared at the man; he glanced away. Guilty! However, the dog intervened once more, barking a warning. Definitely! There was something brown in his left hand.

Unwilling to surrender her hardly worn expensive sandals, Laurel planned a second sortie. She wheeled around; he was fifty or sixty yards away. The mutt, believing it had seen off the aggressor, had trotted out towards the sea. She made a wide approach to be sure that they were her sandals, nicked for some nefarious purpose. If the old perv intended to get himself off by sniffing her footwear, he had another thing coming. Fury mounting, Laurel overtook him; then, lurching to her right, she turned sharply on her heels, blocking his progress.

Barely two metres of beach lay between them. Her nostrils were flaring, her eyes flinty. Alarmed, he shouted nervously, "What do you want? Leave me alone!"

"My sandals... have disappeared... not where I left them. Have you...?" she panted, pointing an accusing finger at the man's left hand, which he instinctively moved behind his back. "I need them... to get back to my hotel. Really, I need them back."

"Your shoes! I'm a married man," he gasped, "Benji! Benji! Come here, boy. Home!"

Still looking bewildered, the walker turned. Only then did he bring his hand back into view. And only then did Laurel realise that he was holding a small plastic bag, in which he was carrying Benji's morning doggy-do.

"You can look inside there if you want to," he sniped, proffering the bag. Laurel immediately caught the acrid whiff of its contents.

"Sorry," she mumbled, wishing that the beach would become quicksand and devour her.

Crestfallen, Laurel climbed the steps up to the promenade and walked on the asphalt, as far as the main road. Wincing at the surprising sharpness on the balls of her feet and her heels, she gingerly picked her way across. Never before had she considered how unsmooth a road could be.

She stroked her feet lightly across the Cumbria's coarse doormat, removing painful little chippings. Alerted by the sound of her key in the vestibule door, Doug came out of the breakfast room.

"Oh, good morning. Have you been out for some exercise?" He glanced down at her feet. "You needn't have taken your shoes off, though. You can't have got them muddy in this weather." Laurel smiled weakly and hauled herself up the stairs, her tortured soles relieved and soothed by the soft carpet. "Breakfast's ready any time you want it," the genial proprietor called after her.

Laurel showered quickly and, once dry, threw on a thick cotton T-shirt — the only other one she had — and a skirt with a blue and white geometrical pattern and a wide elasticated waistband. Stepping into her ballerinas, she almost skipped downstairs, her appetite whetted by the seductive aroma.

It was almost ten thirty by the time Laurel left the B&B, having spent some time chatting with Doug about the state of trade. She would have one last look for her sandals, then make for the pier and the other places she had known since childhood; nostalgia and the hazy sunshine would console her. She strolled through the empty car park and down the path she had taken four hours earlier.

Approaching the sands through the low dunes, she planted her feet carefully among the small ridges and troughs. Then, as her leg stretched out to step down onto the beach, she noticed something brown, partly concealed by the long grass. There, in the little depression where she had secreted them, were her sandals. She stooped and grabbed them, almost in disbelief. But how?

Only when she had walked twenty metres or so down the beach, twice punching the air for joy, did she grasp the truth. There were two paths that emerged from the car park onto the sands: she had been looking by the wrong one! The sandals that she was clutching tightly in her hand had not been disturbed by anybody, foot fetishist or not. She felt really guilty. *That poor man, Laurel! You'll have to avoid Benji's terrorised owner for the rest of the week.*

Laurel climbed up to the promenade and passed the rows of chalets, whose occupants were sitting in deckchairs, enjoying the morning sun. Stopping to gaze seaward, Laurel saw that she had been wrong earlier, when she had assumed that the tide was out. In fact, the sea was now so distant that it was barely visible.

She passed the small boating lake, where, at four and five years old, she had counted the motor boats being brought out of their house every morning, refusing to go back to the hotel for breakfast until they were all accounted for. Steps led her onto the beach. Skirting around a group of young children on a school outing, she strode out, across the immense sand flats.

A faint breeze, imperceptible on the promenade, toyed with the ends of her hair. The worm casts seemed far fewer than she recalled from forty years earlier, maybe because the sea did not come in as close to the built shoreline as it had then. After walking out for five minutes, Laurel felt that she was no nearer to the water. On she walked, fascinated, lured by the great stillness and emptiness of the landscape; she was already beyond the present pier head, and even the original one, now memorialized in massive wooden monoliths.

Reaching where the sand was wetter from the last high tide, Laurel kicked off her ballerinas; she then pushed her footies into the toe of one slipper. The ribbed sand, where hardened, was a little uncomfortable on the soles of her bare feet. Fifteen minutes out now, she glanced back at the promenade, where the strollers

48

seemed tiny; ahead of her, only two people, far apart from one another, were walking slowly.

Here, the apparent wasteland was lush with worm casts and shells, whole and perfect. Some were in beautiful delicate hues, many almost pearlescent, smooth and fragile; others were much more rugged and opaque, rough to the touch; fine porcelain and rustic earthenware. *Gather some and take them home, Laurel, as you did when you were young.*

Home — for what? To be stuffed inside a drawer and forgotten? To be made into some trashy artwork? Why detract from nature's richly random carpet? As a child, Laurel had picked flowers to make daisy chains, or buttercup necklaces. Other kids had scoffed, but they had hung prettily. Once, made to remove the precious garland, she had cried herself to sleep. The next morning, she had awoken to find a limp string of withered flowers, which her mother had promptly binned. Hadn't they been prettier in the field?

And now, out on the sandy wilderness, Laurel trod carefully, trying to avoid crushing the shells, feeling guilty when something crunched beneath her foot. The metaphor struck her at once. *Laurel, you've spent too much of your life treading carefully — on eggshells; too long being self-conscious; too concerned with what others might think; too afraid of somebody's censure.*

She waded into the softer, muddy sand. It felt cold, but good; messy, but stimulating. Being so far out from the promenade, she could see around the curve of the coastline to Blackpool, its celebrated tower and the large rollercoaster at the Pleasure Beach thrusting through the haze. The sun felt warm on Laurel's shoulders: warm and comforting, an affirmation. She was glad and right to be here.

And yet, at that moment, she became acutely aware of her solitude. She was probably a mile or more from the promenade, within shouting distance of nobody; alone in a vast expanse of flatness, bare flatness that stretched for ever.

Another more soul-baring metaphor struck her; this was her life, her relationships, her lack of someone close, someone to hold, someone to lie beside. The cast of lost loves rolled through her mind like the credits of a movie. They were all distant memories, contact broken; they had wandered away to the grey, misty shadowlands of her life, the desert of dead done dreams.

She had reached the sea proper, which now appeared to be in flow. On such a flat seabed, the Irish Sea might progress quickly and cut her off; it was already sweeping around both ends of a nearby low sandbank. The tide had turned; and so, she decided, must she.

The outward walk had been a whimsical adventure to find the end of the sand and the beginning of the sea. Her return strides were strong and purposeful, not to escape the encroaching water, for she was quickly clear of that; but they were an expression of her altered mindset. She would forge ahead resolute, determined, with a definable goal: to find the end of her wilderness and the beginning of... something. Something new.

Enlivened by the walk, and emboldened by her positive outlook, Laurel sat down at the edge of the sand hills, forty or fifty metres to the west of the pier. She had no idea of the exact time, and she had no need to know; it was lunchtime-ish, she guessed. She let the sun dry her feet, so that she could more easily brush off the soft sand before she put on her sandals.

Drawn to Ashton Gardens, she entered by a walkway lined with tulips, in alternate beds of rich Roman purple and white; a rogue yellow, a bold sunny yellow, gleamed from one of the purple beds. Daisies and dandelions proliferated on the sunken lawns. As she approached the war memorial, Laurel's body demanded caffeine. She walked past the nearest café, whose extensive outside seating area had once been a pavilion theatre.

She had never been in that café; she never could. She and her parents had been at the theatre one Friday evening, watching a local amateur society performing *Carousel*. During that night, she had been disturbed by a bad dream, in which the theatre had burned down. The following morning, the local radio announced that the Ashton Theatre had, indeed, been gutted by fire. For months afterwards, she had been racked with guilt, fearing that her dream had caused the conflagration. Even forty years later, Laurel still got goosebumps about it.

She knew of a café just across the road from the park. While she was crossing the street, a lump came into her throat. Her last visit to the New Market Café had been with her father, on the final day out they had ever shared. She breathed in sharply, steeling herself, and entered. Playing subtly and gently was baroque harpsichord music: possibly Telemann, too uncomplicated to be Bach. It was restful, calming and ordered: something to quell her emotional turbulence.

The tall dark-haired proprietor brought her coffee and toasted sandwich to the table. Then, he got on with wiping and cleaning, preparing for the end of his day. Perhaps that was something she might do: open a café somewhere, just like this one; with tasteful décor and a genteel and discerning clientele, a pleasant environment to work in.

Back in the gardens, she noticed people playing bowls in the afternoon sunshine. Folk had been bowling on that day in September, nearly three years before; she and her father had paused to watch them. Laurel had borrowed a wheelchair from the care home because he was no longer able to walk very far; but he had been determined that day, and had used the chair as a support, pushing it slowly to the rose garden.

She was wowed by the perfume of the bluebells that were growing in great profusion beneath the mature trees, on the bank above the neatly designed garden. Nearby, a hawthorn bush, in blossom, was adorned like a bride. It was, of course, too early in the spring for the roses to be showing much colour. She stepped down, nonetheless, amid the geometrically arranged beds.

Her father had loved this place. He had loved that precious day out, when they had laughed that the roses, fading and falling, were like him, their best days behind them. Now, in this moment, she felt close to him, so close that she imagined she could touch his brown leathery skin; so close that she could almost smell his Brylcreemed hair that had stayed sleek and black until he was more than seventy. He had pottered steadily among the tapestry of roses, occasionally stooping to take in their fragrance; still awestruck, after a lifetime of gardening, at the beauty and complex simplicity of a rose.

That day, like this one, had been wonderfully blue and clear. In the open air, released from the care home, he had revelled in the reminiscences. Out on the seafront, once or twice, inspired by memories of days long gone, he had asked Laurel to help him stand; and he had walked fifty yards or so. Then, tired, he had sat recalling family holidays and his beloved garden and greenhouse, until the sun had grown feeble and the air had taken on an autumnal chill. She had pushed him back to the car, and they had driven back to Blackburn through the twilight, heading east in the smothering nightfall.

Laurel felt the weight of memory and the pain of loss. She sat down on a bench and wiped a couple of tears from her cheek. She wished that she could tell her daddy one last time that she loved him. That thought broke her. She sobbed, at first uncontrollably, almost chokingly; but her crying was interrupted by an afternoon breeze on which was carried the faintest aroma of hair cream.

"Are you all right, love?" Laurel turned and saw one of the council gardeners wheeling a barrow, a few metres to her left. She nodded and croaked her thanks. The stocky man, older than Laurel by ten years or so, paused his trundling and shook his head kindly. "Don't fret, love. There's many folk as comes in here for a little cry. Full of memories, this garden is." Laurel smiled through her watery face. The gardener continued on his way.

Daft cow, Laurel, making an exhibition of yourself. Then, she reproached herself again. Why shouldn't she cry? The man was spot on. This place was teeming with memories, and as pregnant with emotion as with rosebuds.

Having recomposed herself, she stood up, whispered on the breeze her love for her father, and walked calmly out of the rose garden. Without consciously thinking 'retail therapy', she made her way up Garden Street towards the main parade.

Noticing a rail of clothes outside a boutique in Orchard Street, Laurel sauntered over, making sure her hands were clean before touching. Between some boho lacy dresses and blouses were several Italian cotton and linen mix, sleeveless handkerchief dresses, all with a large floral print: one a peach ground, another white, another blue. A light grey one attracted Laurel: grey was versatile, and the colours of the flowers — red, yellow and blue — were set off stylishly. The butterfly thus drawn to the flowers, clutching the hanger, she entered.

A woman with short blonde hair showed her to the fitting room. Perfect. The A-shape flattered her relatively small hips. And at £25 for a nice dress, it was a no-brainer. *Wear it out this evening, Laurel.* Re-emerging, she glanced around the shop; there was some lovely stuff. *Must come back.*

New dress meant new nail varnish; the two she had brought would not really match. Ever since childhood, Laurel had fawned at the rainbow of nail paints in stores. She chose a fuchsia pink, to bring out the shade at the centre of some of the large flowers, and a silvery grey. Her dark blue M&S open-toed shoes, with a moderate heel, would complement the blue petals.

Back at the hotel, Laurel felt tired and drained; an emotional day, but a cathartic one. A lot that needed to come out had been released. After a rest, she showered, then painted the silvery colour on her toes and the fuchsia on her fingers, both the quick-dry type. Laurel decided that she needed tights, the evenings still being cool.

It was still broad daylight when she strolled to the only pub along St Anne's seafront. With a white summer jacket over her dress, she was confident of her attractiveness. A group of middle-aged bikers, gathered near the entrance, eyed her up. Should she sit outside, inviting further attention? Who knows, Laurel? One of them might be HIM, the ONE. Flicking her hair, she scanned the array of leathery, hirsute manhood. Nah. In any case, it was a bit chilly for outdoor quaffing.

Although the hostelry was a Toby Carvery, Laurel had no urge to eat; so she sat at a small table with a large glass of Shiraz, facing a window that looked inland. In front of that window sat a couple in their early seventies, whose middle-age spread had morphed into septuagenarian obesity. They ordered bar snacks.

"Chef's put some extra roasts with your turkey bap," the server announced, plonking a plate before the woman. As if she needed extra potatoes. At this point, the husband hauled himself up and lurched towards the toilets, knocking Laurel's table as he passed. Luckily, she had already drained nearly half of the wine from her glass, which she managed to steady before it toppled. Only a little spilled as a result of the jarring.

"Sorry," the man muttered.

"Don't worry," Laurel replied, hastily examining her new purchase, before adding caustically, "I've had this dress for hours." The waspish remark was lost on its intended target.

'Find us on Facebook,' the food menu directed. Taking another sip, Laurel considered the banality of most of the stuff that colleagues and their 'friends' posted on social media. She had always firmly believed that she had been sensible in avoiding Mr Zuckerberg's empire.

As she sat there, however, gradually mellowing, she relived that moment out at the water's edge, when she had decided that she needed to turn. She mentally scrolled down her litany of old relationships; one, in particular, had haunted her for twenty years. Would he be on Facebook? Other people had reignited old flames that way. Was it time to consort with the devil? She found and downloaded the Facebook app.

FOUR

After breakfast the next day, Laurel called at the post office to get a postcard for Aunty Hilda, her favourite relative, and the only one she was really in touch with. Eccentric Hilda, who was not actually Laurel's aunt but a cousin of her mother's, had retired to a bungalow in Southgate, on the Gower Peninsula, even though she had never been there in her life before that. It was Aunty Hilda who had taught Laurel to play the piano when she was a child.

Now, in her early seventies, Hilda entertained neighbours and locals at monthly soirees. A dozen or so would cram into her living room, a third of its space being occupied by the grand piano. Hilda provided finger food, while her guests brought copious amounts of alcohol. On Sundays, she played the organ, refusing to accept payment, at a church on the outskirts of Swansea. Being sprightly, Hilda walked the couple of miles there on fine days; she was usually driven home by a parishioner, for whom Hilda cooked lunch.

After posting her card, Laurel noticed a girl manoeuvring an A-board onto the wide pavement outside a hairdressing salon. "Are you busy today? Do you have a free slot?" Laurel asked.

"What do you need doing?" asked the girl, who was sporting quirkily styled bleached hair, with pink streaks.

"Oh, just trimming the ends and tidying up really."

"I can do it now if you like. My first isn't for another half an hour."

"Fine."

A quick wash, clip and blow dry. Laurel leaned back, her head over the basin.

"Haven't seen you before. On holiday?" the girl asked, running her fingers through Laurel's hair under the tap.

"Sort of. I've been a bank manager in London for years. I just needed a break from the stress of the job." Even as Laurel finished uttering those words, she knew that she hadn't been wholly truthful. And, after all, wasn't a salon chair the nearest thing to a confessional?

"The fact is," she sighed, settling in front of the large mirror, "I've had enough; time for a change. So, I came here because we always came for holidays when I was a kid."

"There's not much point looking round here for a different job — not a good one, anyway. Some of the banks have shut and that big insurance place at Lytham went a few years ago. And Blackpool is getting awful. My partner's job isn't that safe, either. This place just about makes a profit; but I have to keep the prices lower than I'd like because most of my customers are grannies."

"Thanks a lot!" Laurel joked.

"Oh, I didn't mean you." The girl laughed, nudging Laurel's shoulder. "Nice thick hair," she said, seemingly enjoying the sensual pleasure of Laurel's chestnut mane in her fingers.

Laurel raised her eyes and studied the girl. Despite the heavy make-up and the arsenal of piercings, she had a pretty face. Their eyes met in the mirror. Laurel smiled quizzically. The hairdresser was the first to break the mutual gaze, but then she looked directly into the mirror again, tilting her head alluringly.

Was she? Laurel's sexual interest was becoming aroused. Uncertain how to ask the question, she had finally decided on a neutral question, 'Your partner?' when the hairdresser broke the electric silence.

"Single?"

"Very," Laurel replied. "For a long time."

"There must be a Mister Right out there somewhere." Pause. "Or a Ms Right," the girl ventured, trying to sound matter of fact. Was she just being even-handedly PC, or was she hinting?

"Whatever relationship I get into, I seem to screw it up," Laurel confessed, deliberately avoiding gender.

"You sound just like my best friend. She's hopeless. Two young children by different men; now she's living with another guy, but that's going wrong. The father of the baby keeps going round there and demanding to see his kid, at all hours. He kicked the front door in the other night. They had to call the police.

And her new boyfriend is a really nice guy. I've known him for years. He did my piercings — and most of my tattoos."

"You've got quite a few," said Laurel, smiling.

"My mother hates them, of course. But my partner paid for this," she said, sticking out her tongue to display a gold stud. "Thought it would add an extra thrill. You know…" The girl winked. Laurel's own tongue involuntarily flicked her lip. She began to imagine the studded tongue exploring her intimately. She had to know.

"Your partner?"

"Chris. We've been together for three years. Works as an engineer at the airport; although since Ryanair quit, it's only executive jets and helicopters to the oil platforms." Laurel was conceiving a butch Christine arriving home, oily and sweaty, to be greeted by the eager studded tongue and induced into screaming orgasms, when the girl added, "He's ten years older than me. Keeps talking about getting married, but I'm happy as we are."

A bell jingled. In the mirror, Laurel watched the entrance of an elegantly dressed woman, probably in her late seventies. The door was being held open for her by a similarly well-clad man, the solicitor Laurel had met on Monday evening.

"Now, call a taxi when you're all done, Mother; don't try and walk home."

"There's no need to fuss, dear. I'll be quite all right," she assured him.

"Ah, good morning," Bertram Simmonds said, recognising Laurel and nodding. Laurel smiled back, without moving; the hairdresser was, at that moment, trimming the ends of her hair.

"Morning, Mrs S," the girl said, beaming. "You just make yourself comfy. I'll only be a few minutes. Would you like a cup of tea while you're waiting?"

"No, thank you, dear. I've only just had breakfast," the elderly woman said, through tight lips that flexed and pursed, as if she had the remnant of a hazelnut lodged between her front teeth. Her son left.

Satisfied with her trim, Laurel stood up, reached for her bag and paid the hairdresser. She noticed the elderly woman perusing her features.

"Do you know my son, then?" Mrs Simmonds asked kindly.

"No, not really. We happened to start chatting at the pub the other evening. He gave me his business card."

"Ah, I didn't think it would be socially. He prefers other company." Pushing herself up from the chair, she added confidentially, "He's a bloody poof!"

The two younger women could not stop themselves laughing. Laurel thanked the girl and said goodbye, highly amused by the elegant older woman's rather inelegant comment.

It had not been major treatment, but as Laurel strode down the street towards the main square, she felt better and more attractive. Even a small amount of pampering was good. She giggled inwardly at the way Bertram's mother had described him. *Maddie would have enjoyed that; you'll have to tell her!* Reaching into her bag, Laurel caught sight of her footwear. No!

Across the square stood an inexpensive shoe shop, where she found a pair of white open-toed shoes, with a low wedge heel; they would complement her jacket. A few paces confirmed they were as comfortable as they looked, fine for strolling along the Fylde coast. While paying, she remembered the previous morning's hairy episode. Trainers! Oddly, this took longer: some were nice but tight; others were comfy but heavy. Her choice was limited by her needing a size eight; but she finally settled on some pale pink ones.

Where to go next? A double-decker, the number eleven to Blackpool, stopped on the far side of the road. Laurel had not visited Blackpool for ages; was it really as bad as the hairdresser had suggested? She hopped on and rode, for a few minutes, to Starr Gate, where she transferred to a sleek new tram.

Laurel sat down in a comfortable seat. There were only three other passengers when the tram moved off smoothly and almost silently. She paid the conductor for a day ticket, which would allow her the freedom to get on and off as the mood took her, anywhere between here and the old port of Fleetwood.

As the tram journeyed northwards, Laurel noticed how drab and run-down much of the famous seafront had become. Even the Pleasure Beach looked gloomy; and the Golden Mile had lost its lustre. The once tempting amusement arcades and booths, which had seduced generations of young and not-so-young, now assumed an insouciance, their managements resigned to: 'Come in, if you are so minded'.

Laurel alighted in the shadow of the great tower, the once vibrant and self-confident resort's homage to Paris. Wandering around the town centre was a grim experience. Gone were most of the good shops like Lewis's, its once hip 1960s building now stunted to two storeys shared by Poundland and Harry Ramsden's chip shop. Vaping outlets, charity shops and one-pound shops comprised most of the current retail activity.

The brightest moment came with the onset of drizzly rain. On the promenade, opposite the Tower, was the Comedy Carpet, a huge, tiled tapestry of funny lines from many of the comedians who had filled Blackpool's theatres in palmier days. Alongside Ken Dodd's *'TATTIFILARIOUS!'* section were some of Les Dawson's famous quips; at ninety degrees to them were the words of the funniest woman ever, in Laurel's eyes: *'Not bleakly, not meekly, beat me on the bum with a Woman's Weekly...'* Recalling Victoria Wood's drolly delivered lyrics set Laurel laughing in the rain, which was now heavier; and she ran to the nearest tram stop.

By the time she had reached Fleetwood, the sky was brighter. Although a shadow of its former self as a fishing and ferry port, Fleetwood was not quite so depressing. The tram terminated near the imposing North Euston Hotel, a symbol of the town's former glory. It had been built by the railway company as an overnight resting place for travellers between London and Scotland who, at one time, had to detrain there, continuing their journey by sea to Ardrossan.

Laurel remembered her father taking her on a day trip from Fleetwood to the Isle of Man, sailing out past the town's fishing fleet. The Manx ferry and the fishing boats were gone, although the service across the estuary to Knott End was still operating. She considered taking a trip, but there was little to do once over the water.

Pleased with the feel of her new shoes, Laurel followed the curve of the promenade until an interesting hillock, topped by a generously glazed building, came into view. She climbed one of the paths that led to the summit of The Mount, stopping once to gaze across Morecambe Bay, beyond which the great hulks of the Lake District were but pale grey shadows, partly shrouded in mist and murk.

In the summer house, Laurel found a class of school children, aged eight or nine, busily drawing what they could see. While walking around, she became aware that one girl's eyes were tracking her. She stopped, looked down and smiled. The girl smiled back and showed her work to Laurel.

"That's very good," she said, making eye contact with a heavily pregnant young woman, obviously their teacher, who nodded permission for the conversation to continue.

"But it's not right, is it?" the child pleaded. Impressed by the child's self-critical awareness, Laurel scanned the landscape.

"Well, I think this church tower is a bit too big, compared with the other things," Laurel suggested. The child rummaged in her pencil case for a rubber, which she immediately handed to Laurel, with an imploring look on her cute face. They sat down together.

"Carla, leave the lady to look around on her own," the teacher said softly. "She's a real perfectionist, that one," added the mother-to-be.

"It's okay," Laurel assured her. Then, turning to the child, she said, "I was useless at drawing when I was at school, honestly." The girl took back the eraser and began to rub. "See, that building is about as tall as the length of my thumb; and the church is only a little bit taller." The child's head bobbed up and down in agreement and she copied Laurel's actions. She handed her pencil to Laurel, who began to sketch faintly, then stopped. "It'll look better if you do it," she said, returning the pencil. "Just go over where I've drawn, nice and firmly."

Three other children had gathered around them. One of them asked Laurel if she was going to be their new teacher. Before Laurel could deny it, the child

66

explained, "Miss is going to have a baby on Friday." At that, the teacher howled with laughter.

"No, Samira, I'm not having my baby on Friday. I'm finishing as your teacher on Friday." Turning to Laurel, she mouthed, "Six more weeks."

"Good luck," Laurel replied.

Carla, gap-toothed and smiling, presented her altered drawing. While Laurel was still inspecting it, another little girl skipped over and thrust a paper in front of her face. It was a hastily drawn portrait. "Who's that?" Laurel inquired, half expecting the answer that she received.

"It's YOU!" said the girl, giggling. Laurel laughed kindly and handed the picture back to its creator. "It's for you," insisted the child, pressing the paper into the stranger's hand.

"Thank you," Laurel replied, touched by the child's spontaneous kindness.

Slipping the artwork gently into her bag, Laurel walked down the slope, her spirits lifted. Could she retrain as a teacher? The government kept screaming for people to do so. She had even considered it many years ago. Primary school only, though: children of that age were delightful; teenagers might not be so appealing.

Her phone bleeped, alerting her to a text from Maddie.

Didn't hear from you yesterday? You OK?

Yes, hon. In Fleetwood, just met the sweetest school kids.

Fleetwood! Played there once with the band.

Gonna bite the bullet and phone HR tomorrow. Everything OK there?

Quiet. Trevor Rhys from Knightsbridge branch phoned this a.m. to check we were coping. Nice man.

Yes, he is. Will let u know what HR say tmrw. X

After a light lunch in a nice café only yards from the tram terminus, Laurel climbed aboard to ride back. She had just settled on the seat when a thought struck her, one so blindingly obvious that she berated herself for not coming to it before. 'Of course, Trefor's a nice man; and you, my girl, are cute, single, a good laugh and a bloody good friend.' Her mind was in devious overdrive.

Tref, thanks ever so much for phoning Maddie at the branch. She's a great friend — hilarious at times, but very capable. She might need some help with the monthly return. Could you poss spare half an hour after work tmrw? Don't come all the

way over — she could meet you in the Grapes.
Told her to phone you if she has a problem.

Next, Laurel typed a quick note to her friend.

Maddie, Trefor from K'bridge needs to give you
sth. Can u meet him in the Grapes at 5.30 tmrw?

Sure, will do. Not busy tmrw eve.

As the tram rumbled up the rise to Bispham, Laurel sat
back, impishly hopeful about her matchmaking. Well,
Maddie deserved someone solid and reliable.

Maddie's love life had often been turbulent. She
had become a mother at just seventeen. The father of the
baby had hung around for a while after the birth:
"Twenty-eight minutes to be precise," she often
recalled, as a punchline. She had been a talented
clarinettist, progressing to the county youth orchestra.
Later, she took up the saxophone and jazz, playing in a
semi-pro band. Having settled down and married a
steady guy with a steady job as a lab technician, who
gladly accepted her child, she found her own steady job
in the bank.

Then, after ten years with Mr Steady, and around
the time she met Laurel, she was on tour in Europe with
the band when she fell for Husband Two, a Dutchman.
She was then in her early thirties. He moved to the UK,
then lost his job and went back to Utrecht, but not before

fathering Maddie's second daughter. Returning from maternity leave, Maddie applied for a transfer to the small branch where Laurel had recently assumed her first managerial post. In tandem, they turned around a struggling office; and within weeks, Laurel was babysitting whenever Maddie was playing a gig and her elder daughter refused to.

Back at the hotel, Laurel opened her new Facebook page and uploaded a better profile picture. It was a selfie she had snapped at Fleetwood, with sandbanks and the Irish Sea as a backdrop, and the fresh breeze blowing through her hair. It screamed FREEDOM. She was amazed and girlishly delighted by the suggestions for possible friends. How clever this Mark Zuckerberg was!

Golly, how some of her old colleagues had changed in ten or twenty years! Others looked exactly as she remembered them. She tapped in the names of old schoolmates, or colleagues from her early days in the bank, in Lancashire. There was one name she wanted to search for above all, someone she had once felt very close to. She typed ADRIAN WILLIAMS, then hesitated, twitching over the button. Did she really want to see what he looked like twenty years on? Did she need the disappointment of finding out that he was happily married?

Lured by hunger, Laurel entered the pub. After a passable prawn cocktail, she moved towards the carvery counter. "Excuse me, love, a moment," a voice chirped.

"I'm just going to refresh the veg. Do you mind waiting a couple of minutes?"

Laurel hung about, wondering what the process of 'refreshing' vegetables actually entailed. Finally, she was beckoned towards an unexciting selection of meat: a wizened, dried-out bit of gammon, probably enough for one person; the remnants of a lump of pork; and some beef, which appeared to be the only edible offering. Among the vegetables was a dish of carrots that had been cooked to a pulp. Refreshed? They were well beyond being refreshed, revived or resurrected.

"Is everything all right?" asked the waitress, as she flitted past, not pausing for a reply.

"Yes," Laurel said vacantly. She rationalised her response by thinking, 'If you and the goon in charge of the kitchen can't see that this bland garbage isn't all right, why should I bother to tell you?' Even the Shiraz was characterless and devoid of spiciness this evening.

It was all served against inane techno-babble music, whose manufacturers would not know a harmonic progression if it smacked them in the face. What a contrast with the little café the previous afternoon, where she had sat enjoying the baroque harpsichord music!

Still, her stomach was full and the view was nice enough. The low evening sun accentuated the dips and rises of the pitch and putt course, the shadowed miniature valleys versus the golden green of the sunlit slopes. Multifarious worm-hungry birds swooped or

71

strutted to one lush daisy-clad slope: five ducks, a large family of starlings, a couple of rooks and a solitary magpie. *You can't spit at it from a carvery window, Laurel!*

She paid her bill and left, taking a lingering look at the seascape. To her right, the low tangerine sun was serenely descending towards the sea. Ahead, the mountains of north Wales, more clearly visible than she could ever remember, hung like pale grey clouds above the slate blue of the wide estuary.

Her phone bleeped. Trefor! A pang of apprehension suddenly struck her: he hadn't replied immediately and now she feared that he had rumbled her. He was a very intelligent man, though a little timid around women. Laurel began to think she had done the wrong thing. Was it too soon? Perhaps she shouldn't have interfered. She lit a cigarette. *Too late to worry now.* She opened the message.

Hi Laurel, Yes, OK. I'll meet Maddie. Isn't she the bubbly little blonde?

Promising. Laurel pictured the two of them meeting in the pub. How would that go? And how, she wondered, staring at the darkening sea, would her call to HR go tomorrow?

FIVE

After venturing out for a run, and successfully avoiding Benji and his owner, Laurel showered and flumped down onto the bed. The email to Human Resources at the bank's regional head office could not be postponed any longer. Anyway, she knew the woman who managed the department.

Come on, Laurel; steel yourself and get it done before breakfast. Tell them you just got over-stressed; you need to speak to someone, and you'll be available all day.

She hit 'send'. Relieved, she sighed, grabbed her cigarettes and skipped downstairs to the car park. She inhaled deeply, with a feeling of satisfaction. The ball was in their court for now.

Feeling energetic, and with a weight off her mind, Laurel set out to walk to Lytham. Perhaps her earliest memory was of visiting a dark, pipe-tobacco scented room during the last days of her great-grandfather, who had lived, in Lytham, to the age of ninety-eight. Her mother had always dreamed of retiring there, but had died very suddenly, without ever having the opportunity.

Laurel walked so briskly that, within an hour of leaving, she was browsing the shop windows in Clifton

Street, Lytham's main shopping area. There was an interesting parade of independent retailers, especially on the sunny side: a few nice cafés, a butcher's, traditional shoe shops, like Clarks, and the odd charity shop were happily juxtaposed with bijou boutiques.

Led by memory, Laurel walked past the closed down library and turned left into Station Road. Beyond the railway bridge and avenues of trees in their spring green, lay one of her favourite spots. It was a park where, as a child, she had often played on the rickety old swings. The area had been much altered and improved, with new equipment and a café with its own kitchen garden.

"If you want to sit outside, I'll have to give you a paper cup," the serving girl informed her. Laurel did not want to sit indoors on such a glorious morning, nor did she want to drink from a paper cup.

"I promise I won't drop the cup on the ground. I won't break it over the head of a toddler, and I'll even bring it back in when I've finished," she said politely but firmly. *I'm a forty-eight-year-old woman, for heaven's sake.*

The girl hesitated, looked behind her towards the kitchen, checking that she was unobserved, and shrugged. "Okay then, I suppose."

Laurel had just settled on a picnic bench when her phone rang. It was from a London number, but not one that she recognised. "Laurel Ashworth?" asked a male voice.

"Speaking."

"My name is Rupert Framlingham-Smith. I'm calling from HR at RHO. We received your email this morning."

"Oh, yes," said Laurel, a little surprised. "Sorry, I was expecting Alison to call me."

"She's on secondment to Debt Recovery for three months. It's a head office initiative. I'm the temporary manager's assistant."

'Another bright idea,' Laurel kept thinking, as the stand-in, who sounded no more than an adolescent, repeatedly pressed for a date when she would be returning.

"I'm sorry. I don't know."

"It's very important that there's a responsible person in charge, so that all the necessary reports are filed." Typical head office lackey. Laurel's frustration with the twerp was near breaking point.

"I'm sure that the entire financial framework of the western world isn't going to collapse because one manager of one smallish branch in one corner of London isn't at her desk for a few days. In any case, my assistant is quite capable of holding the fort; and Trefor Rhys, from Knightsbridge, has promised to keep an eye on things."

"That's all very well; but Mr Rhys has his own responsibilities, and we really need a timescale," he drawled superciliously.

First, the girl in the café, now this officious idiot; they summed up Britain in 2019.

"Look, if you're so concerned, you could try to prise your backside off your swivel chair in the bunker you inhabit, get out to the branch, and meet some real customers yourself."

"Oh. I… I don't think there's any need for that," said the voice, in a shaken tone. He was probably going to run home to his mummy after this conversation. However, she could ill afford to get reported for bullying a pen-pusher.

"I apologise," she said, "I've been under a lot of stress." She breathed deeply. "I have an appointment to see the doctor tomorrow," Laurel fibbed, "So I'll probably have a better idea of 'when' after that."

That was how things were left. Laurel realised that she needed confirmation from a doctor that she was not able to work. Tomorrow, she would pop into the health centre and see her father's old GP, before raising merry hell at the lettings' agency. She finished her coffee, then dutifully returned her undamaged cup to the counter.

Later, she began her walk back to St Anne's via the Lowther Gardens, another place that evoked long and deep memories. Every year during the Spring Bank Holiday week, her mother had brought girls here to compete in the annual dance festival, usually commandeering the gents' toilets as a dressing room.

The lawns were fringed with trees in blossom. It was not their scent, however, that infused her senses:

closing her eyes, she could smell the Leichner stage make-up and the Elnett hairspray of the dressing room. She reached the pond, with its fountain formed from the slightly grotesque figure of a Lytham shrimper, the water falling from the tines of his rake. Sparkling in the bright sunlight, the drops of water played on the surface of the pond like golden jumping beans. Mesmerised, Laurel stood there for several minutes, oblivious to everything else around her.

She sat down on a wooden bench, in the very spot where, nearly three years earlier, she had composed the eulogy for her father's funeral. That day, she had sat surrounded by memories, even ghosts; and she had drawn on them for both inspiration and strength. In front of her, on the two bowling greens, men and women were in the early stages of a match; there had been people bowling on that emotional day too.

Laurel reached into her bag for her cigarettes, but her hand initially touched her phone, which had been mercifully and strangely quiet. No wonder: it was switched off. She must have done it after the conversation with the twit from HR. There were three text messages, one from Trefor and two from Maddie. *This should be interesting, Laurel.* Maddie's more recent text simply asked whether Laurel was okay, as she hadn't responded to the first. Next, she read Trefor's.

Met up with your friend Maddie. She didn't seem to need any help from me. Neither of us sure what you meant. Spent an hour chatting though. Told her to call me if… You were right, Laurel — she's quite a peach.

Laurel beamed, her heart racing, unable to wait a second longer to open Maddie's message.

Had a good old chat with T. He's really sweet. And a real gent. Didn't have anything to give me, though. Seemed puzzled. But I got his mobile number.

Excellent.

Laurel was still giggling when, thirty seconds later, her phone bleeped.

OMG!!! Did u set us up?

XXX!

"YES!" Laurel screamed at the top of her voice, punching the air, just as a woman was delivering a bowl from the nearest corner of the green. The bowler turned and glared, uttering an exasperated, "Ooh!" as the wood travelled fast and wide of the jack, finally thudding into the ditch.

"Sorry," said the matchmaker, standing up. "Just had some good news." She walked away briskly, not daring to glance back, but heading through the car park, across the main road and onto the broad expanse of Lytham's famous green, where daisies, white clover and the first buttercups adorned the lush carpet.

Her walk back to the B&B was a happy one. The promenade was temporarily closed beyond the western end of the green, so she took what she had always known as the Sandy Path towards Granny's Bay. There was some more banter with Maddie, which began with a comic threat:

Laurel Ashworth, just u wait!

The next morning, Friday, was dull and drizzly, a suitable day to head inland to Blackburn. Dr Shaw, a kindly man nearing retirement, was both surprised and delighted to see her. He had been her father's GP for many years and seemed happy to reminisce for a few minutes. It was to this room that Laurel had brought her father four years earlier, concerned that he was losing track of what he was doing. The initial tests were inconclusive. "He's borderline. I'll need to have a proper assessment done," the doctor had said.

"So, what brings you here today? I thought you lived in London."

"I do. It's just that…" Laurel hesitated. *Aren't you a fraud? Do you really need a doctor?*

"Go on. I can see that you're tense. What is it?"

Laurel really tried to hold herself together, but the pent-up stress and emotion breached her flood defence. The physician pushed a box of Kleenex across his desk.

"It sounds as if you need a break. It's probably been building up for a long time: your father and work and… Are you with anybody — in a relationship?"

"Don't ask," Laurel replied, managing an ironic laugh as the tears subsided.

"I'm going to sign you off for two weeks. I think you've done the right thing to get away from the bank and from London. Maybe somewhere that isn't loaded with so many memories might have been better, though." He smiled. "Do you have other friends or relatives who you can visit, somewhere different?"

"Apart from a slightly mad aunt in South Wales, not really."

"Well, think about it. And try and do something completely new. My daughter has taken up something called zumba. Heaven knows what it is, but she enjoys it!"

The girl in the letting agent's feigned surprise that Laurel had not been receiving regular payments; as usual, the accountant was blamed. It was only when Laurel mentioned the County Court that a phone call was urgently made, as was a solemn promise that the matter would be dealt with that day.

The sky remained grey, increasing Laurel's gloom. In The Mall, she flicked carelessly through a few rails in H&M; then she took the escalator down into the market, which seemed to have more unoccupied stalls than ever before, and where an Asian stallholder flattered and cajoled her by turns. She had bought from him before and his stock was enormously varied. He was eager to move some lace dresses, in a variety of bright colours; but Laurel escaped, more practically, with a pair of jogging pants and a lightweight jumper, with broad stripes in pastel shades.

Depressingly, she was in the town where she had grown up, yet she did not see anyone she knew. She called up an old school friend and arranged to visit him after work. Joseph was a gay man who lived alone and did not enjoy cooking. By five fifteen, she was waiting in the Italian takeaway near to Cherry Tree station, clutching a bottle of red wine from the Sainsbury's Local nearby.

For more than three hours they sat talking about old classmates, and Laurel was able to pour out her frustrations with her job and her life, especially relationships. Joseph had done some professional training as a counsellor, so he was a good listener; and, with no possible romantic complications between them, Laurel opened up to him.

"What about that good-looking boy you worked with at the bank in Darwen? The one who played cricket. You were always very interested in him, I seem to recall," Joseph said, with a grin. "You used to go out to pubs together, didn't you?"

"Adrian? I haven't seen him for over twenty years. We lost touch not long after I moved to London. To be honest, I was about to look him up on Facebook the other day."

"Yes, I noticed that you'd finally joined the twenty-first century," Joseph replied with mild sarcasm. "And?"

"And what?"

"You didn't look up him?" Joseph said, jokingly. They had spent a good deal of their time at school exchanging double entendres and slightly risqué quips. It was good to be with him again.

"I got cold feet," Laurel admitted, after an embarrassed pause.

"Whatever for? He wouldn't be able to see that you'd looked at his page! You're hardly going to be arrested for stalking," Joseph exclaimed, with mock outrage that Laurel should be so tech-green.

"I don't know. I looked at others. It was just his — I felt... I don't know what I felt: nervous, unsure. Cowardly, I know, but I didn't want to be disappointed."

"Well, he's never popped up on Grindr, if that's what you're worried about," said Joseph, laughing.

"Not that!" said Laurel, throwing a cushion at him.

After batting the soft missile away with his forearm, Joseph looked at her sternly. "Well, what then?"

"I just don't want to rekindle all those ancient memories and the wasted opportunities, only to find that

I'm staring at a photo of Adrian hugging a gorgeous wife and three teenage children."

"I'm not interfering, but you'll never know unless you find out."

Laurel went to the bathroom, knowing that the journey back to St Anne's would take well over an hour. She touched up her powder and lippy, then stared at herself in the mirror. *He's right. Stop being so... so Laurel! Even if he's happily married, you'll be no worse off than you are now.* She would check out Adrian's profile when she arrived back at the Cumbria.

The living room was darkening, but there was enough daylight to see the mischievous grin on Joseph's face. "He's divorced."

"What?"

"Adrian Williams. He's divorced."

As much as Laurel tried to concentrate on the evening landscape through the train window, she could not. Her mind was in turmoil; her stomach was all butterflies. Should she contact him? After twenty years, would Adrian even remember her? Would he want to? After moving to London, she had allowed the friendship to fade. Later, the pain of separation had revealed the depth of her feelings for him. Despite pining, she had made no move to contact him.

She was pleased when, at Preston, she had to focus on walking from the south end of the central platform, down the steep slope and under the tracks to platform one. "Ridiculous, fanciful," she muttered, willing herself to dismiss all thoughts of fanning warmth into what had probably turned from embers to ash many years ago.

By the time she stepped out of St Anne's station, she had convinced herself to drop the whole silly notion. She stuffed the new clothes into her large tote bag, thus leaving both hands free; for she had learned how to protect herself by not looking vulnerable and being able to repel an attacker. Even in St Anne's, she was not going to take unreasonable risks.

Safely in her room, Laurel kicked off her shoes and lay down, phone in hand. No more messages from Maddie. She opened her Facebook. There were messages and friend requests from several people; they could wait until tomorrow. She typed Adrian's name into the search box. A few accounts appeared in a list, the first two were both in the London area. Then, she saw the word 'Darwen'. That must be him. Turning to jelly inside, she tapped the screen.

She stared at the profile photo. It was clearly him, but he had put on weight. The sleek jaw line was flabbier. He worked in Bolton for a firm called Atkinson. There was very little recent activity on his page; and the only other picture was of a cricket team composed almost entirely of middle-aged men. But the one word she wanted to see, yet which somehow frightened her, was plain enough. Adrian Williams was, indeed, a divorced man.

Laurel's finger hovered over the Messenger icon. What on earth could she say? How do you open a conversation with someone you drifted apart from two decades ago? 'Hi, remember me?' Trite. She plugged the charging lead into her phone, and slobbed into the bathroom.

SIX

Saturday dawned bright, the sun warmly streaming through the blind. Laurel sent messages to Maddie and to Trefor, letting them know that she had been signed off for two weeks. Feeling guilty about the twelve-inch pizza the previous evening, she was about to get ready for a run when she noticed that it was already after eight o'clock. And she needed something for breakfast, even if it was just a bowl of cereal.

"So, are you heading back to London today?" Doug asked nonchalantly as Laurel entered the breakfast room. She stood there, frozen for a moment. *Honestly, Laurel, you can be so stupid at times!*

"Actually, would it be possible to stay longer?" Doug breathed through his teeth. "Sorry," she said sweetly, "I've been so busy that it just slipped my mind."

"Yeah, I can do that. I had someone booked into your room for the next two nights. But we aren't full, so I'll move him. I've got five guests arriving today. It's a bank holiday weekend, of course."

"Thanks. I'll get my credit card," Laurel said, turning to leave the room.

"It'll do after you've finished your breakfast." Doug laughed.

After posting off the doctor's certificate, Laurel walked briskly to the far end of North Promenade, her swimsuit in the bag that swung from her shoulder. She returned along the beach, barely slackening her pace. In a seafront hotel, she had a salad lunch; then, she went to reception to pay for access to their pool.

"You take here the lunch, have no need to pay, madaam," the dark-haired, olive-skinned manager assured her, exuding Mediterranean charm. "Is not busy. You wanting the towel?" Laurel patted her bulky bag to indicate she was replete in the necessaries, thanking him. Although the pool was indoors, there was a sunlit outdoor seating area affording a view of the swimmers. To one side was a lounge with large windows, where she read a magazine until she felt ready to swim.

A family was using the pool area. A girl, about sixteen, was sitting in a corner of the overlooking terrace, deeply engrossed in a textbook, probably revising for GCSEs. Her tall elder brother was in and out of the pool; the father had a short swim before returning to the sunny chairs, where his wife was sleeping.

Laurel sauntered through to the changing rooms. Her swimsuit was a scoop-neck one-piece, with a daring Brazilian cut, whose slender V-shape exposed the full curve of her equally slender hips. At the back, the strip of material lodged tightly in the valley between her buns, baring them completely. She turned and glanced in the long mirror. Not bad; the exercises had paid off.

Walking the long way round to her seat, via the sun terrace end, Laurel was immediately aware of being eyed by the portly middle-aged father. Turning, she smiled at him and flicked her hair. *Go on, look.* Detected, the man shifted his attention back to his newspaper, turning a page so hurriedly that he ripped it. His wife, alerted by the sound, momentarily opened one eye.

Laurel slinked to her place, tying her hair in a ponytail. She dipped a toe, then her lower leg into the water before bending down and splashing her front. Warm enough. The young man, swimming smoothly and persistently, completed another length, launching himself back in the opposite direction by pushing his legs against the wall. He glided underwater for a few metres; then, the back of his head appeared above the surface. Laurel admired his elegance and grace as he planed through the water. He passed the only other occupants of the pool, an older couple, who were chatting together, resting their forearms on the edging tiles.

As she had learned many years earlier, Laurel dived sleekly into the water, and began swimming at a leisurely pace. The keen boy overtook her a couple of times. Neither swimmer paid much attention to the other, though Laurel noticed that the father's newspaper had lowered to a position from where he could peer over the top.

After a few minutes, the boy — probably about nineteen — stopped and rested at the shallow end. Still swimming as gracefully as she knew how, Laurel neared him, noting his broad shoulders and his practically hairless chest. His face was handsome. She looked away. It was wrong to stare; and, anyway, he was far too young for her to be ogling. On the return length, however, sheer devilment made her wonder how much the newspaper would start flapping if she, with her almost bare derrière, approached the boy flirtatiously.

Arriving at the terrace end of the pool, Laurel glanced up at the family group. The man, having given up all pretence of reading, was focused on her. This time, he did not avert his gaze when she looked at him; but a moment later, his pleasure was interrupted. "Dad!" The daughter, pausing her cramming, had clocked her father's fascination with the woman in the pool.

Laurel smiled knowingly at them and, using her arms, propelled herself back towards the shallow end, from where the young man lunged forward, breaking into an energetic butterfly stroke. She had only just reached the end of the pool when the athletic swimmer completed his second length.

Climbing the stainless-steel ladder, Laurel squeezed the water from the foam cups of her swimsuit. She was tempted to glance along the pool to see whether

89

Peeping Tom had witnessed that moment, but thought better of it. She wrapped herself in the large towel from the B&B, unbound and shook her hair; then, she settled down into her chair.

The splashing became louder as the tiring boy, arms beginning to flail, finished a sixth length of butterfly. He pushed himself up and out of the pool, shaking the blinding water from his head. Realising he was very near to Laurel, he smiled pleasantly; and it was then that Laurel gave a slight gasp. He was so much like Adrian, the Adrian she had known twenty-odd years ago, that he could almost be Adrian's son. Dark brown eyes, a straight nose; even the jaw line and the chin were similar. Taller than Adrian, this lad was about six foot two. Her eyes flashed across to the rest of the family. No way could the leering father be Adrian unless he had lost his hair and gained far more weight than even his Facebook image suggested.

"You swim very well," Laurel said, alarming herself, not having consciously decided to speak to the boy. And he was, after all, still a boy.

"Thanks," he said, smiling; and, rather embarrassed at being admired by an attractive older woman, he lowered his gaze and headed away to his family.

While the boy was drying his top half vigorously, Laurel lay back and closed her eyes. She saw, in her mind's eye, the young man in her room, dutifully attending his first lesson in lovemaking, nervous as she unbuttoned his shirt, exposing that smooth chest. She saw her hands roaming across its plains, a fingertip toying with one of his nipples. She could feel herself pulling him towards the bed and allowing him to fall onto her. She writhed a little as his virgin breath warmed her neck; and his hands, now eager, instinct aroused, pressed and caressed her satin-draped breasts. In the half moment before their lips met, she opened her eyes. Adrian! This was a sign.

Laurel pushed herself upright, took hold of her bag and shuffled into the changing room. Adrian, Adrian! She dried off and dressed hastily, a woman with a mission. Single-minded for once, she strode back to the Cumbria. Throwing her bag — wet towel, swimsuit and all — onto the floor, she dived onto her bed and opened Facebook.

She keyed ADRIAN WILLIAMS in the search box and jabbed the icon. Selecting the right one, determination trumping apprehension, she started to type.

Hi, Adrian. I don't quite know how to start, and I know we haven't spoken in a long time, but I'm in Lancashire and it would be great to catch up. Would love to see you again.

She deleted the last sentence, and then retyped it. Was it too much? Did it say enough? *Oh, for heaven's sake, Laurel, just hit SEND.*

Laurel dropped the phone by her side, ran her fingers through her hair, leaned back and sighed. It was done, out of her hands now. Whatever happened, she couldn't take it back. What would he think when he saw it? For perhaps a quarter of an hour, she lay in tense anticipation, partly willing the phone to bleep, partly terrified of it doing so.

When the phone did sound, her stomach leapt into her throat. She grabbed it. A message from Maddie. Deflated, yet relieved, Laurel opened it. Maddie was apologising for not replying sooner: she had been busy at work, particularly since some bod from regional office had visited to check that things were running properly in Laurel's absence. That evening, Maddie's band had a wedding gig in Tunbridge Wells.

Hope it goes well, sweetie. Will call you Monday. XX

Laurel felt uneasy at being so laconic, but her mind was elsewhere. Eventually, resigned to not having a swift response from Adrian, she sorted out her bag, had a quick shower, hung her swimsuit from the shower head to dry, opened the bathroom window fully to admit the breeze, and made a cup of coffee. Later, she lay on her bed, rehearsing what she might say to him if he ever answered.

There was still no reply when she checked her phone during breakfast the next morning, for the sixth time since waking up. It had been a nice day yesterday; perhaps, after playing cricket, he had stayed on for a few beers.

Laurel felt that she needed some peace, space and time to enjoy what promised to be another fair day. The first bus that came past the bottom of the road was bound for Lytham, so she rode to the town centre. A peal of bells began nearby; and as she strolled along Clifton Street, it became clear that the tones were ringing from the tower of the red brick church a little further down, on the opposite side of the road.

It was the Catholic church and Laurel had been baptised a Catholic. She had also taken her first Holy Communion and had been confirmed; but that was a long, long time ago. Apart from the odd wedding or funeral, she had not darkened a church door for years. About to turn away, and trying to decide where to walk next, she was alerted by a frail, thin voice.

"Is the road clear, dear? I can't see properly, you know. Only shapes, when they're near to me."

"Shall I help you across?" Laurel asked, offering her arm to the elderly woman.

"Oh, that's very kind of you. Are you going to Mass too?"

"Erm." Laurel hesitated. *Why else would you be hanging around a church in a quiet little town?* "Yes. Yes, I guess I am," she replied, looking carefully before they crossed the road.

Oddly, accompanying this octogenarian seemed a most natural thing to be doing. In leading and guiding her across the road, Laurel was allowing herself to be led and guided, surrendering to the moment. As they entered the nave, a nun took charge of the elderly lady and took her to a front pew. Although politely invited to sit with them, Laurel opted for a safer position, a few rows further back.

Memory kicked in. She knelt, made the sign of the cross and closed her eyes. She had almost forgotten how to form prayers, but she breathed deeply and tried to clear her mind of clutter and external distractions.

Sitting once more, she took in the beauty of her surroundings. The church was nice and light. The stained-glass windows on the south side glowed richly as the sun illuminated the warm colours. As the church was dedicated to St Peter, Laurel reasoned that the balding man featured repeatedly was the ex-fisherman.

The large candlesticks on the altar were probably by Pugin, or at least Puginesque, as were the carved wooden panels that framed and separated the Stations of the Cross. Above the chancel arch, a fresco depicted Our Lady rising to heaven.

Her gaze lowered. Moving into the pew in front was a young woman in a nice dress. She had shoulder-length dark hair, slightly wavy. Her face was cute and pretty, in a Rubens sort of way; her body was curvaceous, even voluptuous, her bottom large and round. Chastening herself, Laurel looked away to her left, where a much smaller woman, seated next to a grey-haired man, was smiling at her.

At the Peace, the petite woman made the effort to leave her pew, crossing the aisle to enfold Laurel's hand between hers. "Peace be with you," the friendly stranger said. Laurel reciprocated and sat down, but then realised that everyone else had remained standing. She rapidly rose to her feet again, wishing the grey-blue carpet would devour her. Furtively, she glanced around. The woman across the aisle smiled kindly.

Unable to make a quick getaway, as people were filling the central aisle, Laurel waited patiently for a gap in the human traffic. The couple sitting opposite moved towards her, the woman handing her hymn book to her husband.

"I don't think I've seen you before. Are you visiting, or have you moved here?" The woman's enquiry, like her smile, was warm and genuine; she had traces of an accent that was not British. Laurel replied that she was staying in St Anne's for a few days.

"I'm Stella, and this is my husband, Don. We've only been coming here for a couple of years. We moved from the Bolton area. A nice Mass. Father David is very good. We like him, *ta'*." The last syllable was uttered with a rising tone, as if to prompt agreement. Her husband nodded.

"I'm Laurel. I'm afraid I'm rather lapsed — dreadfully, actually. I don't really know why I came," she said nervously. The woman maintained an interested posture. "Maybe I needed to get in touch with something. Things have been getting on top of me lately," Laurel volunteered. "I didn't plan to come. I was just in the street and the bells started ringing; and then suddenly an old lady was at my side, needing help to cross the street. And here I am," she added, affecting a grile — something between a forced grin and a smile.

Stella studied Laurel's face with kindliness and also, Laurel felt, with the focus of a trained professional. "Are you here on your own? *Mela*, why not come and join us for a cup of coffee? We usually walk to the park over the bridge after Mass on fine days. There's a little café, with decent coffee; and I love watching the children playing there."

"Oh, the one called Park View? Yes, I know it." The woman, probably about retirement age, trim and little more than five feet tall, seemed truly nice; and the place was pleasant and familiar to her. "Sure, why not? I'd like that."

While Don walked an infirm parishioner home, the women strolled towards the railway bridge. They chatted about Lytham and its attractiveness, especially in the middle of spring; and Stella wondered why Laurel had chosen to stay in the area.

"You've come to find something: something that you think you've lost," the older woman said. Laurel was intrigued by her perceptiveness. "It's written all over your face, *ħanina*."

"We spent so many happy holidays here. A lot of my childhood memories are connected with Lytham and St Anne's. It's strange, but I feel whole again here." Laurel paused to breathe deeply and to smile at Stella, who was nodding in an interested way, like a counsellor pleased that her client is opening up.

"People think Lytham St Anne's is very staid and boring — God's waiting room; but the people here are more... real, I suppose — normal, relaxed; they smile at you." The happy squeals and laughter of young children greeted them as they descended the steps from the road.

"Do you and Don have children or grandchildren?"

"No, darling. No." Laurel detected a crack in Stella's voice. She wanted to kick herself for asking. "I lost two babies," the petite woman explained, crossing herself. "Then, they told me I was unlikely ever to carry to full term. And thirty-five years ago, *mela*," she added, "There wasn't so much science and help available. It was difficult, but we settled our minds to being childless."

"I'm sorry," said Laurel, holding the swing gate open for her new friend.

"We weren't blessed in that way; but we always have children around us," Stella said, her face instantly animated. "Our neighbours have two sweet little girls. I look after them sometimes. They love coming around — Nanna Stella, they call me. If I know they are coming, then I hide a bar of chocolate somewhere; and

97

I leave them a little note with a clue. The older one is very bright, *mela*; I'm having to make the clues more difficult. Don helps me — he's good at crosswords. What about you?"

"Oh, I can usually get through the cryptic ones," Laurel answered glibly.

"No, not crosswords." Stella laughed. "I meant children, a family. Have you had children?"

Guarded for a moment, Laurel hesitated. "Erm, no. No. I couldn't have children either. To be honest, my relationships never lasted long enough to consider it." Another grile.

"And do you regret that?" Stella's eyes seemed like lasers, piercing Laurel's defences. "Forgive me, sweet. It's not my business."

"No, no. It's fine. I don't know, Stella," Laurel said, as they entered the café. "I don't know whether I'd have coped with bringing up kids."

Laurel ordered the drinks, insisting on paying, despite Stella's reasoning that she had made the invitation. They had only just sat down when Don arrived. "Here he is. My toy boy," Stella said, laughing. "You wouldn't believe that he's a couple of years younger than me, *ta'*," she continued, smoothing her husband's ash-coloured hair.

Between them, they related the unusual circumstances of their meeting. Stella was Maltese; she had trained as a nurse and had moved to England during the political unrest and violence of the Mintoff era. She had been working on a ward in a hospital near Manchester when Don was admitted following a serious motorbike accident.

"It was my lucky birthday."

"Sorry, your what?" Laurel asked.

"In Malta, your lucky birthday is when your age is the same number as the date of your birth. It was October the twenty-fourth; and I turned twenty-four that day. He'd been brought in the day before, unconscious most of the time. Everything happened that day. My parents arrived from Malta — a total surprise: they just walked into the ward. And there was Don, one arm and one leg broken; and a face like he'd gone ten rounds with Mohammed Ali. I didn't tell my parents what had happened to him because my brother had been killed riding a motorbike. I didn't want to ruin their day." Stella crossed herself when mentioning her brother.

"We seemed to hit it off straight away," Don continued, putting his arm around his wife's shoulders. "I always looked forward to the time when Stella would be coming on shift. I was almost sad to be discharged; but on that last morning, I plucked up the courage to ask her out."

"I looked up at him and, wagging my finger, I said only if he promised never to ride a motorbike again," she added sternly.

"I didn't, either. Didn't dare to after that!"

As they strolled along a path that led towards Lytham Hall, Stella asked about Laurel's job and the causes of the stress that had culminated in Monday's flight north. "Living in London, too. That would drive me crazy for a start," she sympathised. Then, in a second, she turned and put her hand on Laurel's forearm. "*Isma'*, why don't you come home with us for lunch?"

There was no good reason to turn down the invitation from this pleasant, open, easy-going couple. Laurel thankfully accepted, and they continued walking. Don suggested 'the leafy way' home, through the Witch Wood. Despite her many visits to Lytham, Laurel had never been there before.

"So, how did you come to be living in Lytham?" Laurel asked, settling onto the sofa in the living room.

"We've always loved it here. And we promised ourselves that if the opportunity came along, we'd grab it. Well, about two years ago, shortly after Stella's mother died," Don continued, "I took early retirement from my job as a company accountant. They were restructuring after buying out another business, and the offer was too good to turn down. Now, I do three days a week at a small firm based near the old Preston Docks; easy to get to from here."

Stella explained that they had considered keeping the old family house in Malta as a holiday home; but the Maltese economy had been strong, property prices were high, and someone had been keen to redevelop it. They had added Stella's half of the proceeds to the profit on the sale of their house in Bolton; and they had bought the bungalow in Lytham when Stella retired.

"Would you like an aperitif?" Don asked, opening a door in the centre of a large teak display cabinet.

Stella, who had already gone through to her kitchen, sang, "Yes, please, darling." Don chuckled. "I know you would. I was asking our guest." Using the lowered door as a shelf, he poured a pale-dry sherry into three crystal-cut glasses.

As Laurel received her glass, something standing among the ornaments on the mirrored unit caught her eye. It was a framed and engraved silver plaque, a presentation to Don on his retirement. What piqued her interest most of all, however, was the name of the company: ATKINSON & CO, Bolton. That rang a bell.

"Ah, part of my leaving present," Don smiled. "Thirty-two years I worked for them. These glasses were another part of the gift. Cheers!"

"To a new friendship," Stella said, raising her glass.

"Yes, cheers!" Laurel nodded.

"I think an old friend of mine might be working for Atkinson's," Laurel said, glancing back at Don's plaque. "An old colleague from Darwen. He's called Adrian. Adrian Williams. Did you know him?"

"Adrian! Yes, we know Adrian. In fact, he took over from me when I retired. He'd been my assistant for several years. Darwen, eh? Yes, he still lives in Darwen. Good heavens!"

"*Hija dinja żgħira*, it's a small world," observed Stella, providing her own translation. "*Ara!* Look here," she continued, putting down her glass and reaching for a bundle of photographs that were propped against a Mdina glass vase. She flicked adroitly through the pictures, quickly finding the one she wanted, which she thrust into Laurel's hand.

It was undoubtedly him, taken around the same time as the image on Facebook. There was a second person in the picture, a young girl. Stella noticed where Laurel's attention was focused and the distracted look on her face.

"That's Emily, his daughter. He has two children — well, they're teenagers now, *mela*. The boy is the elder one, but I don't really know him. He can be a bit surly, I think. But Emily, she's a real sweetheart. A lovely girl, but we haven't seen her for…"

"I suppose it must be eighteen months," Don interrupted. "We couldn't go to the Christmas do last winter because Stella came down with the flu. I had to nurse her," he chuckled.

"*Uwejja!*"

Laurel barely noticed what was being said, still trying to process the fact that Adrian was the father of teenagers. She reached into her bag for her phone, begging her hosts' pardon. There was no reply to her Facebook message.

Stella provided a lovely meal, revelling in the opportunity to entertain a guest. When Don opened a bottle of wine, Laurel apologised for not bringing anything. "Don't be silly. After all, we practically kidnapped you." He laughed.

She offered to help with the washing up, an offer that was accepted by Stella, who said, in a stage whisper, "If you bring those things through, we'll talk while Don has his nap."

The kitchen window looked out onto a small garden and, beyond it, the trees of the Witch Wood, their spring leaves enchanted by the sunlight. Stella loved her kitchen, especially on sunny days, as it faced south — home. It was her space and she had decorated it with pictures and mementoes of Malta. The generous area had enabled Stella to have a breakfast bar, with two stools, at one end.

As they washed and dried, they chatted about Laurel's plans and dreams. In the safe environment of this open stranger's home, Laurel was able to articulate her desire for a severance deal from the bank, enough for her to return to Lancashire and start a business. "Just now, I feel as if my future is up here, not in London." Laurel sighed.

"Sit there, and I'll make us some coffee," Stella said, putting away the last of the pans and dishes. While the Maltese woman busied herself with the coffee maker, and Don snored lightly in the next room, Laurel checked her phone for any activity. Two more friend requests, but no response from Adrian. Surely, he had read her message by now. *He doesn't want to know, Laurel.*

"Growing up in Malta in the nineteen sixties, I was brought up on good Italian coffee," Stella said, filling the two cups from an Italian machine. "I can't abide instant. Don drinks Nescafé. Ugh!" She shuddered theatrically, then inhaled the aroma. "Mmm!"

"So, how well do you know Adrian?" Laurel asked, anxious for any information about his recent history.

"We keep in touch. He's been over here a couple of times. He popped in last summer while Emily was playing in a netball match somewhere in St Anne's — she's very good at netball, *ta'*. The divorce was unpleasant. It all happened just before Don retired. We like Adrian a lot; he's a nice man, kind and polite. How long did you work with him?"

Laurel related the story of twenty-odd years before. They had spent lunchtimes together, had gone for drinks every few weeks on a Friday evening; she had watched him playing cricket. And yet, they had never been more than friends. She had been transferred to another branch in Lancashire before moving to London a year later. Eventually, they had lost touch.

"I never met his wife," Stella said. "She never came to the staff parties. I think they weren't happy for a long time. Even Don could tell there was something wrong. We all need to feel loved, *mela*."

Laurel smiled awkwardly. There was a pause, a long pause. Stella put down her cup and studied Laurel's face. "You care about him, don't you?"

"Him?"

"Adrian," Stella said gently, but markedly.

"Erm," Laurel hesitated, defensive. "Well, yes. No — not... I thought I did once, deeply. But that was twenty years ago."

Stella smiled knowingly. "So, why did you ask me about him just now? It wasn't just idle curiosity. I can see it in your eyes." Laurel lowered her head, abashed. She had been read. "And you're both single; and too young to be so. Check your phone, *ḥanina*; he might have replied," the retired nurse urged. There was nothing new. Laurel shook her head. "*Isma'*, if he hasn't messaged you by tomorrow, let me know. I'll give you my mobile number."

Several hours later, Laurel sat at a table, gazing into a glass of Shiraz. Its hue was comfortingly rich, enhanced by the glow of the setting sun. She imbibed generously, almost recklessly, allowing the wine to tingle satisfyingly before it slid down her throat. Drawing deeply on the fresh evening air, she leaned back and closed her eyes. Peace, serenity, wholeness. The breeze gently chilled her bare arm; it was not yet summer. She pulled on her cardigan.

Laurel's mind replayed the remarkable day, not only the novelty of going to Mass, but meeting such a genuinely nice couple there; and the coincidence of Don

105

being Adrian's former boss! She checked her Facebook; still no word from him. Stella, almost carried away by her enthusiasm, had twice made Laurel promise to let her know by Monday evening. *Only a few days earlier, you were playing matchmaker for Maddie.*

She took a more measured sip, reflecting on the momentous week. Exactly seven days ago, lounging on the sofa in her London flat, she had been pouring wine down her gullet while dreading the prospect of another week of stress, targets and infuriating solicitors. She had been a bit irresponsible; but she was single, with no dependants. It was her life; and if she wanted to, she would stack shelves in B&M Bargains at the end of the square; and if she had to, she would rent a one-bedroom flat above a café.

Lighting a cigarette, Laurel realised that it was her first since early morning. She had felt no need, being so occupied and relaxed. Writhing in the smoke, the stress and cares of a week ago drifted away on the breeze. She knew that she would have to face reality: to deal with the bank, and to find a future occupation. Yet, there was a temporary reprieve for her, the next day being a holiday. She could do nothing about the bank until Tuesday.

SEVEN

As bank holiday weather goes, this was normal. The breeze had strengthened into a moderate wind that carried in sharp showers from the Irish Sea. And yet, between the bursts of rain, the sun shone brightly. Laurel made up her mind to take the train to Preston. The shops would be open, affording shelter from the weather.

Laurel wore the longer skirt that she had travelled north in, along with a fairly thick cotton top in spring colours. Without a proper coat, as she hadn't planned to stay this long, she put on her white jacket, making sure she took her umbrella. She messaged Maddie from the train.

How was the gig Sat?

Brill. Booked us for 2 more — one just b4 Xmas.

Great. Heard from Trefor?

Yesterday. Meeting Fri after work. Just for a drink.

Hmm. Excited?

U know me.

She also called a couple who had been friends with her parents, asking if it was okay to pop in and see them. She had last seen them at her dad's funeral. Walking towards the bus station, she was shocked by the number of people who were begging, in a modestly sized city like Preston.

Laurel popped into Booths supermarket for a nice box of chocolate biscuits. In the few minutes that she was inside, towering clouds moved across the sky. The house was only three hundred yards away; she would probably get there before it rained. Wrong. She sprinted the last part as the squall threatened to soak her, but she dried off over coffee and reminiscences.

"After you phoned, we were trying to remember if it's one or two years since your father died."

"It'll be three years next month," Laurel replied quietly.

It was good just to sit and chat for an hour, catching up on their news. On the bus back into town, she mused on how remarkably the human mind manages to bend time: the memories of the people and incidents they had been chatting about stretched back twenty or thirty years, yet seemed like recent events.

Back among the high street stores, Laurel wandered into Debenhams, past some ditsy dresses that looked nice, but felt horrid, even at thirty percent off. Ugh! She shuddered as the chiffon ran through her hand, reminded of an ex: by the end of the three-month affair, just about the only thing they had agreed on was a hatred of chiffon.

Upstairs, in the lingerie department, colours drew the butterfly to a luscious part of the garden: lilac, with swathes of a richer purple and flashes of a deep rose colour, abstractly colouring flowers that were outlined black, like pen and ink drawings. Lighting on a set, she felt its sensuous silkiness, the cami top finished off at the bust with white lace, and matching French knickers.

Excited by the mere anticipation of wearing them, Laurel tossed her chestnut mane confidently, flaunting her femininity as she approached the young man at the till. She felt attractive, smiling as she placed the garments in front of him. Perhaps not wholly comfortable at being stationed in that part of the store, he avoided her gaze. He was dark-haired and quite good-looking, but seemingly inexperienced. *Leave him in the nursery, Laurel.*

Her original urge satisfied, however, she swung lightly out of the store, fully intending to go back to St Anne's and curl up on or in bed, clad in her gorgeous acquisition. *Come on, Laurel, gorgeous for whom?*

Encouraged by the bright sky, she took a walk to Avenham Park. She stood, awestruck, above the lawns that rolled down to the majestic curve of the Ribble, its broad turquoise line bordered by a magnificent avenue of trees. In the large hollow to her right lay the Japanese garden, the architectural shapes of its trees and bushes only trumped by the spectacular palette of their leaves and blossom: dark reds, pinks, brilliant whites and a hundred shades of green.

Laurel sat on a bench close to the top edge of the garden. Sitting two benches away to her right, she noticed a woman with a pretty, pixie-like round face; probably in her late thirties, she had collar-length bobbed hair that was likely mid-brown, but which was lightened by the May sun. Gazing in Laurel's general direction, she smiled; it was a sweet smile that produced dimples.

Not wanting to be obvious, Laurel did an optical sweep of the horizon before glancing back. The woman, too, turned her head away. She had nice round boobs, accentuated by the strap of her shoulder bag that crossed her chest diagonally. Laurel's mouth was watering.

The cute woman was sitting with a man, nearly bald, his remaining ginger hair shaved short. He was not turned towards the woman, but sat looking straight ahead, towards the river. Making several more scans of the scene, Laurel observed that the two made little eye contact. They were talking, but not intently; neither paying much attention to the other.

Laurel, aware that she might have feasted her eyes too long on Cutie's face and boobs, resumed her wider people watch. A jovial-looking black man walked by, talking to a thin, rather eccentrically dressed woman in semi-walking gear. Both in their sixties, they did not appear to be a couple. He was, apparently, a creationist.

"Someone, some great mind sat down and designed all this. Look," he said, gently holding a limb of a white flowering shrub. "Feel," he said, stroking its waxy foliage, and encouraging his disciple to do the same. She said something about Big Bang. "I cannot accept this as random," he insisted. The remainder of his exposition was lost to Laurel as the pair walked on.

Another walker crossed Laurel's line of vision. In her mid-twenties, with a Pomeranian on a pink leash, she was wearing skin-tight exercise pants, which hugged her firm curves. Her boobs stood out, perky and prominent, from a white T-shirt. She was not particularly pretty, but her body was absolutely edible.

Once again, she caught Cutie looking in her direction. Had she clocked Laurel's lustful gaze at Ms Pink Leash? Laurel allowed her eyes to flick over the vista of Cutie's front. Her grey cardigan was pulled part way across her white top, its open edges draped seductively across the centre of each boob. Tempting. Should she? Could she? Laurel turned back to the statuesque line of trees and, above them, the confused sky: blue and cloud.

She waited for a few moments before glancing to her right again. When she did so, she observed a cloud of smoke rising from the other bench, then dispersing. *Way In: pretend you need a light, Laurel.* Grabbing her cigarettes, Laurel stood up, slung her bag over her shoulder, and walked elegantly towards Cutie's bench. However confident she may have appeared outwardly, she was fluttering inside.

"Hi, sorry. Could I borrow your lighter? Seem to have left mine at home," Laurel fibbed.

"Sure," the cardie cutie replied, smiling as she handed it over. *Eye contact: positive.* Standing in the lively afternoon breeze, Laurel managed to light her cigarette at the third attempt. Baldie offered no help.

Laurel returned the lighter, lingering as her fingers slid against Cutie's while performing the simple exchange. It was only a second or two, but it was longer than necessary. And Laurel gazed into the woman's eyes as the transfer happened. Involuntarily, the tip of Cutie's tongue licked her bottom lip. *Very positive.*

"Nice boots," Laurel said, hoping that she had pronounced the word clearly; it was not Cutie's calves that had attracted the butterfly to the flower.

"Thanks. Had them ages; but they're comfy to walk in." Baldie gave a little snort and continued looking into the distance.

"Been shopping?" Cutie asked, nodding towards the Debenhams carrier bag.

"Good old Debenhams. They've got some decent reductions: thirty per cent," Laurel replied lamely. At least, she thought she sounded lame.

"Bought anything nice?"

Bingo! With feigned coyness, Laurel opened the bag, turning her back towards Baldie. It was a girlie thing to share. "I love satin when I'm in bed, don't you?" Laurel said, pulling the cami from the bag to invite Cutie's touch. Her fingers stroked the slinky material, sliding it against Laurel's hand.

"Nice," Cutie said, before suggesting capriciously to the man: "You can take me to Debenhams before they close."

"Okay, if you want," he grunted.

As the women exchanged glances, Cutie shifted along the bench to make room for Laurel. *Opportunity knocks.*

"Husband?" Laurel asked quietly, when Baldie had resumed his tree gazing.

"Boyfriend. Early days, you know. Three weeks," the girl replied.

"Congratulations." Laurel smiled, still curious about the pair.

"Thanks," said Cutie with a slight giggle. *Delve a bit more, Laurel.*

"Previous?"

"Disaster. Both of them. I swore I wouldn't again. But, you know," added Cutie.

Oblivious to the conversation, her boyfriend lit another ciggie. Then, his eyes followed a young girl of fourteen or fifteen, who passed by, holding hands with a boy hardly any older. The girl's buttocks and curves sheened in her tight leggings, and her cropped T-shirt exposed a teasing line of bare midriff. Both women noticed how Baldie's attention had been piqued, and they reciprocated knowing looks.

"Like I said, we've only been going out three weeks," Cutie said almost apologetically. Baldie's stare was following the tight-arsed teeny up the path. *I wouldn't give it much longer if he's into meat as tender as that,* Laurel thought.

"If you don't want to take me shopping, you can buy me a glass of wine," Cutie said, as the three walked towards Fishergate. Laurel learned that her new friend was called Claire, and that she was thirty-seven. Baldie's name was Dennis. Laurel paid little attention to him, partly because he barely merited any. He had little conversation to offer, his teeth were quite goofy, and there was something shifty about him. He had rarely looked at Claire while sitting in the park; even now, his odd utterances were unaccompanied by visual contact. Maybe he was just desperately shy.

Claire, on the other hand, was a sweet, giggly, open woman. She described her job as a lead teacher in a kindergarten. She loved young children.

"Have you got kids of your own?" Laurel asked.

"No," Claire replied, wrinkling her snub nose, "Never been the right time. I was expecting once, with my first husband; but I lost it — her."

"I'm sorry." Laurel replied. *Second time in as many days you've put your foot in it with that question, Laurel.*

"It's years ago," Claire shrugged. "I'm over it; but I would still like kids — even one. You know, just to be a mother."

Laurel did know. At times, she had felt the empty, nagging hunger for parenthood. Claire still had time on her side, though. Just.

"You need to get your skates on, girl," Laurel said smiling. She turned her face from the cute woman towards Dennis. He grunted and eyed up more teenage flesh across the street. What on earth would the spawn of Dennis turn out to be?

"Are you joining us?" Claire asked, as they approached a bar.

"Let me get mine," Laurel offered.

"Don't be silly. You're our guest. He gets paid enough." She laughed. "He's an administrator for the county council."

The bar was not busy, as its regular clientele were mostly professional people from the offices nearby. A couple of oiks were drinking beer at one table and talking loudly about a football match. Three men at the bar, though casually dressed, appeared to be talking business and were focused on some documents. One of them, the only clean-shaven one, caught Laurel's eye; he had dark wavy hair, greying at the temples, and backcombed. Probably married, Laurel decided; he's far too dishy to be single. She smiled back and flicked her hair. *Anyway, Laurel, you've already selected a flower whose nectar you hope to savour.*

Claire plonked herself onto a bench seat in a quiet corner. Laurel thought about sitting facing her, but then decided to slide in next to her, allowing Baldie a better view of the TV screen; the world snooker final was in its second day. Laurel sometimes watched snooker, but the better-looking men had lost in the semi-finals. Neither Judd Trump nor John Higgins really floated her boat; but Dave Gilbert and Neil Robertson — she wouldn't have kicked either out of bed.

Having ordered, Dennis returned, instantly locking onto Judd's break. Claire rolled her eyes, a gesture clocked by Laurel, whose appetite was growing with every glance; and every glance was more lingering than the previous one. She hardly noticed the waitress placing their drinks on the table. The women clinked their glasses; then they talked about Preston, shopping and favourite clothes before they got back to relationships.

"So, what about you?" asked Claire, angling her head seductively.

"Single. Never married. A comedy of errors; with both women and men," Laurel ventured, then anxiously looked at both Claire and Dennis. Had she dipped her toe too far into the water? *Typical, Laurel, suddenly becoming self-conscious!* Dennis was oblivious to everything except Judd's clearance; Claire, taking a good mouthful of wine, had a sparkle in her eye.

Applause from the TV; the frame was won. As the likely winner of the snooker championship went to relieve himself, Dennis did the same.

Laurel took a gulp of wine and slid her free hand along the bench seat. She paused for a moment. *Come on, Laurel, this is it.* Scanning the bar room, she stretched her arm out, so that her fingers alighted on Claire's hand. She sensed the initial tensing reaction, but almost immediately, Claire's hand relaxed and her fingers parted to admit Laurel's between hers. Their eyes surveyed one another's.

"You've got a really cute face, especially your little nose," Laurel said softly. Their heads moved closer together. Laurel's heart was racing. It was that now or never moment; that moment she'd held back from so many times in her life, worrying what people might think.

About to move in for the kill, Laurel was taken by surprise. It was Claire who moved more quickly, planting her lips on Laurel's. The older woman gasped, then recovered, sampling the softness of Claire's lips, moist and fruity from the wine. Laurel gently nibbled at Claire's bottom lip, then raised her head slightly. The lips of both women parted. The butterfly's proboscis explored the petals, then the depth of the sweet dewy flower, their tongues in combat to prove whose was the more eager. An electric tingling coursed through Laurel's whole body.

Seconds passed: ten, fifteen? Who was counting? Then, as suddenly as she had advanced, Claire froze and pulled back. Dennis was standing a couple of metres from the table. For the first time that Laurel could remember, he was looking fixedly at his girlfriend. His face was a study of shock and bewilderment; he was a human statue.

Laurel grabbed at her glass and raised it to her mouth, avoiding eye contact with either of them. The handsome guy at the bar, who had glanced back at Laurel while the women were kissing, gave a rueful smile and shook his head, either in disappointment or reproach.

"Erm, it's not... We just... It just happened," Claire stuttered. Baldie twitched and flinched, unsure what to do. Laurel felt guilty, even rotten, for a moment. How deeply had he been shocked? Had his manhood been rejected? He had returned from the gents to find his girlfriend snogging another woman.

"Come on. Sit down," Claire pleaded. "We were just..." Dennis drained his beer glass, muttered that he would call her later, and left.

"I'm so sorry, Claire. I feel awful," said Laurel. And she did. Claire swigged her Pinot Grigio.

"Oh my God!" She giggled. "Did you see the look on his face?" The giggle became a laugh, which Laurel emulated.

"Well, that got his attention away from the snooker," the barmaid smirked, collecting Baldie's empty glass.

"I need a cigarette," Claire said, heading for a door that opened onto a small garden area. Laurel avoided the handsome guy while walking as elegantly as possible to the toilets. She had no desperate need to go, but neither did she want to sit alone in the bar after the little drama. *Anyway, touch up your lip gloss, Laurel; you'll look more succulent.*

"Do you need another drink?" Claire said when she returned, noticing that Laurel's glass was empty.

"No, thanks. Are you sure you do?" Laurel smiled.

"Not really," the kindergarten teacher said, giggling. Knocking back the remainder of her wine, she added, "One's enough."

Laurel kissed her new friend's ear, whispering, "One? Depends what we're talking about."

When they hit the breezy street, the alcohol hit Claire. "I should have had a proper lunch." She laughed. "That's gone straight to my head." The two walked arm-in-arm along Fishergate, Claire leaning into Laurel's side.

"Where do you live?" Laurel asked. "I'm not inviting myself in, but do you want me to see you home safely?"

"Not far — a few minutes' walk beyond the station," she replied.

"And, yes," Claire added, gazing into Laurel's eyes. "Yes, why not?"

Objective in sight. It was nearly all spoiled, however, when a taxi driver swung around the corner, having to brake sharply to miss them. He shouted some abuse, but Laurel gave back with interest, which set Claire off giggling again. Soon afterwards, in a quieter side street, Laurel felt hungry. Pushing Claire's back against a garden wall, she plunged her tongue deep inside the cute woman's mouth.

They reached a house which, like many along that Victorian row, had been divided into flats. As soon as they were inside the communal hallway, with the front door closed, they kissed again. Passion was running so high that they tried to continue kissing as they made their way up the stairs, but wisdom ruled they should wait until safely on the landing.

"Why don't you put those on while I go to the bathroom?" Claire asked, tugging teasingly at Laurel's carrier bag. Laurel watched her new friend's bum wiggling as she headed out of the living room; but before she disappeared, Claire glanced back and giggled again.

Laurel stripped off, fumbling occasionally in her excitement. Desiring to be perfect when Claire returned, she hurriedly bit through the plastic tag. She felt the satin slinking against her hands. *So, you aren't going to be gorgeous solo, after all.*

She looked at her boobs in the mirror; not bad. She had never been huge, nor had she ever wanted to be, but her B-cup breasts had remained pert and rounded. Her rose-pink nipples were already swollen and hard; and they thrilled to the feel of the cami as it glided over them.

She tossed her pink cotton pants onto the sofa, and pulled up the new French knickers. She had only just pinged them at her waist when the door opened. Claire, stripped to her underwear, was all woman. White and lacy, her thong crowned voluptuous thighs; above it, her tummy was ample enough for the waistband to pinch and create small love handles. Her breasts, which had attracted Laurel in the park, were pushed up into tantalising spheres of flesh, her deep cleavage demanding attention.

Laurel advanced slowly. "You're gorgeous," she said, admiring the moving, breathing, boob-heaving work of art.

"Gorgeous yourself," Claire replied. They kissed again. Laurel could not deny her hands the pleasure of grabbing at the lace-bound breasts, the lace worked into a rose pattern. The butterfly had landed on a most succulent flowering shrub.

Claire's hand went straight to Laurel's pubic mound. "Hmm, you don't beat about the bush," said Laurel, as her new lover pressed the satin, drawing it slowly and sensuously over her smooth mons.

"Not much bush there," Claire answered cheekily. She started to giggle again, and Laurel thrust her tongue deep into Cutie's mouth.

Claire, two or three inches shorter, dragged the willing Laurel to her bedroom. They fell onto the bed, hands, fingers and tongues exploring every contour and crevice.

A full hour later, panting and drenched in perspiration, they settled back on a sheet, its centre soaked with the nectar of their passion. Laurel lit a cigarette and placed it between Claire's lips. Then, she lit one for herself. They lay there, nestled together, blowing smoke rings towards the ceiling.

"God, that was good; the best I've had for ages," Claire said, kissing Laurel's cheek. Then, she giggled. "I could've put a fire out with that."

"Not my fire," Laurel replied tenderly, rubbing her nose against Claire's earlobe. "In the three weeks, have you... with Dennis?" she enquired.

"Twice." Claire exhaled.

"And?"

"Not bad," she said grinning. "He's pretty well hung; but..." She sighed and drew on her cigarette. "He hasn't got me going like that." Clearly, the guy needed training.

"You've got to sleep on this later." Laurel smiled. "Do you want me to help you change the bed?"

Claire shook her head. "It's nearly all mine, I think," she said in a pointedly questioning tone. "Was I not …?"

"You were perfect," Laurel said reassuringly. Their lips met tenderly. "Perfect. It's just that…"

Claire's phone bleeped. Laurel watched admiringly as her lover's breasts settled while she was perusing the screen. *A repeat performance in the near future wouldn't be a bad idea, Laurel.*

"It's a text," Claire said. She seemed unsure whether to check it or not.

"Go on," Laurel said. "It's probably from him."

ARE WE STILL TOGETHER?

Four words. Economical, even for a local government administrator. Claire glanced at Laurel, as if seeking advice.

"It's your call," the visitor said. Claire's chubby thumbs tapped the screen.

SURE, IF YOU CAN HANDLE IT. I WARNED YOU I'M UNUSUAL.

Time to go. The butterfly flicked its lilac wings, shedding their satin sheen. Minutes later, she was dressed and walking back towards the station. At Claire's request they had exchanged Facebook details and mobile numbers. "Call me," she had said, before closing the door.

To get to the platform, she had to climb steps and go over a bridge. Up and down again. Laurel appreciated the irony: still able to taste Claire's piquancy that had gushed over her face. She was on a sexual high, but an emotional low. Again.

It was only when she had made herself comfortable on the train seat that Laurel noticed a slogan at the bottom of the Debenhams bag: 'DOING OUR BIT'. The carrier, apparently, was made entirely of recycled plastic, but Laurel's mind was elsewhere. She had certainly done her bit to brighten up Cutie's afternoon. Would there be a message from Adrian to brighten her evening?

EIGHT

The daylight was fading fast by the time Laurel flumped onto her bed at the B&B. It had been quite a day. She imagined Cutie remaking her squirt-soaked bed; and her olfactory memory recreated Claire's sweet and heady scent.

Her phone alerted her to a message. Adrian? No, just Maddie saying that she and her younger daughter had been on a shopping trip to Bluewater, with photos of a dress and a summer jacket she had bought.

Nothing from Adrian. He isn't interested. He moved on a long time ago. Why would he want to be bothered? Probably far too busy as a single parent, with a daughter who needed ferrying to netball matches. And the son didn't sound much fun. Maybe he was having problems. *Aren't you just daydreaming, Laurel, wishing things and time undone? Just acting out a plot in your head, as though you're part of some lame Hollywood rom-com. Drop it, Laurel. Plenty more fish.*

She took a gulp of coffee. For the second time in a week or so, she found herself asking the same question: 'What is it that you do want?' Two hours after having the hottest sex for a long time, with the delicious Claire, why was she moping over a man she had not seen for two decades?

Stella! If only out of politeness, she must text Stella. Laurel had not been chased for an update; she realised that the Maltese woman was too wise to interfere pushily.

Hi Stella, Thanks again for yesterday. No news from Adrian. Guess he doesn't need another woman in his life.

Laurel, sweet. A good woman is EXACTLY what he DOES need. Shall I message him?

Laurel paused and laughed. *As a devout Catholic, you wouldn't have called me a good woman if you'd seen me three hours ago!* Thinking more deeply, however, she realised that the perceptive Stella would hardly have befriended her and offered to help if she was beyond hope.

Why not, if you don't mind. Sorry it's so late. I was in Preston.

No problem. Only watching TV — Brexit again! Will do it now. Fingers crossed.

During her morning run the next day, Laurel resolved to try a partial detox. She would keep off the alcohol for a couple of days. Declining Doug's offer of an English breakfast, she plumped for a mini-box of Special K and unbuttered brown toast. Still, there was no need to be totally ascetic, she convinced herself, as she spread some raspberry jam very thinly across the bread.

After the roughage of the cereal and the wholemeal toast, Laurel needed a refill of coffee. As she stood up, the only other guest in the room, a balding man of around sixty, cast his eyes in her direction. While replacing the coffee pot, she accidentally dislodged a cereal packet, knocking it to the floor. She bent down to retrieve it, which took a few seconds, because it had landed some way under the table. Laurel became keenly aware that the man was leering at her bum. Still crouching, she turned her head so quickly that he had no time to react. Caught!

"I… I'm sorry," he mumbled, his face flushing. "Can't resist a well-formed bottom."

Standing up, Laurel said, "Me too." Puzzlement momentarily crossed his face. Should she extinguish his little flame? "Especially one in a tight skirt," she added coquettishly.

"Ah!" About to make a further observation, but too embarrassed to do so, he returned to his breakfast. Had he been twenty years younger and drop-dead gorgeous, Laurel might have offered him a more tactile appreciation of her derrière.

The morning was cool, with the threat of showers, so Laurel washed some clothes at a nearby launderette. Waiting outside, she had taken two long puffs on a cigarette when she remembered her resolution to cleanse her insides; she absolved herself, reasoning that there was precious little to do during a wash cycle.

A pleasant man in his thirties wished her a good morning as he arrived to open his printing shop. She strolled along the parade a few moments later and noticed that he also made roller banners. Perhaps she would have one made that read, 'GOOD WOMAN AVAILABLE FOR LOVE.' She could erect it opposite Blackpool Tower, or at one of the main London stations, and see what luck she had. Stubbing the ciggie on the nearest litter bin, she glanced at her phone once again. Nothing.

There was still no reply when she checked after returning to the room with her clean laundry; nor after she had put it all away; nor when she had changed out of her running pants into her long skirt. She stuffed her swimsuit and a towel into her bag, intending to have a healthy lunch and a swim at the hotel where she had been a few days earlier.

The olive-skinned manager was hovering behind the counter, which made Laurel suspect he had a thing for the blonde receptionist. Smiling at the girl first, Laurel addressed the man directly, reminding him that he had kindly allowed her to use the pool on Saturday.

"Of course, madaam," he replied, grabbing a leaflet from a plastic holder. "But if you are staying longer in St Anne's, why you not take a room here? I can make you very good price, even with the sea view."

"Well," Laurel began, "I have to go back to London in a few days, but I'll certainly bear you in mind the next time I come up here." A fib, but with the sole intention of avoiding further pressing. It failed.

"And you know, madaam," the keen manager continued, thrusting more information into her hand, "We have the spa, with all kind of treatment for the beautiful laidees; and the sauna, Jacuzzi, the gym — I can make you special membership. Just come and see me; and we have the good deal, no?"

Eleven out of ten for charm and effort, but this guy would be trying to sell her the entire hotel by mid-afternoon. The fitness classes looked interesting, however. Laurel nodded and, thanking him, moved on into the bar. Her mouth watered as a home-made burger was carried past her, but she subdued the temptation, ordering a grilled chicken and avocado salad instead. In any case, she'd have to wait even longer before swimming if she stuffed herself.

Before and after lunch, Laurel checked her phone. Nothing from Adrian. Facebook had flopped. *Work, Laurel: the bank; your job.* Although the doctor's note would cover her for another ten days, this was a situation that she had to deal with.

Having checked with Maddie that everything was okay at the branch, she emailed a request for a meeting with the regional manager, rather than going through young Fartington-Smith, or whatever his name was. Her room at the Cumbria was paid for until Saturday morning, so she suggested any day the following week. She would travel to London over the weekend.

Laurel spent the next half hour mulling over the various possibilities and potential outcomes of her meeting at regional office. Could she negotiate a reasonable severance package for herself, or would she be more open to staying on, having had a break from work? Would she accept a different job within the bank? Or did she really, truly need to walk away? Was her visceral reaction last Monday her honest feeling about the bank? Was it over? If so, what would she do?

Emerging in her slinky swimsuit from the changing rooms, Laurel noticed that the older couple she'd seen on Saturday were in the pool. They were celebrating their ruby wedding and his retirement. Laurel congratulated them both as she slipped into the water. The man swam a circle of a few metres in a doggy-paddle style.

"We came here for our honeymoon. He wanted to take me to Spain, but I was scared of flying at that time — all them hijackings and crashes. No way was I getting on a plane unless the RAF flew with us all the way." Laurel smiled. "Any road, you came in for a swim, didn't you? Don't let me stop you."

Laurel swam a few lengths, taking care to time her stroke in order to avoid a collision with the woman, who was moving in a laboured fashion across the pool. After a rest, she changed to backstroke. Feeling she had done enough, Laurel hoisted herself onto the poolside.

"Oof," the woman panted, stroking her ample belly as she climbed the ladder, "I've gained a fair few pounds since that honeymoon. We both have. You want to see our wedding pictures — he was as thin as a rake!"

They invited her to sit in the lounge, and Laurel was persuaded to try a scone and strawberry jam with her tea. What is it about deciding to go on a strict regime? Someone always comes along and leads you off the straight and narrow. *Relax, Laurel, you've just swum twenty lengths — four hundred metres. One little scone won't hurt.*

"It's more modern and probably a bit cleaner than it was forty years ago," observed the woman, glancing around. "But it's lost something — the family touch. Still, we're having a good time, aren't we, Jack?" He nodded. She leant towards Laurel and winked confidentially, "Rekindled his flame."

"Good for you," Laurel replied. "I wish someone would do the same for me. I'm trying to fan the embers of an old fire, but I'm not getting far."

"Well, keep fanning," the woman advised. "When did you last see him?"

"Twenty years ago."

"Twenty! No wonder it's hard work! The fire's probably gone out by now." She cackled.

"It was never really a fire; we weren't much more than colleagues and friends. He was fairly quiet; and I was too afraid of taking the next step and scaring him away. There was one night, the last time we met... And

I just lost my nerve." *Why on earth are you revealing all this to two strangers, Laurel?*

"Well, if it's meant to happen, it will," the woman concluded.

Laurel insisted on paying for the tea and wished them a happy end to their second honeymoon. The effervescent manager was not around when she passed the reception desk. Phew! She paused in the foyer to check her messages. A reply from Maddie and one from regional office. Nothing from Adrian. The woman had been right. The fire was dead.

Through heavy drizzle, Laurel strode back to the Cumbria, where she opened the email from regional office. An appointment had been arranged for next Tuesday, 14th May, at ten o'clock. Would she please confirm. She did so in one sentence, relieved that it was fixed. All she had to do over the next week was to make up her mind what she wanted.

Laurel Ashworth stood in the car park, drawing heavily on a gasper while gazing into the clearing sky. She would take charge of her future; she would be strong, logical and clinical; she would reassess her priorities, and formulate plans and goals for the next five or ten years; she would put Adrian and the other lost hopes behind her and move on.

Flicking through the TV channels, she found a documentary about an inside job bank robbery. It reminded her of the Friday afternoon when she had been asked to break the bank rules and deliver one set of the dual control keys to Adrian, who was on leave at his home, while she was in possession of the other half of the keys. A total no-no, but she had been the only one with a car. On the way up to his house, she had briefly thought of nipping back to the bank, emptying the safe and disappearing to Spain with the loot. But Friday was a paying-out day and there was never much cash in the safe over the weekend. Afterwards, laughing at the ludicrous breaking of the bank's protocol, they had jokingly planned a getaway route.

In those days, Laurel had never been prone to taking risks. Her mind drifted back to a scene in a pub car park, the last time she had seen Adrian. It had been one of those moments in life that requires blind faith, standing on the edge of a chasm, knowing that the leap might end in the disaster of rejection, but that the prize might be happiness and fulfilment. Trembling, wanting, willing something to happen, she had ultimately stepped back into safety, into the coldness and aloneness; she had let him go away and out of her life.

The decision to stay safe, avoiding risk and hurt, had proved more damaging and painful than any rejection, for the self-recrimination and regret had been an open sore for twenty years. Eventually, gradually, she had learned from the experience: had she not dared to seduce a woman in front of her partner only yesterday? But she was still unfulfilled, tormented by an aching void.

Laurel was roused from semi-consciousness by a message alert. She groped lazily along the bed until she located the device. It was probably only Maddie. Squinting at the screen, she let out a gasp. ADRIAN WILLIAMS.

Fumbling nervously, she read the text.

Had a message from you, but I didn't recognise your name or photo. A friend, Stella, called me last night and said she had met you. I see we've worked for the same bank, but can't remember anyone called Laurel. Sure you're contacting the right person?

Of course, Stella only knows me as Laurel. But surely, he could work it out. Maybe not Adrian: a really nice guy, but not much imagination.

Haven't you read my profile? Not enough clues? We used to talk cricket — even watched you play a few times. We used to go out to pubs in my car Friday nights.

She bit her lip and added another clue.

Bringing both sets of dual control keys to your house???

She clicked on the 'send' button. And waited. The air was loaded; her hands were shaking. It seemed like hours before the phone burst into life again.

JEEEEEZ, Lawrence. Is that you?

PART TWO

Butterflies have developed several passive methods of protection; they may become inconspicuous by using camouflage.

NINE

That WAS me, yes! This is me now. Sorry for the shock!

There was another long pause before the next message arrived.

I can't believe it! What happened?

Well, they lopped some bits off here and enlarged other bits there — and you won't believe what they used my scrotum for!

Laurel was about to hit 'SEND', but reflected on the content. She deleted the last phrase. After all, if she was serious about renewing this friendship, taking it where she had not dared when they were in their twenties, she ought to be less flippant and more sincere. She added another paragraph.

Getting away from home helped me find my real self. I used to stare into the mirror, realising something was wrong. I started to experiment with make-up and a wig and the right clothes. After trial and error, gazing at my reflection, I felt different, lighter, right. So, I talked to doctors and other people, started transitioning — testosterone blockers, oestrogen, dressing and living as a woman. Finally, the surgery. Don't ask about the pain! But I found myself.

She swallowed hard before adding a final thought.

And twenty years after losing touch with you — through my own stupid fault — I've found you too. I'd love to meet up.

No, Laurel. Too heavy, too much. Delete.

Would be really nice to meet and catch up while I'm up here. Have to go back to London early next week.

Laurel paced nervously up and down the bedroom. Why was he taking so long to reply? She filled the kettle. Something stronger needed. She looked at her watch. The off-licence around the corner would still be open; detox can wait. When she arrived back, a few minutes later, there was a reply waiting for her.

Wed. no good, netball. The same on Sat. Fri evening? Meal? Where are you staying? Do you have a car up here?

Although booked at the Cumbria until Saturday, she could hardly expect Adrian to drive thirty miles to the coast; and she didn't want to have to rush away to get the last train back to St Anne's. She asked Joseph if she could kip at his place Friday and maybe Saturday, until she went back to London. That sorted, she told Adrian where she would be staying.

Pick you up from there at 7 Friday. We'll have dinner somewhere.

It was done. All aquiver, her brain spinning, she shakily filled a mug with wine. It was only when she sat down that she realised how terrific a shock she had probably given Adrian. Never mind her own jitters! After no contact for twenty years, his former colleague Lawrence had suddenly shown up on his Facebook — as a woman!

Nicely brought up, Adrian, in his twenties, had been fairly quiet and well mannered, with none of the rough womanising binge-drinking qualities that many young men boasted; he was neither gregarious nor overtly macho. When the office talk had got a bit sexual, Adrian would usually smile and get on with his work. He had always been well turned out, his dark brown hair tidily cut, clean shaven. He was slightly taller than Lawrie and more than passably good-looking, though he would have modestly blushed had anyone remarked so. Maybe he had presented as a little vulnerable, not hardened by experience.

With shared interests in cricket, real ale and music — Adrian played the classical guitar quite well — they

141

had gone out about once a month, chatting about sport, beer, holiday trips and colleagues. Like many young men, however, they had rarely ventured into such dangerous territory as emotions, sexuality and gender. Why had that been so?

Sipping her wine, on the bed in St Anne's, Laurel could not recall any single moment when she — or he, as Lawrie — had first been aware of an attraction to Adrian. Nor could she remember ever having sexual thoughts about him; the romantic feelings, the dawning that there might be an unrequited love, had only become evident and acute after moving to London. How had she reached the point of hoping, as a woman, to win a guy she had failed to win in a cack-handed attempt as a young man?

Her thoughts took her back to one night, after seeing a pantomime. Little Lawrence, aged eight, had lain in bed, the scenes fresh in his memory, and had snuggled down, imagining that he was one of the characters: not Buttons, or even Dandini, but Cinderella. As imagination slipped into dreaming, night after night, he wore the drab, patched-up dress, swept the kitchen floor and, ultimately, was transformed into a sparkly-gowned, tiara-wearing princess, dancing with her Prince Charming, whose velvet tunic was short enough to show off a pair of gorgeous legs in white tights. Alone in that safe, small bedroom, young Lawrie had stepped into a world halfway between wake and sleep, between reality and make-believe; halfway between male and female.

There had been other influences, too, of which the greatest, perhaps, was Mum's ballet school. Leotards, tutus, tights had been ever present around the home. At festival times, these were supplemented by costumes, the magic enhanced by the smell of Elnett hairspray and make-up, especially the old-fashioned Leichner sticks that his mother had applied to little girls' faces. The effect, both cute and glamorous, had made Lawrie wish to look like that too.

Aged about ten, Lawrie, together with a schoolmate and the boy's slightly younger sister, used to make up little plays and perform them to their mothers. One day, the girl had moaned about being bored with playing the princess. "Just because I've got long blonde hair. Let me be someone else."

Lawrie had volunteered to swap roles and, after they had got over the bashful giggling, the girl had gleefully thrown to him her beige ribbed tights and a dress. It was the first time he had put on a pair of tights. They had felt wonderful.

"Whatever made you want to dress up like that?" his mother had asked in a prickly voice on the way home.

"Harriet didn't want to be the girl," Lawrie had answered, half honestly. Had he been able to articulate the whole truth, it might have eased the journey to self-discovery over the ensuing years.

"Well, I don't think your father would approve," she said.

It was only much later in life that Laurel realised this had been a kind of projection: Mum putting her own doubts and prejudices onto her husband, who would turn out to be surprisingly relaxed about Laurel's decision to transition, shortly after Mum's sudden death.

Only months after the ribbed tights incident, young Lawrie had another shock, whose visual impact remained seared on his memory. He noticed one day that his thighs had become fatter, and that mounds of soft flesh had developed on his chest, together with puffy pink nipples. Changing for the next PE lesson at school, he had peeped at other boys' chests. His was different. In innocent confusion, he had panicked, wondering if he was changing into a girl. His nipples had remained that way; and at secondary school he was very self-conscious about his chest, envying the flatter brown ones of other boys.

In his early teens, he started spelling his name 'Lori' on his written work, until admonished by a teacher. "You're not the manliest boy in the school as it is; if you spell your name that way, they'll treat you like a sissy," the former army captain had warned him. "Nicknames acquired at school stick with you long afterwards," the red-faced, moustached man, aka Captain Mainwaring, had added sternly.

When Aunty Hilda moved away to the south of England, the ballet class was suddenly without a pianist. Lawrie, having reached grade six, was asked to step into the breach; so, his world became increasingly centred on the ballet school, tights and prettiness. He had never been laddish, nor rough and rugged.

"You should have been a girl," his mother would say, always in a mildly joking way; but it was a phrase Lawrence became used to.

There had been the occasional flashpoint during Lawrie's mid-teens. During a dance festival at Lytham, two little girls had come to him in a panic, asking where his mother was, as they had to be hurriedly made up for their next dance. One child's mum, thinking on her feet, said, "If I do my Zoe's, can you copy and do Cathy's?"

More concerned with being helpful in a tight situation than anything else, Lawrie followed the instant tutorial successfully. Naturally, the nine-year-old girl revelled in the close attention of a tolerably good-looking sixteen-year-old boy and went through every flirtation she knew.

"What on earth are you doing?" Lawrie's shocked mother asked, as he was finishing the child's lips.

Zoe's mum explained, adding, "Hmm, hasn't done a bad job, has he?"

While the little girl was admiring herself in the mirror, her teacher paused long before saying, "You should have come and found me. It's not something for a boy to be doing."

No more was said, and Lawrie had never been able to understand what he had done wrong, or why there had been long awkward silences in the car during the drive home to Blackburn. Perhaps, he concluded much later, his mother had already recognised the danger signs of her son being around make-up.

Laurel yawned. It was after eleven. After using the bathroom, she nestled herself into the bed. Forty years earlier, as Lawrence, she had pulled the blankets snugly to her neck and dreamed of being Cinderella; tonight, she would go to sleep hopeful that dinner with Adrian might be the beginning of her own happy-ever-after story. *Laurel, you might just be on your way to the ball!*

In the same positive spirit, Laurel limbered up the following morning, more determined and focused than ever. As she ran, she formed a strategy: she would not get herself into a tizzy, like a fifteen-year-old schoolgirl asked out for the first time; she would play it cool on Friday evening. After all, she had to return to London on Sunday or Monday. All being well, she would be laying the foundations of something.

She was not alone in feeling chipper. Doug, effusing superlatives in the breakfast room, was excitedly regaling a guest with the highlights of Liverpool's astounding four—nil win over Barcelona the previous evening. His only regret was that he had been unable to get to Anfield.

"Full English, Laurel?" Doug chimed cheerily, re-enacting the quickly taken corner that had produced the crucial fourth goal. "Sure. Why not?" she replied, not wishing to dampen the mood. *Hold the detox, Laurel; just do without lunch.*

Out on the pier's breezy deck, she tried to rationalise her future. *What kind of business would work, Laurel?* The tempting notion was to focus on what St Anne's did not have; but she knew professionally that one of the first rules of lending money to a 'new business idea' was to ask why nobody was already doing it. She noted, too, the demography of the main square. Retail was clearly under pressure, much of it seasonal; the rag trade was sufficiently supplied. If she chose the food sector, she would need a chef or a cook. Add value to something extant, Laurel; maybe make the music-loving Frenchman an offer.

She sipped a large cup of baroque coffee while observing Patrick's clientele: what they ordered and, particularly, how much they spent. Customers, generally elderly, trickled in and out, with few spending more than a fiver. Some pushed the boat out and chose cottage pie or eggs and chips from the limited selection; most opted for a sandwich, toasted or not, and a beverage. At one point, the harpsichord music gave way, somewhat racily, to operatic arias.

"Hi, kiddo. It's your Aunty Hilda." As if she needed to add the second phrase! Hilda was the only person who ever called Laurel 'kiddo'. "I tried to call you at your office, but they said you were off sick. Are you OK?"

147

Laurel, sitting in the rose garden, explained that she just needed some time away from work, in a different environment.

"I keep telling you, don't I? You work far too hard. You always did. I'm surprised you're still in St Anne's, though. Where are you staying?"

"Well, most nights I sleep under the pier," Laurel began.

"Go on with you," said Hilda, laughing. "You could have come here and slept on the sofa bed. But you were always fond of St Anne's. That's why I'm calling, really, to thank you for the card."

"You didn't need to phone my mobile for that, Aunty. It's expensive."

"Well, you know me, kiddo. It's nice to have a chat. And living alone, you know…" She tailed off to a pause. "Actually, I've been quite busy. I have a new friend, a woman from the church. She's the one who drives me home. She's in the little choir, sings quite nicely too; alto, but not heavy." As Hilda barely stopped to draw breath, it became clear that the main reason for the call was to talk about her friend.

"She's a pleasant woman, and I can't help feeling sorry for her. She's been abandoned by her husband. He's taken up with a younger girl doing some research at the university, supposedly." The last word was given barbed intonation. "I told her, Rosemary — my friend — it'll just be a flash in the pan; one of them will soon get bored with it. What is it with middle-aged men?

They become like teenage boys again, thinking with their you-know-whats instead of their brains." Laurel shattered the tranquillity of the rose garden by shrieking with laughter.

"He'll soon be back, I told her, once he gets tired of paying the bills on her flat. And she's quite a good-looking woman, Rosemary is. A little plump; well, you know, curvy. Ooh, should I be saying that?"

"Why not? She's your friend," Laurel assured her.

"Well, you haven't met her, have you? And she likes to talk. If it's fine, we walk along the cliffs after Sunday lunch; and we just talk. She's good company — intelligent, educated. She used to have a little bookshop, but she had to close down. She started coming to church again after many years away, just to have a social life, I think."

After saying goodbye to her aunt, Laurel returned to contemplating her future. A bookshop, a small café, a hairdressing salon in a town like this, all traditional businesses steadily becoming less remunerative. She would have to think harder if she were to invest her capital in something that provided a living.

It was hardly focused strategic planning, however. Her thoughts kept roaming back to Adrian, no matter how much she tried to rein in her nervous excitement. What should she wear on Friday? It was difficult to decide, not knowing where he was planning to take her. Probably nowhere too swanky. The one worry she did not have was wearing the same outfit as she had on the last evening they had spent together!

Later that evening, Laurel got a text message from Stella, suggesting coffee the next morning. She smiled at the Maltese woman's tact; Maddie would have been far more direct, pestering until supplied with all the gen: 'Did he call you? What did he say? Where's he taking you? How are you going to play it?'

Would love that. Had a text chat with A last night. Tell you all about it tomorrow.

She would keep Stella in suspense for another twelve hours or so.

"Look at you!" Stella squealed with delight, as Laurel entered Caffe Nero. Going onto demi-pointe, she kissed the younger woman on both cheeks. "How radiant you look, *ħanina!* So different from Sunday! Come, tell me everything."

Laurel, who could not help laughing at Stella's girlish enthusiasm, summarised her Messenger chat with Adrian, concluding, "So, we're having a meal on Friday evening. Do you think I should wear a dress?"

"*Mela*, wear whatever you're comfortable in. Smart casual. He'll probably be wearing an open-necked shirt and a jacket; and I expect he'll take you somewhere like a nice pub in the countryside, rather than anything exotic. I know he has very traditional tastes in food, like Don."

Replying to Laurel's enquiry, Stella said that Don was working. "So, I have the morning to myself; then there's a bowls match in Kirkham this afternoon. A friend is picking me up at one thirty. Talking of being picked up, where is Adrian going to meet you tomorrow? And how are you going to get back here?"

Laurel explained carefully about Joseph and her arrangements for the weekend. "Do you think I ought to tell Adrian about him being gay? He might not remember from all those years ago. It'll sound odd that I'm moving from here to stay with one man, but going on a date with another."

"Just say that you're staying with an old friend. Adrian isn't very sympathetic with all that; he's quite conservative in his views. If you don't mention a name, he'll naturally assume your friend is a girl."

"Have you spoken to Adrian since Tuesday night?" Laurel asked, anxious to know exactly what information he and Stella might have exchanged.

"No, I haven't. He simply replied to my message, saying he would contact you. If I'd followed it up, it would have looked like we'd been plotting the whole thing." Stella smiled. She really was quite astute, Laurel realised.

"Do you think he'll tell his kids that he's meeting me?"

"You're like a butterfly in the garden, nervously flitting from one flower to another," said Stella laughing while placing a calming hand on Laurel's. "One question, one aspect of tomorrow, to another."

Laurel sighed, "I've been trying not to get overexcited, but I want to get it right, Stella."

"You will, *ħanina*. Just stay calm and collected." Pausing, she looked earnestly at Laurel. "*Mela*, it's natural to feel excited about a date; but don't expect too much. It's been a long time; and it's come right out of the blue for Adrian. After all those years, it must have been quite a shock when he got your message, *ta'*."

Laurel smiled; but inwardly, it felt more like a smirk, as she thought, 'Yes, and you don't know half of the shock he's had.' It did not seem the right moment to tell her. Far more important was how to prepare herself for tomorrow evening.

TEN

When she woke the next morning, Laurel felt drowsy. She couldn't recall her sleep being fitful, but she wasn't well rested. Had her brain, weary of being told not to get excited about Adrian, rebelled overnight? She spent ages trying to decide what to do, what time to leave for Joseph's, whether to go for a run or a long walk, glancing between the leaden sky and the weather app.

She had a quick shower and, dressed in her pastel jumper and joggers, took the bus to Blackpool. Returning three hours later, with nothing more than a dark blue scarf and a set of bangles, she climbed a St Anne's sand dune, where she munched her salad in the breezy sunshine. After eleven days here, this would be her last lunch on the Fylde coast for a while. She recalled her first evening, an escapee from the bank, enjoying her 'freedom meal.' Then, she had been running away; now, she was heading towards... *No, Laurel, don't get all silly. It's just dinner with an old friend.*

On the train, Laurel tried to analyse the history of her twenties, especially around relationships. Lawrie had dangerously allowed himself to be seduced by a fifteen-year-old boy, a pupil at the ballet school, their occasional trysts narrowly avoiding detection. There had been girlfriends too, some of the relationships passionate and physical; others so tentative that they had never reached first base. None had endured for more than six months.

Lawrie had developed itchy feet, partly due to ongoing doubts about sexuality and gender. His parents' home had become like a psychological open prison. He had started to wear make-up and more androgynous styles, but had often got cold feet about entering bars and clubs. The odd proposition had come from some sad, overweight bloke in his fifties or sixties, the type that Lawrie waspishly nicknamed 'Ichabod.' One evening, getting ready to meet Adrian, Lawrie had discreetly made up his eyes with liner, the darkest shade of a 'nude' palette, and mascara. If he had noticed, Adrian had said nothing.

Was that, Laurel wondered, the evening when they had chatted about buying together a house that was being repossessed? The bank wanted very little for it, easily within their reach. Although the three-bedroom terraced home was in Burnley, Adrian had been open to the idea; the drawback was that he could not drive, which meant a long train journey. If only…

And so, with mounting irritation at home, believing that he would be breaking out of the cocoon to spread his still youthful wings to attract whoever they might, Lawrie had seized the opportunity of moving to London, where the bank needed more staff. Despite a bigger swarm of potential mates, however, it had been difficult to form solid relationships.

During the first few years in London, he had rented a room from an elderly couple, who had a garage but no car. Every six or eight weeks he drove home for the weekend; if possible, he took a half day on the Friday, enabling him to set off around two o'clock. Normally, he would call Adrian at the beginning of the week and arrange to meet up on the Friday evening.

Their last meeting had been on such an evening, six weeks before Christmas, and their first time together for months. It was chilly, slightly foggy; damp and dank, but not actually raining. Adrian had suggested meeting at a pub called the Handel's Arms, at Eccleshill, just outside Darwen.

The mood had been more tentative than usual. Was life taking them in different directions? Were they doing this as a mere ritual? Or, Laurel thought, years later, was it because their expectations had been different? But they sat down with a pint each, talking and catching up on gossip and minor scandal from the bank.

A live Premier League match drew an animated crowd into the bar. Adrian was not much interested in football, Lawrie a little more; but he was trying to focus on Adrian's words and ... yes, on Adrian. Lawrie had missed him; he tried to discover whether Adrian had found a girlfriend, a boyfriend even? His probing questions had been deflected, or answered in a noncommittal manner. Adrian had other acquaintances, clearly; but there seemed to be a void in his life.

As they sat there, mellowing comfortably, at a corner table, Lawrie realised that the aching gap in his own life was sitting opposite. But how to approach it? The background noise swelled as the second half of the match got more tense. Lawrie's unease and apprehensiveness mounted as the conversation dwindled or turned back to meaningless stuff, only half heard above the din.

They even thought about going elsewhere; but the game ended, and most of the football drinkers moved on. Two of them remained, however, and the bank clerks became briefly involved in their conversation about the respective vicissitudes of Blackburn Rovers and Bolton Wanderers.

The evening was wearing on. Lawrie's mind refocused on Adrian, rehearsing possible lines. 'Why not come down to London?' No, too direct. Eventually, Lawrie bit both his lip and the bullet, and he asked, "Have you thought about working in London? They pay more there. We could find a small flat to share — remember we once talked about buying a house." He trod carefully, not wanting to cause alarm. There was none; Adrian ummed and ahhed a bit, then became quiet again. Had Lawrie gone too far?

They left the pub before chucking-out time. Outside, the cold air was still and dense; frost was forming, and they watched their breath mingling with the fog.

Adrian was quiet as they walked, but he had never been garrulous; Lawrie was a bag of nerves and confused urgency. How long would it be before he saw Adrian again? If he didn't express his feelings and stake his claim tonight... Yet, he was wary of making the wrong move and destroying the friendship. They sauntered to the car, Lawrie dragging his feet, weighing up the odds, risk and reward.

Only yards from the car, time, distance, everything was closing in. Lawrie was desperate to say something. What, though? Was it love? Was it affection? Or longing? How could he put this visceral thing into words that made sense in this context?

They reached the car, and they stood facing one another. Lawrie needed to touch him, to tell him... to kiss those gentle lips. Yes, those manly, but not rugged features that framed those kind dark brown eyes. The air, time, everything hung there, pregnant. Lawrie felt his mouth going dry. Could he? Dare he? On the precipice.

He stepped forward, detecting that Adrian was bemused by the hiatus. Voices, men's voices: the two football pundits. Lawrie withdrew a couple of paces and fumbled for his keys. The men passed by. Another opportunity, one more attempt; but it was do or die in the next moment. He couldn't make Adrian stand pointlessly outside the car any longer.

"Adrian," Lawrie began, but failed.

"What?" Adrian asked, baffled at the other's unease.

"I... I just miss you. I miss seeing you. Since I went down south, I've realised..." Lawrie sensed his legs shaking and tremolo in his voice. "I really miss you. I just want to spend more time with you and... I think..." Could he say it? Could he use the word 'love'? Was that what he meant, what he actually felt? He hesitated, lost; a drowning man surrounded by debris, not knowing which thing to clutch at for salvation. His whole body was like jelly, a quivering mass of tension.

"Can you hold me?"

"What?" Adrian replied, startled.

Lawrie stepped nearer, within touching distance. This was it; this had to be the moment. "Hold me. Just put your arms around me," Lawrie pleaded, tears filling his eyes, his voice betraying the desperation of his heart and mind.

A car engine started. Light from its headlamps flooded the stage of Lawrie's climactic scene. There was no hiding place now. All was open, laid bare. Instinctively, the pair pulled back, apart. The engine revved; gravel crunched.

"See you, lads!" called one of the football aficionados.

"I'll walk home. It's okay," Adrian said, once the car had passed. Yet, he did not turn.

"Don't be silly. It's horrible." Although the night was nasty, Lawrie, emotionally wracked, knew that he had not meant the weather.

Deflated, Lawrie unlocked his door, climbed in and pulled up the button of the passenger door. The drive to Adrian's home took three minutes; it seemed more like three hours, in torturous silence. Lawrie wondered whether he should apologise; he felt he should, but for what? For trying, however badly, to say that he was falling in love? Confused, frightened and ashamed, he was trapped into silence.

After Adrian had got out of the car, thanking Lawrie civilly for the lift back, they had never seen each other again until now, twenty years later.

A car horn blew. Laurel glanced out of Joseph's front room window. Her heart jumped into her mouth. "He's here," she announced, in a deadpan voice.

Joseph easily saw through the feigned insouciance. "Have fun. And if you're not in bed by ten, come back. He isn't worth it," he quipped. Grabbing her bag, Laurel turned and stuck out her tongue at her oldest friend.

Checking her appearance in the hall mirror, she skipped out in the floral dress she had bought in St Anne's. Over it, she was wearing her white jacket, finished off with the new scarf, the bangles in three-coloured gold, and the appropriately spring-like scent of Mark Jacob's Daisy. The passenger door of Adrian's car was slightly ajar; and he waved a beckoning hand.

"Hello, stranger," he smiled, putting the car into gear.

"Hi, Adrian. Thanks for picking me up," she said. For a moment, she thought about leaning over to kiss his cheek, but he was already completely focused on the junction at the end of the road. *Remember, Laurel: play it cool.*

Cool it was as they drove along. Slightly awkwardly, both former colleagues were 'feeling' for each other, with Laurel instigating most of the hesitant conversation.

"What a coincidence that I met Don and Stella last weekend!" she opened brightly.

"Yes, my old boss." He laughed.

"And you took over his job," Laurel added lamely.

"Sort of. After the merger, they gave me a fancy title — Chief Finance Officer — but I'm little more than a company accountant," he confessed modestly. "There's one girl who works under me."

"Lucky girl," Laurel joked, smirking. Adrian didn't pick up the innuendo. He had never been very sharp at that.

"This seems strange — you driving me," Laurel smiled.

"Yes. I started after the bank transferred me to Bolton."

Silence.

Laurel thought awhile before asking, "Can you remember the last time we were in a car together?"

"It was probably a Friday night at a pub," Adrian replied casually.

"Handel's Arms," she added.

"Really?"

No recollection, apparently, Laurel. Typical man. Had he forgotten that night? Had she been needlessly beating herself up about that awful scene for twenty years? Had she refrained from contacting him over embarrassment about something that had made no impression on him — over nothing?

"I booked a table. It gets busy here at the weekend, especially on nice evenings," he said, as they parked outside a pub that was pleasantly situated by the Leeds and Liverpool canal, next to the topmost of the seven Wheelton locks, between Chorley and Blackburn.

They were seated close to a table occupied by a woman with two boys. The waitress returned moments later with two tall burgers, served on small chopping boards, with the chips in a metal beaker. She then brought a bowl of pasta for the smaller child, who looked about six.

As Adrian and Laurel scanned the menu, the younger child seemed more fascinated by Laurel than his dinner. Time was, during her transition, when she would have been terrified of scrutiny, fearing that even a child might read her and blurt out something mortifying.

"It's my brother's birthday," the little one confided to Laurel, edging closer along the bench seat. How lovely to have no social fear, to be open to anyone! Laurel engaged with the cute curly-headed youngster, enquiring about the elder boy's age.

"He's eleven."

At the mention of the number, the older brother glanced briefly towards Laurel, who mouthed 'Happy Birthday.' The boy, who had learned the reserved behaviour of older children towards strangers, smiled weakly and turned back to his meal.

"Jayden, leave the lady alone, darling. Come and eat your dinner."

Laurel, not at all bothered by the child, was about to tell the mother that it was fine, when she thought better of it. The woman wanted him to get on with his food; so, Laurel stroked his hair and said, "That looks yummy; you'd better eat it before it goes cold."

Dutifully, the sweet child shuffled back to his place, where his mother was twisting spaghetti onto his fork. The women exchanged smiles. The waitress reappeared and took their order. Laurel chose a lamb curry and a bottle of cider; Adrian opted for steak and kidney pudding, chips and mushy peas from a section called 'Home Comforts'.

Halfway through his spaghetti Bolognese, the child became bored and, with sauce coating his small hands, approached Laurel again.

"Jayden!" yelled the mother, horrified, as the boy made a beeline for Laurel. "Don't put your hands on the lady's dress!"

Laurel, who had already seen the potential danger, grabbed a paper napkin and caught one hand inside it, while holding his other wrist. She wiped both hands clean.

"Sorry," said the mother, with a comic grimace. "He's a bit over friendly."

"No problem. He's adorable." The child looked up with big eyes, not understanding the word.

"My daddy lives in America," the child disclosed.

"America?" Laurel hesitated, not wanting to say the wrong thing, and looked to the mother for clarification.

"He doesn't live there, stupid," the elder brother snapped.

"Kyle, there's no need for that. Daddy doesn't live in America, Jayden; he's working there for a few weeks, that's all."

Comprehending, Laurel turned to the small child. "It probably seems like a long time to you. I'm sure he'll be home soon. Are you missing him?"

The child thought for a moment, then shook his curly locks. "No, 'cause I can sleep in Mum's bed," he announced gleefully, then returned to his dinner. Adrian, who had remained a passive observer throughout, laughed at the innocent remark.

"You've got a little character there," Laurel said to the woman, at whom she had taken only passing glances until that moment; now, she recognised the considerable attraction of curling up alongside her. Her low-cut top revealed a cleavage to die for; and young Jayden had

163

inherited his mother's large deep blue eyes. Slightly wicked thoughts were running through Laurel's mind.

"Emily was a lot like that," a voice said. Laurel blinked, startled from her reverie.

"Sorry? Oh, your daughter." *Pull yourself together, Laurel! You're sitting opposite the guy you've been longing for, and your eyes are all over another woman's boobs.*

"Are you okay?" Adrian asked.

"Yes — yes. I was miles away. It's been a long week," she added distractedly, glad to see the waitress approaching with their food.

"Tell me about Emily and her brother. Sorry, I don't know his name," Laurel said, anxious to get Adrian to open up more.

"Martin. He's sixteen, almost seventeen. We don't get along brilliantly. He lives between my house and his mother's. He's having to retake some of his GCSEs. But Emily is a different person altogether. Good at school; good — very good — at netball."

"Yes, Stella said so. And you? Do you still play cricket?"

"Once in a while. We have a veterans' team." Laurel had to laugh at the label 'veteran'.

"I'm a little out of condition these days. You were stockier than me all those years ago. Now, I'm the portly one; and your body…" He stopped, unsure; a smirk formed on his wide lips.

"Do you like it?" Laurel asked unnecessarily, for his facial expression had already betrayed him. She gazed intently into his eyes while giving him a flirty smile. A pause.

"To be honest, yes. Yes, I do. You look great, fabulous. Really attractive."

From any other man, she could have smiled and accepted the compliment as commonplace. Not that she was vain, but she knew that such words are often cheap. For some reason, however, she felt her heart racing. All of a sudden, she was the one at risk of losing her composure. *Cool, Laurel, stay in control.*

Unable to speak, with an audible intake of breath, she placed her hand on his and stroked his fingers. He did not flinch. It was the first tender physical contact between them. Ever. How she — or Lawrie — had longed to make that simple gesture of affection when they had been young men, especially on that dreadful evening at the Handel's Arms! She smiled at him, a watery smile through the welling tears. He placed his free hand on top of hers, pressing gently, softly, kindly, warmly. The dam burst.

"Heavens, Adrian," she spluttered, after the initial cascade. "If you only knew how long ago, I wanted you to do that. And to say that." Laurel was shaking inside, a tangled mess of emotion. She dabbed her eyes. "I'm sorry. Excuse me." She grabbed her bag and made straight for the ladies' room. Hot, bewildered, her feelings in turmoil, as if she were inside a tumble dryer during a major earthquake, Laurel began to fix her make-up.

"Are you okay?" Laurel turned. The woman from the next table was in the doorway, her face concerned.

"I'm fine. Thank you. Perfect, in fact." Laurel smiled. "If only he'd said that twenty years ago…"

"That's men all over," the mother nodded, as they left the restroom. "Mine's the same: the strong, silent type. He isn't your husband, then?"

"No. No, he isn't. We're just old friends, really; just met up again. I came over all emotional," Laurel continued as they returned to their tables. She felt the woman's encouraging, sympathetic hand on her back.

The smaller boy beamed at Laurel. "I'm going to have choc-lock ice-cream," he announced.

"Chocolate, silly," his elder brother corrected. Out came the younger boy's tongue. Their mother shook her head in resigned exasperation.

"Enjoy it, then," Laurel said, retaking her place.

"Are you all right?" Adrian asked gently. "I'm sorry if I…"

"Don't be silly. It was all those years ago, so many emotions and memories swirling around in my head. You should have known me when I was on the hormone treatments. I could burst into tears reading a bloody recipe book!"

The conversation became easier when they reminisced about the bank and laughed about old colleagues. Then, the talk turned to Laurel's situation.

Practical and accountant-like, Adrian asked, "But what would you do for income?"

"Don't worry," she said laughing. "I'm not going to sponge off an old friend. That isn't why I tracked you down. I have some income from what my dad left me and, who knows? I'm seeing the HR people next week, hopefully to try and negotiate a severance package."

Mopping up his last drops of gravy, Adrian glanced up and enquired, "So how did you choose your name? The closest to Lawrence?"

"Um, I guess Lauren would have been closer. But yeah, I wanted to stick with an 'L' name; and I made a list of a dozen or fifteen names. Then I kept saying them in my head and looking at photos of me *en femme*; a whole evening, with Bach's forty-eight playing in the background. Finally, Laurel sounded right, natural: more like me." She breathed deeply.

"And you have to use your tongue twice to make it," she added, leaning forward while licking her bottom lip seductively.

There was no pick up again; he had not changed in two decades. With time-honed instinct, the tip of Laurel's tongue trilled across both lips. The penny dropped. "Oh, that's gross!" he exclaimed.

Somewhat taken aback by his reaction, Laurel absolutely had to know. "You didn't ever go down on … your wife?"

"Pauline. No. We weren't very adventurous or… experimental," Adrian replied coyly, raising his pint glass to his face, as if trying to conceal himself inside it.

Laurel could not avoid laughing. "For God's sake, Adrian, licking your wife's pussy is hardly pushing the boundaries of sexual deviance!"

Concerned that her voice might have carried further than intended, Laurel quickly scanned the nearby tables, especially where the two young boys were tucking into ice-cream. No reaction. There was too much general hubbub, in the midst of which Rick Astley was tirelessly promising never to give somebody up.

"She… she didn't like it… I don't think," he hedged, in little more than a whisper. "We tried it once or twice, but…" He shrugged his shoulders.

"It's no wonder…" Laurel began boldly, then checked. *Might be hurtful, Laurel. Alternative approach.* "Maybe you just need a bit of training." *Steady, girl.*

Adrian's eyes darted around, seeking rescue. "Can we talk about something else?"

"Of course," she replied. A pause; a long pause. Laurel studied him, challenging him to bring up a different topic.

"Would you like a dessert?" he asked lamely. Laurel sniggered; this was the Adrian she remembered.

"Actually, I'm quite full," she answered truthfully. Intuition made her realise that her questions had gone a little too near the bone. It was, after all, their first

168

meeting in over twenty years; moreover, she had completely transformed herself.

"Why don't we take a stroll along the towpath while there's still daylight?" she suggested. "You can tell me more about your children."

"Okay," he replied, his expression lightening. *Right move, Laurel.*

'You can make steamy passionate love to me on some grassy bank.' For a moment, she considered giving utterance to that thought; sensibly, it remained tacit. Instead, she reached into her bag for her wallet and produced a twenty-pound note. "That will cover mine."

"Certainly not," he replied. "I'll get this." The true gentleman. Laurel had expected no less, though she had been genuinely prepared to split the bill. "If you're sure…"

"Sure."

The path was wide enough for them to walk side by side, though not touching, towards Blackburn. The cool dampness of the Lancashire air chilled Laurel. She wriggled her forearm between Adrian's arm and body. He tensed initially, but he relaxed and allowed her to stay there. With their flanks now touching, she was warmer, protected. So close, Laurel felt something stirring: a discernible current was flowing between them.

That had been so easy; so different from the haunting night outside the Handel's Arms, tremulous with nerves and trembling in fear and the frosty air. The canal ahead stretched into the glow of evening; Laurel glanced behind, into the deepening blue-grey gloom.

"Perhaps we'd better turn round," she said, stealing a glance at his face. Uncontrollably, she was drawn back, like a moth to a candle. The setting sun, almost vermillion, shone in his eyes. He was fuller in the face than when he was twenty-two; and the hair on his temples was now greying; but the clean, straight line of his nose, the kindness of his eyes and the broadness of his lips were the same as Laurel — or Lawrence — had gazed at, in hopeless confusion, on that fateful night. He was still a handsome man; and her right arm remained wrapped inside his left.

Suddenly, Adrian's free hand reached across his middle and enclosed hers. Laurel's heart clicked up a gear. In auto-response, she tilted her head to rest on his shoulder. The stirring morphed into a surging. They had stopped walking.

"You do remember that night, don't you?" she said, lifting her eyes to study his expression. *Careful, Laurel. Here is something more precious than the casual lovers you've had recently; here is something fragile; manly, yet vulnerable.* He merely nodded and lowered his gaze, as if in apology.

Fluttering within, her stomach a swarm of butterflies, she immersed herself in the lakes of his gorgeous eyes. She was standing on the precipice again. Was this the moment? Should she take the lead? Should she kiss him?

ELEVEN

Suddenly, they were walking again, still arm in arm. Adrian seemed lost in thought. Halfway back to the pub car park, where the lamps had come on, Laurel broke the silence. "It's such a lovely evening, and somewhere nice to stroll. Good choice."

"We used to come here often when the kids were younger. Martin liked watching the boats rising or sinking in the locks and Emily loved the ducks and swans. I wasn't sure that it was a good idea to come back, but…"

"Well, I've enjoyed it." She leaned into him gently. "And it's wonderful just to meet up again." Slightly awkward for a moment, Adrian turned his gaze away from her and down the canal.

"Thanks for the dinner and… and this moment." *Yes, this moment, Laurel, now.* Pressing still closer, she kissed his cheek. He stiffened at the touch of her lips on his face. "What's wrong?" she asked softly. She moved in front of him, but again he averted his eyes.

"Nothing, I…"

She grabbed his hands. "You can kiss me back, Adrian. Being a woman isn't a disease." *Careful, Laurel! Where on earth did that come from? Don't screw this up.* "And after all I went through, I don't think anyone would doubt that I am."

"It's just that it's all such a shock. How long is it since...? Twenty years?"

"Something like that."

She pulled him closer. She was treading dangerously, but this was not the Handel's Arms; and they were no longer two gauche young men.

"You do look nice, really nice," he said; and thawing in the warmth of their closeness, he kissed Laurel's cheek. "Mmm, you smell nice, too." Progress. Laurel's pulse quickened. She felt heady. Was this the moment she had dreamed of?

At the sound of footsteps on the path, Adrian pulled away, instantly bashful; an involuntary reaction, as though he was embarrassed to be seen kissing someone. An older couple approached and, as they passed, commented on the pleasantness of the evening.

So close! Yet, as they got into Adrian's car, Laurel's mild disappointment was eclipsed by elation. Those minutes on the canal bank had been the most tender and warm that she had ever known with Adrian. There was hope.

"So, when are you planning to go back?" Adrian asked, as they joined the main road.

"Probably Sunday, maybe Monday morning, whichever trains are cheaper," she replied in a matter-of-fact way.

"And are you really thinking of moving back up here?" The unexpected question made Laurel turn and study his expression. Was he possibly thinking they might have a future?

"That's the idea. It depends on what I can get from the bank." He nodded. Silence again. Was that it? No follow up?

"What?" she asked, scrutinising his face, which betrayed nervousness. "Erm, well," he began, before slowing down and pulling in. "I've enjoyed this evening; and I'd like to see you again before you go, but tomorrow…"

"Netball, I know." Laurel smiled. Inside, she was positively beaming.

"It's a county match and they're playing away — in Cumbria. And it's my turn to drive Emily and her friend."

"Sunday, then?" *Strike while the iron's hot, or at least warm, Laurel.*

He nodded. "Maybe, it's supposed to be nice over the weekend. We could go for a walk."

"I'd like that, Adrian."

Pulling out into the road again, he added, "We've got a cricket match arranged, but I can cry off." *Wow, Laurel! He's prepared to forego his veterans for you.*

As they stopped outside Joseph's house, Laurel placed her hand on Adrian's, just as she had earlier. He did not respond in the same way, nor was there another kiss. Did it matter? She was happy enough that he wanted to see her again.

"Don't pretend you haven't had a good time." Joseph giggled, as Laurel dropped her bag on his sofa. "I know that look. Are you going to give me all the gory details?"

"I need a ciggie. Outside, then." They headed into the small back garden, where Laurel leaned against the kitchen wall and lit up, inhaling massively; then she laughed with girlish delight as she released the pent-up tension.

WELL?

Maddie was up early for a Saturday, too early for Laurel, who had been snoozing when the phone alerted her. Her groan became a snigger when she remembered Maddie's 'date' with Trefor the previous evening. Laurel typed a response.

Well yourself?

You first. How did it go with A?

Fine. Seeing him again Sunday, so travelling Mon. Trefor?

Had a really nice evening. Dinner and wine bar. Got on great.

And?

Next week again. Agreed to take it slowly.

That was a novelty for Maddie; and it was probably Trefor's suggestion.

Laurel's thoughts remained in London. Laurel, still Lawrie, had moved south at the age of twenty-six, having always been excited by the vibrancy and the cultural life of the capital. The bank, unable to recruit from the millions who dwelt there, had enticed staff from the provinces, dangling the carrot of a bonus payment on top of the normal 'London weighting' on salaries.

It had also given Lawrie a convenient exit from a dead-end relationship with a girl two years older. Little had they had in common, except a need for sex. She had kept a dog, not a particularly pleasant animal, which had continually licked Lawrie's feet as he performed on the low bed in her basement flat. He had been scraping the barrel; and the sex had been merely functional, devoid of meaning. The girl had possessed a voracious libido, but their clumsy coition had usually left him feeling sullied and guilty, as if taking advantage of a dull nymphomaniac.

After a good run in Witton Park, beside the River Darwen, Laurel showered and raided Joseph's cereal stock. She was still munching when her phone bleeped. Nine thirty. Stella.

How was last night, sweet? Fancy coffee this morning?

Fine. Would love to, but only just having breakfast. And I'm in Blackburn. How about lunch? Meet you in Lytham Square shortly after 12?

Lovely. See you later.

Stella and Don were sitting on one of the benches in the square. They got up as they saw Laurel coming. Don smiled pleasantly; Stella, however, was beaming from ear to ear.

"*Mela*, I don't need to ask if you enjoyed yourself last night. You look radiant, *ħanina*." Laurel, mildly taken aback, wondered how her face was speaking so eloquently. She had not noticed such a change when leaving Joseph's.

Laurel regaled the couple with the events of the previous evening, keeping the scene on the canal bank to herself. Don listened with polite interest, adding observations about the Top Lock pub and Adrian's history. Stella grew increasingly excited, particularly when Laurel added that she would postpone returning to London, so that she could see Adrian again.

"He said he'd even drop out of a cricket match tomorrow," Laurel said laughing.

"How wonderful!" Stella squealed with delight, clapping her hands together. "I'm so pleased for you."

She paused. "Take it easy; *bil-mod, ta'*. He was hurt pretty badly when Pauline left him."

After some persuasion, they allowed Laurel to foot the lunch bill. She had been insistent; it was a 'thank you', not only for Stella's prompting of Adrian, but also for being in her new life; friends for her future. They took a stroll along the green, sharing memories of Lytham. The one awkward moment came opposite the Lowther Gardens, when Laurel mentioned the spring bank holiday dance festivals.

"You must have loved that," Stella cooed, "I bet you were such a pretty girl in your costume, all made up for the stage. I had ballet lessons in Malta for a few years. What dances did you do?"

Laurel bit her bottom lip and mumbled, "Oh, the usual stuff. Classical, song and dance and character. Modern and jazz weren't my mother's forte. To be honest, I preferred playing out here on the grass," she breezed, determined to move the conversation on.

Both Don and Stella hugged Laurel as the train squeaked to a halt. She promised to keep in touch while away in London, hoping to return before the end of the month. A growl, a diesel cloud, and the train edged forwards. She waved cheerily to her friends. Don, smiling pleasantly, raised an open hand; Stella's wave was vigorous, both forearms thrashing away like windscreen wipers on full power.

Taking a break from the Saturday night telly that Joseph was gorging himself on, Laurel was enjoying a cigarette in his back garden when Adrian messaged her.

Hi. Just back from Barrow. 2pm OK tmrw? Will pick u up.

Economical and succinct. Laurel's thumbs hovered over the keypad as she mulled over possible responses. She needed to sound keen and warm, without appearing to be over grabby.

Sure, looking forward to it. Where are you taking me?

How about Sunnyhurst Wood?

Fine. Haven't been there since I was a kid. Won't wear heels, then!

In the sunset glow of the garden, with blackbirds singing, it was impossible to dispel romantic notions of sharing time with Adrian in the woodland that rose above Darwen. *Just keep your head, Laurel, and see what happens.* With his natural shyness, however, she knew that she would probably have to take the next step in developing the relationship, as she had on the towpath at Wheelton.

The next morning, positive and punchy, Laurel's trainers paced the ground through Witton Park and onward, between mature trees, to Pleasington, where she turned and retraced her route. She had run further than planned and, having exhausted herself, stopped on the bridge to rest, gazing into the placidly flowing river.

Her memory carried her to another river, where she — as Lawrie — had stood, on a drizzly Saturday evening, a few months after moving to London. Not having made any real friends as yet, Lawrie drifted through Saturdays, unsure of sexuality or gender, mooching about the West End.

That dank afternoon, Lawrie had traipsed through Bloomsbury, down to Soho, and into one of the last remaining dodgy cinemas. He had sat through a mildly entertaining soft porn film, during which a person had moved into the next seat, rubbing his leg against Lawrie's for a couple of minutes, before reaching out a hand. They had groped, squeezed and teased one another until the closing credits. They had left together, the man, in his late fifties, making surprisingly intelligent conversation until ushering Lawrie into an alley and giving him a blow job. While Lawrie had been zipping up the size ten stretchy jeans he had dared to buy on Shepherd's Bush market, the man had disappeared into the drizzly dark.

Grabbing a takeaway, and feeling cheap and sullied, Lawrie had wandered through Covent Garden, emerging onto the eastern end of the Strand, near St

Clement Danes; he had carried on roaming eastwards, beyond the Temple area, beyond Blackfriars, and down a slope from Upper Thames Street towards the river.

Alone, miserable, in the wintry damp, Lawrie, whoever Lawrie was, had found himself in a car park underneath a modern concrete building, by a riverside pathway; unknowing, unsure why he was there, or exactly where he was; lost, alone. Haunted by the Handel's Arms horror, ten weeks earlier, he had cried out for Adrian in his heart, or maybe out loud. Emotionally out of control, remembering, regretting; a car wreck in a dark, empty car park, a mausoleum of concrete, his mind had only recorded the dark cold aloneness.

There, in desperate solitude, Lawrie had imagined Adrian holding him, kissing him; but the slate-coloured water of the cold Thames had lapped mockingly against the hard, cold concrete in front of him. He had stared out at the water, into the water, almost lured in. Confused, torn between genders, lonely, ashamed, cold. What am I? Who am I? If I just do it, here, now, who will care?

Regaining the present, Laurel shook her head vigorously, as if to rid herself of something nasty, and took a deep breath. The River Darwen flowed untroubled beneath her, the greensward of the playing fields stretched before her, framed by the mature trees of the former Feilden estate and the rise of Billinge Hill.

That was then, Laurel; this is now, your chance to shape the future.

After some warming down stretches, she walked back to Joseph's house, where she showered, before popping out to get something for a brunch. Joseph had gone food shopping and, hailed by his Grindr app, to an assignation with a young man.

Mobile in hand, Laurel found the times of trains to London for the next day. The cheapest fare via Preston departed there at 11.21; the train from Cherry Tree, where she was staying, arrived in Preston at 11.22. Wonderful. The next London train, leaving Preston just before noon, was forty pounds dearer. Cheaper journeys involved changes at Blackburn, Bolton and Manchester. She switched to National Rail's website, where the midday train, plus the connection to Preston, was seventeen pounds cheaper.

She was about to tap on the BUY button when a car horn sounded. She turned and, through the bay window, saw Adrian waving at her from his car. She hurried out in such an excited state that she tangled herself in the long strap of her bag while locking Joseph's front door. *Not very cool, Laurel. Calm down. Don't let him think you're over eager.*

"I didn't dress up, bearing in mind where we're going," Laurel half apologised, which was unnecessary, for Adrian was in jeans and an obviously not new, baggy jumper. He smiled and gently shook his head, probably thinking, 'Would Lawrie ever have said anything like that?'

The drive over Horden Rake and Bog Height Road was more spectacular than Laurel had remembered it from her childhood. They crested the hill, surrounded by lush rolling pasture, before descending to the main road into Darwen. The surface was still wet in sheltered patches after the morning's showers. Now, white and rain-bearing grey clouds were hurled across the sky by a strong breeze. The bright sun on the West Pennine moors accentuated their contours, the patchwork made more complex and dynamic by the trailing cloud shadows.

"Did you tell Emily where you went on Friday? Wasn't she curious?"

"Not really, she was still doing her homework when I got back. I said I'd met an old friend from the bank," Adrian replied.

"And how did the netball go?"

"Very well — won easily. In fact, they were so much better that Emily and the other strong girls only played half the match; they let the second string have a go."

"I met Stella and Don for lunch in Lytham," Laurel said.

"Lucky you." Adrian grinned. "I had a sandwich and an apple in Barrow."

The conversation had been general, rather than focused; ephemeral, rather than intense. They walked down the lane, Laurel waiting to see if Adrian would make any move to hold her hand, or put her arm through his. Nothing. Maybe she was, as Stella had warned her, expecting too much. Maybe, in Adrian's mind, she was just an old colleague. After all, they had only shared a pub meal, a stroll and a coy kiss on her cheek. And yet, he had suggested this second date. Was this even a date?

"I haven't been up here much since…" He paused.

Laurel nodded, understanding exactly what he meant. "It is pretty in the sunlight." She knew he was hurting; it was a pointless comment.

"We… we came up here often when we were first going out. Then, after our first major row, I brought the kids out of the way while Pauline was chucking things around the kitchen. Even then, it was a disaster. Martin flatly refused to get out of the car; Emily and I stood gazing into the stream. Neither of us said anything until she asked me why we no longer liked each other. I couldn't answer. I didn't know. I promised her it would all be okay. I hoped, at the time, that it wasn't a lie. Looking back, I think I knew that it was. We'd been building up to it for months."

Wow! He had opened up like a flower on a May morning. Laurel could not recall him revealing such intimate thoughts, even when they had been working together. She hooked her arm through his.

"Not a lie, Adrian. You weren't wrong to hope." There was sadness in his soul. As they walked on, sensing no resistance, Laurel let gravity do its kindest, her forearm sliding down his until their hands touched. As on the Friday evening, she felt a tense twitching, a momentary freezing; but she did not release him, nor did he struggle for freedom. She slid her fingers between his, not daring to glance at his face. *Another milestone, Laurel.*

"So, where are your two today?" Laurel finally asked.

"Oh, Martin is at Pauline's, and Emily has gone out with her friend's family, her non-netball friend. They were talking about going to Southport. I'm glad she's kept up that friendship; sports teams can become all consuming. Some of those kids don't seem to have a life outside school and netball."

"And you gave up your cricket to meet me." Laurel winked.

"Oh, that's just a bit of fun, really. We're a bit past all that intensity."

The woodland was magically vibrant and vital. The ground and foliage had been freshened by a recent shower; and when the sun emerged from behind towering clouds, the wet leaves sparkled, smelling fresh and alive. The breeze stirred the grass and its spirit rustled the new greenery of the trees. For Laurel, who had not been in Sunnyhurst for more than thirty years, the newness and the enlivening rhythms of nature's spring symphony only heightened the thrill of being hand in hand with Adrian, here in Darwen.

As they turned a bend in the track, while Adrian was gazing into the high branches to spot a tuneful bird, Laurel noticed a dog heading towards them. Never having been a doggy person, she was relieved to see that the black and white creature was being restrained on a leash by one of two teenaged girls. One was an attractive brunette, the other sandy and toothy. Following them were two adults.

"Oh, my God!" Adrian exclaimed, loosening his hand from Laurel's, "My daughter!"

Laurel was tempted to grab his hand again to show the world — and Emily — her prize, but she resisted. Adrian stood stock still; but the girls, led by the dog, continued their advance.

"Dad!" Despite addressing her quizzical surprise to her father, the prettier girl was busily scanning his companion. Scanning, but smiling.

"This is... an old friend of mine, Emily. We used to work together."

Apart from a momentary glance at her father, Emily remained focused on Laurel. For her part, Laurel was doing the same. Yes, this cute kid was certainly the one in the photo at Stella's, though she was now probably three years older. It was instantly obvious that the girl was open, outgoing; there was a positive spark about her. Laurel smiled back.

"I've heard quite a lot about you, Emily. But I thought you were going to the seaside."

"They changed the forecast," the sandy girl's mother intervened. "It didn't look too safe, so we decided on a walk before the rain returned, then the cinema."

"Have fun. Nice to meet you. Perhaps we'll see each other again," Laurel remarked to Emily, before clocking Adrian's bashful grile. The girl beamed and nodded. The two groups moved on past each other.

"She's a really nice-looking girl. Can't think where she gets it from," Laurel quipped, once they were out of earshot. She halted, turned towards Adrian, and was just about to kiss him, when Emily turned around to glance back. Time froze. Laurel held her position, angled towards Adrian's face; the young girl paused too; but, after a second or two, she waved. Laurel waved back. When the group had vanished around the bend, Laurel placed her lips on Adrian's.

"Do you think she saw?" Adrian asked anxiously.

"Saw what?"

"Us, holding hands."

"Would it matter?" Laurel asked, amused by his coyness. He was, at that moment, like someone of his son's age, a gawky teenager caught fondly eyeing a girl.

"I suppose not."

"Okay, so now you've met one half of my family," he said, a minute or so later. "Thank God it was Emily."

"Why? I'm sure your son isn't all that bad," Laurel replied.

"No, he isn't a bad person; he's just infuriating. Which reminds me, he's moving back in this evening. No doubt he'll go on about how wonderful his mother's cooking is and moan about whatever I give him."

"Well, you seem to be eating well enough," she jested, patting his belly.

"Microwavable ready meals from Tesco, mostly. Emily cooks better than me, but she's often too busy with homework and netball."

"Stella was right," ventured Laurel.

"What's that?"

"She said you needed a good woman in your life." *Steady, Laurel. Quick, smile, as if it's a joke!* Too late. Adrian looked away towards the stream, embarrassed. Oops! A step too far? A tense silence. The precipice again. *Grab him and jump, Laurel!*

"Adrian, look at me." Their eyes met. Uncomfortable, he turned away again. With her left hand, she gently turned his head until their noses were almost touching. Her lips parted slightly and landed on his; but this time, with her hand bracing the side of his face, she was in control. She pushed her tongue deep into his mouth. Subdued, his hands helplessly clutched at her waist. Their tongues wrestled.

"Oh God! I'm shaking like a leaf," he gasped. Laurel was quivering, too; a butterfly, trying with utter determination to maintain equilibrium on a trembling bloom. Her heart was pumping madly, noisily, she thought; her legs were about to give way at any moment.

Her breathing became shorter, almost gasping. So too, she realised, had his. She leant into him again, forcing her tongue between his lips.

Light rain was settling on them and on the car, but they remained fixed in each other's arms. The balm of his embrace infused Laurel's body and soul, healing the open wound of that desperate, desolate, drizzly Saturday night twenty years ago. And that, in turn, prompted another memory.

TWELVE

A week or two after that horrid night by the Thames, Lawrie had taken the daring, despairing step of sending a Valentine card to Adrian, addressing it to his home. He had asked a colleague who lived some distance out of London to post it. Hiding a cryptic clue in his little verse, he had tried to be subtle; afterwards, he feared it had been clumsy and obvious.

When he had phoned Adrian a few days before Easter, exploring the possibility of a Friday drink, Lawrie had been rebuffed. At least, that was how he had interpreted Adrian's terse declining. Lawrie, rumbled and rejected, had never called after that.

As Adrian pulled away from their embrace, fumbling in his pocket for the car key, Laurel took a couple of steps ahead and lit a cigarette. There, in the Lancashire dampness that she had known from childhood, the pale grey smoke became the cremation plume of a twenty-year-old corpse.

"You're going to get soaked," Adrian called from the car window.

"Just another couple of puffs," Laurel shouted back. Immediately, she regretted her choice of phrase. Two young men were walking together, not twenty metres from her. The men looked at each other momentarily, then the shorter of the pair scowled at her. Should she apologise? "Er, sorry. I didn't mean…" Laurel stuttered, mortified. They ignored her and walked on. Oops!

She strode over to the nearest bin, stubbed out the cigarette, and shrugged her shoulders. When she reached Adrian's car, he was laughing fit to burst.

"Don't make it worse!" she exclaimed, aiming a playful punch at his shoulder. "What's so funny, anyway?"

"I guess you don't know them. The taller one was Martin's art teacher. It's common knowledge that he's queer."

Even Laurel had to laugh. "Oh, my God! Really? Now I feel terrible," she said, attempting to be serious for a moment. "I hope I won't be responsible for your son getting a D minus," she added.

"Don't worry. He passed his art GCSE. About the only one he did."

After Adrian had listed Martin's academic disappointments, the chat on the way back to Joseph's became more hesitant and staccato. Riding over the railway line at Cherry Tree station, Laurel felt a sickening emptiness in her stomach. Tomorrow she would be taking a train from there, away from Adrian. He, too, was quiet now. She glanced across at him. Although his eyes were focused on the road, his mind seemed to be elsewhere. 'Is he thinking about us?' Laurel dared to wonder.

"Thank you," Laurel began, as they pulled up. "And..." She paused, uncertain.

"I've really enjoyed this afternoon. I haven't laughed like that in a long time," he confided. Laurel placed her right hand on his left.

"I'm glad. Glad that I made you laugh, I mean; not that you haven't been able to." Their eyes met smilingly, deeply. This time, Adrian did not look away.

"When... when do you think you'll be back up here?"

Laurel felt herself tremble, simply at the fact that he had asked that. "Soon, hopefully; as soon as I..." She stopped. He was still gazing at her face. "Why?" *Dumbass question, Laurel; but I have to know.*

"Erm, nothing, really. Erm," he hesitated, as if preparing to step into something that might be quicksand. "I'd like to..."

Cue, Laurel. Releasing her seat belt, she pressed herself against him, her lips against his. This time, though, her tongue met some resistance, a reticence that she recognised and partly understood. Like a pair of teenagers, they drew apart when a neighbour slammed his front door shut.

"It's a pity you have to go back tomorrow," Adrian said, almost apologetically, she thought.

"Well," she sighed, "I don't absolutely have to go tomorrow. I can put off regional office until later in the week," she appended, mildly frustrated. Her eyes continued to explore the window to his soul. "I'm signed off until Friday after all."

"But, your future with the bank…"

"Bugger the bank! I want a future…" She checked. *Too soon, Laurel?* "I'd love to see you again before I go back," she said, kissing his forehead, then his nose, then his lips. *Inspiration! Risky, Laurel, but you're on a roll.* "Why don't I come and cook for your son one evening?"

Adrian pulled back slightly, surveying Laurel as if she were showing signs of insanity. She stared back confidently. A pause.

"Okay. You're on! How's Tuesday? Emily always has tons of homework on Tuesdays. I usually have to cook."

"Tuesday it is, then." Laurel nodded.

"Are you sure?"

"Are you? They're your teenagers, and it's your home."

"Well, Emily's met you already. And…"

"And I'm just an old friend from the bank," Laurel winked, opening the car door.

'*I'm walking on the air, dear.*' That old song from *Show Boat* came into Laurel's head as she entered Joseph's house. Unwittingly, she started singing to herself, dwelling on Ravenal's responding couplet: '*In this sweet, improbable and unreal world, finding you has given me my ideal world.*' At the age of seventeen, Lawrie had been in a school production, understudy to the boy playing the gambler. '*Why do I love you? Why do you...*'

"Someone's happy," Joseph called out, in a mildly ironic tone, above the theme music to *Hollyoaks*. He was catching up on the week's episodes. As she floated into the living room, the unmistakeable smell of lube hit Laurel's nostrils. She sniffed theatrically.

"Had a good time yourself, then?"

"Well, he didn't complain about the service. We came back once I realised that you'd gone out. Easier than in the back of the car. Too many ramblers around country lanes on a Sunday. And before you say anything, I'm not really into dogging," he chuckled.

"How old?"

"Twenty, or twenty-one." Laurel was just about to speak when Joseph added, "And if you call me a dirty old man, you won't get any dinner." They both laughed; they had known one another most of their lives.

"What about you?" he probed.

"We didn't get as far as shagging in the bushes, but I'm going round to his house on Tuesday."

"Tuesday! I thought you were travelling..."

"Oh, sorry, Joseph. He looked all wistful and asked me if I absolutely had to go back tomorrow," Laurel said exaggerating. "Is it okay if I stay till Wednesday or Thursday?" Joseph, being generally laid back, acceded to her request. "And luckily, I hadn't quite bought a train ticket when he arrived."

Laurel was still in a jolly mood when she messaged Maddie that evening.

Practically invited myself by promising to cook for them Tues!! Can't always read him — a bit bashful at kissing. Surprised he agreed to me going up there. And u won't believe it — we bumped into his daughter!! Must have seen us holding hands. Sweet smiley kid. Dreading the moody son, though.

You'll be fine. Just give him your stern manager face. LOL

Any more from Tref?

Hmmm.

Don't tease!

We went to the cinema. Held hands, cuddle in the back row. Like being 17 again!

In bed that evening, Laurel spent a few moments assessing her situation: new friends, work, love. Was it love yet? Even though he was still shy of displaying affection, maybe unsure of his affections, she had made solid progress. Everything was to play for. She would actually be inside Adrian's house, for the first time ever.

The satin of the green French knickers caressed her hips as she turned onto her side; her fingertips gently stroked the rose-patterned lace; then, as she imagined Adrian's bedroom, they burrowed inside, deeply within.

Waking in a bullish mood, and with the spring sunshine filling the room, Laurel decided that she would go over and confront the letting agents. Her visit, eleven days earlier, had yielded nothing; despite their promises, no payment from them had hit her bank account.

She strode purposefully along the canal to where the Albion Mill had recently been demolished. Arriving at the shop a few minutes later, she was not overly surprised to find the metal shutters still down. Eventually, about twenty minutes late, a woman appeared and opened up. Laurel introduced herself and said why she was there.

"Oh," the clerk replied, eyes cast downward. Silence. Laurel realised this reaction was a well-rehearsed one. There were obviously more clients who were owed money by this outfit. "Is there any more than 'Oh'?" Laurel demanded, with measured frustration. "Like six thousand pounds more than 'oh'? I've been standing out there waiting for you to arrive, and waiting for my money for more than a year; and the best you can manage is 'Oh'!"

Laurel plonked herself down on a chair, declaring that she would wait there all day if necessary. And there she sat all morning. During the long wait, Laurel sent a message to the bank's regional office, apologising that she had to postpone the Tuesday appointment, and suggesting Friday instead.

"I'm still waiting for that money you owe me from last year," Laurel announced pointedly, on each of the three occasions when someone entered. The stand-off continued until about one thirty, when the clerk's mobile rang; after a brief exchange, she handed the device to Laurel. All apologetic, not knowing how it could possibly have happened, and confirming he had made an electronic transfer to Laurel's account, the proprietor of the business promised that everything would be handled better from now on. Within minutes, Laurel saw that half the outstanding money had reached her. That would suffice for now.

Waiting for the bus into the centre of Blackburn, Laurel updated Stella on the Adrian front. "I'd love to have seen his face," Stella chuckled, when Laurel described the accidental meeting with Emily. She was delighted and astonished when Laurel mentioned she was going up to Adrian's house. "You've got the magic touch, *ḥanina*. Well done!" They both laughed.

"Don is whisking me away to Coniston Water tomorrow to celebrate our wedding anniversary. He's still quite romantic at heart, *mela*." Stella giggled.

"Well, you have a lovely time. And I'll see you when I'm back up here," Laurel promised.

"Keep in touch; and let me know how tomorrow goes. I'll be thinking of you. Both of you."

Buoyant and pleased with life, Laurel decided to treat herself to something new. Whatever she could not cram into her small case, she could leave at Joseph's, pending her return. Leaving the bus station, her principal target was H&M, via the market. She never made it, her approach spotted by the Asian stallholder who had recently netted her.

"Yes, lady. Come and see. New stock in today. I have the perfect thing for lovely lady." This guy was a professional flatterer. To be honest, the lace dresses she had looked at before were nice. So was the strappy linen-mix summer dress he was entreating her to feel. He ushered her between crammed rails to a small curtained area, deep within his stall. "Yes, please. Try it on, lady."

Five minutes later, Laurel felt she had done well in spending only twenty-five pounds on two dresses. She had chosen the burgundy shade in the lace, which came to a few inches above the knee, and an Indian sundress, vivid in bright green, orange and purple. Leaving, she paused near a rail of summer jackets, but sensing the stallholder's eager advance, she moved on.

A flurry of messages between Adrian and Laurel the next morning helped her plan the evening meal. A packet of minced beef was defrosting; she could do whatever she wanted with it, pasta and potatoes were available.

Emily likes Bolognese. Martin prefers shepherd's pie, but often turns his nose up at anything except chocolate. No hurry, I won't be in till 6.30 or 6.45. Then I can leave early tmrw — netball. Good luck.

Laurel popped into the Sainsbury's Local near the station, mainly because she had smoked her last cigarette after breakfast. While there, she noticed a special offer on garlic bread, so she grabbed a pack of two baguettes; Bolognese was favourite now, so her eyes roamed across the desserts for something chocolaty. That would even things up between the siblings.

Even though it meant changing trains at Blackburn, the railway was the quicker route to the centre of Darwen; it also shortened the climb to Adrian's house. Emily, already changed out of her school uniform, let Laurel in. Despite being in the middle of an essay, she offered to make her a cup of tea. Adrian's daughter was relaxed and naturally charming, easy to talk to; they chatted for a few minutes, mostly about school; and then, after showing Laurel where stuff was kept in the kitchen, the girl dutifully resumed her studies.

Out on the patio, while drinking her tea, Laurel fancied a ciggie, but she didn't want to smoke the washing on the nearby line. She removed the pegs, folded the various garments carefully, and placed them in the plastic basket. Adrian's shirts made her smile:

they would have drowned him twenty years ago, when he was slim and at least two collar sizes smaller. At the end of the line were three bras: a sports bra, which she folded first; a plain white one; and a cute black lacy one. The kid was finding her femininity. 34B, Laurel estimated correctly; for Emily possessed a shapeliness.

Laurel put the basket inside the kitchen, closed the door and, in the lee of the breeze, lit up. A few minutes later, the back door opened.

"Thanks, Laurel," Emily said. "Dad told me to do that when I came home, and I forgot."

"That's okay. I just folded it. Wasn't sure what else to do, or whose was whose. Except yours, of course." Laurel smiled girl to girl.

"Mostly Dad's. Mum does most of Martin's, luckily. Boys' underwear is so gross!"

"I agree," Laurel replied.

As the door closed, she remembered just how much she agreed. At fifteen, Lawrie had started buying his own underwear, with money from his weekend job. Not yet venturing into female attire, which was awkward when changing for PE in a boys' grammar school, he wore pants that were as genderless as possible. His father had ribbed him, calling them 'boy's knickers', and averring that he should be wearing something with a fly, like the Y-fronts that Lawrie's mother was about to iron. Ugh! Horrible! And why did many women feel they had to iron their fella's underwear?

It was after six when Laurel heard the front door thud. She also heard Emily jump up from her chair to explain that 'a friend of Dad's' was in the kitchen, preparing dinner. *First impressions count, Laurel.* She adopted a relaxed stance and what she imagined was a pleasant, unforced smile, waiting to see what Martin looked like.

A rather gangling youth, spotty faced and with mousey, unkempt hair, lurched into the kitchen. "Hi," he grunted, his eyes focused on the fridge rather than on the stranger, who was leaning against the worktop.

"Hi," countered Laurel, extending a hand. "I'm Laurel. You must be Martin."

Another grunt, accompanied by a nod of the untidy head; he opened the fridge door, ignoring the proffered hand.

"Had a good day?" Laurel enquired, as he snapped a row of chocolate from a Cadbury's bar.

"Not bad. What time's dinner?"

"I'm aiming for a quarter to seven. Your dad said he was working late."

"I'm hungry now." He prised open the biscuit barrel, grabbed a handful, slapped the lid closed and slopped out of the kitchen. His feet pounded the stairs up to his room.

'So far, so mediocre,' Laurel thought, as she continued prepping. There was something unmistakeably Adrian-like about him, though she could not remember Adrian being so graceless. *But you never knew him as a teenager, Laurel; he was about twenty-one when you first met.*

Even though the garlic bread was slightly singed, the main course went down well enough. Emily was full of questions about what it was like to work and live in London, especially about shopping and places for recreation. She had only been there once, in awful weather, and she had seen almost nothing. Adrian allowed his daughter to lead the conversation, chipping in with the occasional comment; Martin ate.

"That was lit, Laurel. Thank you," Emily said, as soon as she had finished her last mouthful.

"Lit?" Laurel looked bemused. Concurring with his daughter, Adrian explained that 'lit' was teenager-talk for 'really good'.

Martin grunted and nodded. *As ringing an endorsement as you're likely to get, Laurel.* Knowing that she held a trump card, however, she smiled confidently at the nearly seventeen-year-old.

"I heard you like chocolate, Martin. So, I bought a dessert with you in mind." Adrian cast his eyes around interestedly; but Laurel had carefully hidden the thawing item behind her bag. Getting up theatrically, she carried to the table a chocolate fudge cheesecake.

"Lit! Sorry, cool!" Emily exclaimed.

"You're being spoilt," Adrian said, laughing. Laurel, however, experiencing the novelty of being in a family situation, was focused on Martin. He didn't say anything, but Laurel saw his eyes light up and his tongue flick his bottom lip. *Gotcha!*

Emily was curious about her father's history with Laurel. How long had they worked together? Why had they not stayed friends? Adrian stuttered a couple of responses, but gave little away.

"It was a long time ago," Laurel intervened, helping him out. "I moved south, and I came up here less and less. We just lost touch, I guess. So, when is your next netball match?" Laurel asked, changing the direction of flow.

"Tomorrow, in Preston. You can come and watch." She looked anxiously at her father, fearing she might have said something inappropriate.

"I think," Adrian said tentatively, "Laurel is travelling back to London on Thursday, so…"

"I'd love to. I'll come and cheer you on," Laurel enthused. Martin snorted and, declining the suggestion that he might make coffee for everyone, returned to his cave. Emily, sure that she had caught Laurel's eye, raised her eyebrows.

"I'll do it, Dad," Emily said.

"No, I'll do it," Adrian insisted. "You go and finish your homework. I'll bring yours through."

During and after coffee, Laurel and Adrian sat at the table, talking about work and Laurel's intentions, sketchy as they were. Only once were they interrupted, when Emily rushed in, phone in hand.

"Becca's checking that we can take her to Preston."

"Yes, of course, we'll pick her up at five thirty — no, make it five fifteen."

"I'll tell her that Laurel's coming, Dad's ... should I say Dad's friend or girlfriend?" She grinned impishly at her father before flicking a glance at Laurel, who looked away.

"Friend will do, young lady," he said, with mock sternness. Demurely, the intelligent Emily tapped a reply, giving Laurel a knowing smile as she turned and left the room.

"Sorry," her father began.

"Don't be silly. She's sweet, Adrian. A lot of them are horrid at that age. And she's bright enough to test the water," Laurel observed.

"And you survived Martin," Adrian said, swiftly side stepping.

"He isn't so awful." She paused before adding, "Do you think he's jealous, envious? His most negative reaction was when I said I'd go and watch Emily's match. Maybe he just needs to feel affirmed in something he can do," Laurel posited.

"Maybe." Adrian smiled ruefully. "And maybe you would have made a better parent than me."

"Don't beat yourself up, Adrian. Emily's delightful; and he's probably just going through an awkward phase. He's older; maybe he took your break-up worse."

"Oh, bugger! The washing!" Adrian exclaimed, pushing himself up. "I hung it out this morning before I went."

"It's done," Laurel said calmly, rising to meet him. "I brought it in, and Emily sorted it out." They were suddenly close, too close to resist.

"Thank you," he said. "I didn't expect you to have to…"

"Shut up," Laurel smouldered, her lips landing on his. It wasn't a mega-snog; perhaps that would come tomorrow, when they parted before Laurel's return to London. But she was firmly back in Adrian's life.

THIRTEEN

For the second day running, Laurel had to buy her train ticket from the conductor; the machine at Cherry Tree was out of order again. Despite standing amid a forest of penalty fare warning signs, it failed to supply even the 'intention to pay' ticket. The connecting train from Clitheroe was late, so by the time Laurel had walked to Adrian's house, Emily was in her sports gear, finishing a plate of pasta salad.

"Want some? There's plenty in the fridge," the girl offered.

"Thanks, but I'm fine. I had a late lunch at my friend's house in Blackburn."

"Tea, then. Or juice? I'm having orange juice."

"Juice is good," Laurel replied.

"What's her name?" Emily asked with an air of nonchalance, as she handed Laurel a glass.

"Whose?"

"The friend you're staying with."

"Oh. His name's Joseph."

The teenager screwed up her nose and scrutinised Laurel's face. "Joseph? So, you're staying with a man, but you're seeing my dad?"

"It's not like that, Emily." Laurel laughed. "Joseph is a gay man. I've known him since we were a lot younger than you. I don't have many female friends up here now." *And I'm not going to explain why.*

"Does Dad know that your friend's gay?"

"Yeah, I made sure of that," Laurel smiled.

"Were you Dad's girlfriend when you were working in the bank?" Emily, wide-eyed with curiosity, tilted her head to maximise her cuteness. "Didn't he ask you out?"

"Not really. We were… just friends," Laurel answered truthfully.

"But why? Why didn't he ask you?" A pause. Laurel, just fleetingly, considered telling her the truth. *Consequences? Don't go there, Laurel.* "You're nice and good-looking. I wish he'd married you, not my mum."

Laurel smiled sympathetically and thought before she answered, "Then, you wouldn't be here, would you?" *Careful, Laurel.* "Or you'd be a totally different person. And I like you just the way you've turned out." She patted the girl's nose with one finger. Emily giggled. On the cusp of adulthood, she was a winning mixture of sweet innocence and developing astuteness.

"Do you have to go to London tomorrow?" Emily asked, echoing her father from a few days earlier.

"Yes, for a week or two. I have some important things to sort out."

"But you've only just started going out with Dad," the girl protested; then, she paused. "You two are going out, aren't you?"

Good question, kid. Not sure myself. "Kind of," Laurel replied, guardedly.

"And you're cool." She paused. "You haven't got a boyfriend in London, have you? A not-gay one, I mean?"

Laurel laughed out aloud; then, she reassured her: "You can see all about me, on my Facebook. Are you on Facebook too?"

Emily screwed up her nose again. "Facebook is for old people. Oh, sorry! I didn't mean..." This time, Laurel screamed with laughter, not so much at the girl's tactless remark, but at her contrite little face.

"I know you didn't mean it like that, Emily." They both laughed again.

"I do Instagram and Kik — we have our netball group on Kik."

"I've never even heard of it," the social media novice remarked.

"Look," began Emily, bringing up the app on her screen. There were already quite a few messages on the page, all encouraging one another for that evening's encounter. One of them, directed at Emily, looked less than polite.

"Why is someone calling you a goat?" Laurel asked.

"GOAT, silly. Greatest of all time. You can join Kik and then I can chat with you while you're in London."

A helpless onlooker as the girl grabbed her phone, Laurel was amazed at how quickly Emily got to the upload button. Within a few moments, Laurel was signed up to her second social media platform.

"You two seem to be getting along well," Adrian said, as he entered the room.

"Your daughter has just joined me up to something called Kik, apparently."

"So that we can chat to her when she's in London," the girl added earnestly. Laurel noted the change of pronoun. This kid was intelligent as well as talented and cute. The more Laurel saw of Emily, the fonder she grew of her.

They picked up Emily's teammate just before they reached the motorway. The girls sat in the back, engaged in their own banter about the likely strengths of the opposition; up front, the conversation was limited to comments about work and the road. At first, Laurel put it down to Adrian's concentration on driving; later, she was not so sure.

Even when apart from the girls, Adrian seemed quieter than normal, even stand-offish. He nodded and exchanged pleasantries with other parents, but remained insular. Was it being seen in public with a woman, when he normally arrived alone? Something was weighing on his mind. Once the match had started, he sat with his hands in his pockets, or with his arms folded across his chest.

Laurel sighed. Here she was, at a draughty sports complex outside Preston, sitting on a cracked moulded plastic seat, next to an unaccountably distant Adrian; Maddie's kiss and cuddle with Trefor in the back row of a cinema seemed a million miles away.

All effort and positive calls, Emily, playing Goal Attack, intermittently stole smiling glances at the couple. Each time she did, Laurel smiled back or waved discreetly. Adrian remained fairly aloof, even when Laurel joshed him about the obvious attractions of one of the older girls.

Some of the parents strolled around the court, shouting their encouragement. One mother, about Laurel's age, somewhat overdressed in heels and a low-cut dress, with Ray-Ban sunglasses pushed back onto her head, was showing off her latest acquisition, a rugged beefy guy, probably in his late twenties.

"Did you see what Antonia's mum was wearing?" Emily asked her father, as soon as the post-match debriefing was over.

"Do you mean the dress or the man?" Laurel quipped.

"Oh, I know — that's her new boyfriend. He plays rugby for Wigan."

The woman in charge of the team came over to speak to Adrian. Emily pulled Laurel aside. "Is Dad okay?"

"I don't know. He's been very quiet. Maybe he's tired," Laurel suggested.

"He wasn't holding your hand, like Antonia's mum. And did you see them kissing over there?" Emily asked, with astonishment, as if the pair had been copulating in front of a packed crowd at Deepdale.

"You should have been focusing on the game." Laurel laughed.

"We won, didn't we?" shrugged the girl.

"You did. And you played very well. Not that I'm an expert."

"Didn't you play netball at your school?" Emily asked blithely.

"Erm, no. Not while I was there," Laurel replied diplomatically. *You're talking to someone who went to a boys' grammar school, honey.* "I wish I *had* been able to play netball," Laurel added, with wistful honesty.

"Why doesn't Dad hold your hand and kiss you?" Emily continued, insistently.

"It may be difficult for him… in front of you. And after all, we've only just met up again. But actually, Emily," Laurel confided, "He has. We had a couple of kisses and a hug in Sunnyhurst on Sunday."

"I thought that's what you were doing." She beamed cheekily. Laurel put her arm around the girl's shoulder, Emily reciprocating by placing her arm around Laurel's back. Gathering her friend Becca, they followed Adrian back to the car.

"You can sit in the front, Becca," Emily said, clinging to her new adult friend. If Laurel felt mildly uneasy, it was not so much that Adrian might have been doing the hugging, but that she was sensuously warmed by the touch of the attractive teenager. *Keep in control, Laurel; this is something beautiful and innocent, not something bad. Don't push her away; maybe, separated from her mother, she needs this tender contact with a woman.*

A couple of minutes into the journey home, Emily flopped her head onto Laurel's shoulder. "Tired?" Laurel asked. Emily nodded.

"Why do you have to go away? We're like new friends. I'm just getting to know you."

"It won't be for long," Laurel explained. "And now that you've shown me Kik, we can keep kicking one another. I'll kick you up out of bed every morning if you like!"

"You're funny," Emily giggled. "Kind of uncool, but cool with it." *A compliment, Laurel.*

"Are you sure you haven't got a boyfriend in London? Or a husband?" Emily asked, looking directly into Laurel's eyes.

"Trust me, Emily. There's no one in London. I haven't had a serious boyfriend for nearly two years." Laurel scrolled through the photos on her phone until she came to some of her flat. "That's the wardrobe. Any men's clothes?"

"Nice dresses!" the girl drooled, with excited lake-sized eyes. "Did you get them in Oxford Street? I want to come to London!"

"Maybe you can one day. But I'm planning to sell my flat and move back up here."

"Lit!"

Outside Joseph's house, Laurel kissed Emily on the cheek and gave her one last hug. Then, she leaned through Adrian's window, promised to let him know how her meeting went on Friday, and kissed his lips briefly, but tenderly. She and Emily waved to one another until the car turned the corner.

Closing her eyes as the train sped southwards, Laurel replayed all that had happened. Three weeks ago, she had been sitting at her desk, irritated and disgruntled, with no inkling of what the following week would have in store. Had she really walked out? Had she really intended to ditch her career of twenty-seven years? For what? For whom?

Adrian. What on earth was the matter with him yesterday evening? Okay, he had sporadically shown traces of diffidence when he was a young man, but in his mid-forties? Was he really worth chucking it all in for? She could have wrung his neck last night. And yet.

And yet, after more than twenty years of silence, they were in a relationship of some kind. The very thought of him warmed her, sweetened her. Generally, things had gone well; broken bridges repaired, they had chatted and laughed; they had kissed and he had, albeit briefly and coyly, held her in his arms. She had cooked dinner in his home; and she had definitely made a hit with Emily.

Emily! Laurel snatched her phone and opened Kik.

Hi, Emily.

Erm, what exactly do you need to say, Laurel?

Hope you're having a good day. So glad I met you. Big meeting tomorrow, keep your fingers crossed for me. See you soon.

Prompted by her own words, Laurel's thoughts turned to the 'big meeting'. She needed a strategy; she had to be confident, to appear to know exactly what she wanted. Suddenly business-like, she cleared the space before her, grabbed a pen and a notebook from her bag, and began to list her objectives rationally. *Single-mindedness, Laurel; you have to make this tell.*

She had only been home for a matter of minutes, and had just messaged Maddie and made a cup of coffee, when there was a knock at the door. Mrs H, no doubt.

"I heard a door, and I thought it must be you. Are you all right? I've got a parcel for you. I didn't bring it with me, in case it wasn't you. Oh, and I've got some news. You'll never believe what's happened! I'll just be a minute."

Without getting a word in edgeways, let alone inviting the woman into her home, three minutes later,

Laurel was making another mug of coffee while listening to a convoluted tale of how the man in the flat above had been arrested before breakfast on Monday. It took a lot of persuasion to convince the well-meaning woman to resume her Neighbourhood Watch through the net curtains of her own flat.

Alone again, Laurel exhaled deeply and flumped onto her sofa. Exhausted, she lit a cigarette. Dealing with regional head office tomorrow would be a doddle after that.

Although the meeting was scheduled for ten thirty, Laurel — in a navy-blue M&S suit, a white blouse and a green and navy neckerchief — was still waiting nervously at ten to eleven. When had Personnel become Human Resources? When had persons become 'resources'? Itching for a ciggie, she knew that the moment she headed outside, they would call for her; then, they would be tetchy for keeping them waiting. She fiddled with her phone. Nothing interesting on Facebook. She tried Kik.

Hi, Laurel. Did u get back OK? Dad all grumpy today. U gotta come back, missing u. Love u. XX

Laurel was in a state of semi-shock, tears forming in her eyes, when the heavy dark door opened. *Missing you, Laurel.* The regional manager himself was beckoning her in. *All grumpy today.* Dropping her phone into her bag, she took a gulp of air. *Love u, Laurel.* Teetering on the modest heels of her court shoes, she entered the HR manager's office.

FOURTEEN

A friendly face greeted Laurel from behind a highly polished desk. Even so, she felt as though she was on a fairground Waltzer. After inquiring about Laurel's health and expressing concern at her stress, Alison, the HR manager, asked how they could help her 'going forward'. Another dumb 'in' phrase. *What they're asking, Laurel, is how can they make the future better. So, here goes, girl. Breathe and...*

"The thing is, I haven't felt really happy or fulfilled for quite some time. I don't feel I'm in the right place..."

"I see," Alison mused. "So, is it a transfer that you're looking for? Are there staff problems in your branch?"

"We want to support you in any way possible," the regional manager oozed.

"No, no. The little team there are great," Laurel assured them. "I think the last inspection and the results show that. Just about everyone pulls together. It's not them at all. It's me. I'm jaded, run-down..."

"Well, perhaps if you take a break for three months? Either that, or do something quite different — a head office secondment, perhaps?" the HR manager suggested.

"Away from the cut and thrust of branch banking," the support actor added. The spectre of working alongside several Fart-arse Smyths was appalling, however. There would be plenty of cutting comments, not to mention thrusting probably sharp implements up his Farty rear end.

"I think I need to leave, to do something completely different." A silence. Only seconds, but an eternity.

"Leave, as in resign? Completely?" Alison was, for a moment, floored.

"Oh, but you're much too valuable to lose like that," her senior colleague interjected. "Experienced, well-liked. Look, keep this a state secret, but Hammersmith may be in the offing. There are… issues." He coughed meaningfully. "It needs someone reliable, dependable, like you."

"Normally I would be grateful and flattered, but…" She sighed. *Don't give up now, Laurel; and don't give in!* Emily's message flashed through her brain. "I was really hoping to discuss a severance package."

Replaying the scene in her mind later, she could not remember actually saying those words; the thing she did recall was the bristling reaction of the regional boss and his 'this-is-not-happening' expression. He glanced across at Alison for help.

"There isn't a formal severance scheme at the moment. We are not looking to shed senior personnel," Alison went on, using the crutch of formality for support against Laurel's shockwave. "Certainly not those with

217

your background." Laurel felt and looked crestfallen. She had stepped up, had not bottled it, made her difficult pitch.

"I'll tell you what we'll do," Alison began, recovering her poise. "Let me run an idea past head office. No promises; if there's a chance of something fairly generous, we'll talk again."

"In the meantime," the regional boss posited, "How would you feel about going back to the branch, at least for now? Trefor Rhys has been keeping an eye on things, as you know, but he's been through a lot himself."

"And we don't want two of you having a meltdown." Alison smiled; but there was pith and point in the comment, and Laurel took it on board.

"Yes, he's a good friend of mine. And he's been very helpful," Laurel agreed.

She nearly fell from the two steps onto the pavement of Regent Street. Buses, taxis and vans blurred her middle-distance vision; people flashed across her foreground, jostling her. Recovering slightly, she shuffled around the corner and lit a cigarette. She had played as well as she could; at best, at worst, it was a draw. Extra time needed. *But the most difficult passage of play is over, Laurel.*

The Underground sign invited her to flee homeward. Instead, after a bit of window shopping, she crossed Regent Street and cut through to Piccadilly, emerging by Malta House. Tempting, Malta. *But no,*

Laurel, you've staged one escape; just be patient and deal with the future here.

It was not quite lunchtime, but the spending of nervous energy had made Laurel peckish. Costa, opposite, was usually frenetic and noisy; so, she crossed Piccadilly and entered the churchyard of St James's. After browsing the market stalls, pausing to watch the skilled leather worker, and convincing herself that she needed another belt, she stepped down into the café. It was moderately busy, but she found a vacant spot.

The strains of Vivaldi floated from the church: a cellist was rehearsing for a lunchtime concert. So close to the hectic heart of the West End, this was an oasis of calm. She relaxed, closing her eyes to concentrate more on the music. Peace and baroque music in a café adjoining a small market: St Anne's on a grander stage. If she left London, she would miss moments like this. *Unless, Laurel, you actually take over Patrick's little business.*

She messaged Maddie.

MEET ME AFTER WORK.

Went badly, then?

Not AWFUL, but I need to talk.

OK if T's there too? Grapes, 5.45?

Fine. See you later.

The recital was beautiful, but over all too soon. She still had nearly four hours to kill. Although the day was not overly warm, it was fine; so, she strolled along Piccadilly, and into Hyde Park. Between cloudy spells, the sun bejewelled the Serpentine, where she took photos of the swans and geese, which she sent to Emily.

Trefor and Maddie were already inside the Bunch of Grapes when Laurel arrived. Through the large bowed window, she spotted them before they saw her. For a moment, she observed them, deep in conversation. *Admit it, Laurel; they look like a couple already.*

When she entered, they both threw their arms around her, as if they had not met for years. And with Trefor eager to know about the meeting at regional office, and Maddie demanding a detailed account of her stay in Lancashire, particularly the budding romance, it took Laurel two rounds of drinks to fill them in.

"So, what are you going to do?" Maddie and Trefor asked in unison. They were speaking as one already, even if they were focused on two different decisions that she had to make.

"I've got one or two ideas, but I'm going to wait and see what they come back with before I start making any serious plans. "And," Laurel said, swilling a little Shiraz, "What about you two? I'm not spoiling your plans for this evening, am I?"

"Well, as a matter of fact," began Maddie, looking impatiently at her watch. It was Trefor's guffaw that gave her away, though; and Maddie's pretended irritation dissolved into laughter.

"No, Laurel. To be honest, I'm pretty tired; so, we decided just to have a drink and go home," the Welshman said.

"But we're going out for lunch on Sunday," Maddie added, her eyes sparkling.

The weekend was not easy for Laurel, being in limbo. Should she put her flat on the market or not? Would she have to come down on the price too far to get a quick sale? Would she soon be looking for a small business to run? Could she get something in time for the coming summer?

Fearing she might drive herself mad, she devoted her energy to washing clothes, cleaning the flat, having longer than normal runs and answering Emily's Kik messages. She heard once from Adrian, a succinct question about how her meeting had gone. Not having to drive Emily around, he was playing cricket. *Are you missing him, Laurel, after just two proper dates?*

Sunday evening. The bottle of wine was almost empty. She poured the remainder and, snuggled inside her bathrobe, she nestled herself into the corner of her sofa and began to paint her fingernails.

"Oh, bugger!" she muttered, realising she had forgotten to get a cigarette out of the packet before applying the copper-coloured paint. She tried to shake

221

one out, but the packet was fairly full. Now, she would have to wait until the varnish had set.

She took a generous sip of wine. Three weeks ago, she had sat here, knocking back wine, with Monday looming. Was she back where she had started? No, absolutely not. Walking into that bank tomorrow, dressed in spring colours, she would be doing so in the knowledge that it would not be for ever. Of that much she was certain.

Later, she messaged Adrian, hoping he was okay and wishing him a good week. He had not replied when she went to bed.

Laurel walked brightly and confidently into the branch the next morning. Everyone seemed genuinely pleased to see her; and she was relieved to see just a small pile of paperwork on her desk, some of which were Trefor's notes on an important account. Maddie had mopped up much of the routine stuff. Two appointments had been scheduled, neither of them problematic clients.

Shortly after the first meeting was over, the internal phone rang. Young Steve, one of only two male clerks in the office, announced, "There's a Miss Waterson on the line. Should I put her through?"

"Waterson?" Laurel queried, unfamiliar with the name. "Is she asking for me personally?"

"Yes."

"Oh, go on, then. Laurel Ashworth speaking."

"Oh, hello, kiddo, I hope you don't mind me calling on your first day back."

"Aunty Hilda! Sorry, the lad introduced you as Miss Waterson, not Watkinson. Just a sec." Covering the mouthpiece, Laurel yelled through her open door, "CLOTH EARS! It's my Aunty Hilda!" A couple of giggles from the office. "He's a nice lad, but…"

"Are you okay to talk for a few minutes?" The tone of Hilda's voice prompted Laurel to stretch her leg and close the office door with her instep.

"Sure. Is everything all right?"

"Well, I don't know, Laurel. You remember I told you about Rosemary, the woman from church. Well, I don't think we're friends any longer."

"Oh, Aunty. I'm sorry. What happened? I thought you were getting on really well," Laurel sympathised. Hilda could be a little quirky; perhaps it had been too much for the woman. "So, who upset who?"

"No, I didn't mean that, kiddo. Far from it." Hilda breathed heavily. "Oh, I'm not myself; I'm all of a fluster."

"What on earth's the matter?" Laurel waited for Hilda to compose herself.

"On Saturday, I had another of my musical soirees. And when Rosemary arrived, she looked a bit out of sorts; and every time she started to tell me, while I was putting out the food, someone came in. Anyway, I did the little concert; and at the end of that lovely Debussy piece, *The girl with the flaxen hair* — well…" She paused.

"Well, I noticed she was sobbing into her hankie, all discreetly, like. Eventually, all the others left; it was quite late, and the two of us sat down with a cup of cocoa. She told me that her husband had filed for divorce, alleging unreasonable behaviour. Well, I don't think she's got an unreasonable bone in her body. Honestly, kiddo, he's only doing it so he can marry his bimbo. She was terribly distraught. You see, she'd been hoping he'd get it out of his system and come home; and suddenly, her hopes were shattered. I said, 'Well, I could see you were upset, dear, while I was playing.'

"And then she said, 'Play it again for me. It was so soulful and beautiful that it touched me deep inside.' So, I did. And part way through, she came and stood close by. She was sobbing again, so we sat together, and I just put my arm around her shoulders, as you do; and I said it would all be fine, that she had a friend in me. And then it happened."

"What, Aunty? Go on," Laurel urged.

"Well, it was nothing really, just reassuring her, you know; I gave her a hug and kissed her on the cheek. And then, suddenly, I don't know what came over me… us! The next moment, we were kissing on the lips…" Laurel let out a little gasp, more of excitement than of shock.

"Honestly, Laurel, I've been so disturbed. I've never felt anything like this before; well, not since the chap in the RAF, and that was before you were born. I haven't been able to concentrate, or to talk to anyone else, kiddo; I thought you were the least likely to be offended or shocked."

"Oh, Aunty Hilda! I'm glad you've told me," Laurel said, emotional herself. "And how do you feel about her?"

"Well, I don't know. I'm so befuddled and confused, which is unlike me, as you know. It's so unexpected. There have been a couple of men interested over the years, but I either managed to scare them off, or they moved on when they realised that they weren't getting my knickers off easily. But this, now. And with another woman!"

"Aunty, there's nothing wrong with that," Laurel said, stifling a giggle at Hilda's drollery.

"Don't get me wrong, kiddo. I'm not disgusted with myself, or anything like that. It's just that — well, I think I've shocked myself. Getting all worked up and having these feelings about somebody at my age."

"I wish I could get over there to give you a great big hug. So, what are you going to do?"

"Well, I keep telling myself that it's probably something and nothing. I apologised to her at church yesterday. And she laughed and said she'd intended to apologise to me. And I said, 'Whatever for?' Then we both started laughing. So, we're going out for lunch today; she's picking me up at twelve. We'll be somewhere public, and we can have a good talk about things. I don't want to lose her as a friend."

"I'm sure you won't. It all sounds lovely. Where are…" There was a knock at Laurel's door. Time to get on. "Now, you enjoy your lunch; and let me know!"

Maddie entered, wondering if Laurel would allow one of the small retailers an extra thousand on overdraft until the month end. "They're already more than twenty against a limit of fifteen," she explained.

"Whatever," Laurel shrugged. Maddie looked surprised at her friend's liberal response. "Just remind them not to forget you at Christmas," Laurel laughed.

"It's good to see you here and in a bright mood again," Maddie said sweetly.

"Go on, before I change my mind," the manager winked.

Hilda's news, told in her inimitable style, coloured the rest of Laurel's day. She was still feeling light when a call from regional office came through the following morning.

"Alison, Hi!"

"How does it feel to be back, Laurel?" the HR manager inquired.

"Could be a lot worse," Laurel replied.

"Erm, I'm obviously phoning about our conversation last Friday. I've done what I can, but the offer may not be as much as you were hoping for."

"Hit me with it, Alison."

"Based on your present salary, you would be walking away with between twenty-five and thirty thousand. As I said, there isn't a severance scheme in place at the moment."

Laurel turned the figure over. "Well, it's not great, but it's something. I'll need to think about it."

"The thing is, Laurel, they'd like an answer within a week: Tuesday, as Monday's a holiday."

"Okay, Alison. No problem. I'll let you know by Tuesday morning. Thanks."

Laurel stood up and glanced around her office. Talking numbers had brought the possibility of leaving here for the last time into sharper focus. Would she have enough? She picked up her bag and walked to the back door, where she lit a cigarette.

"Alison at HR?" Maddie asked, having noticed Laurel heading down the corridor.

"Uh-huh." A pause. The question didn't need to be asked. "Not great, but... I don't know, Maddie. I'm going to have to see what I can get for the flat."

Laurel called an estate agency, who eagerly offered her a visit at five thirty that afternoon. She would have to leave work a bit early and wouldn't have much time to tidy up, but she accepted. Should she make an appointment with a rival agency? *Probably, but see how this goes first.*

The agent, Nigel, was optimistic. The building was well maintained, around the corner from a bus stop and local shops, and only a few minutes' walk from the Underground.

"Sorry it's a bit of a mess. I've only been back a few days. Haven't had time to sort everything out," Laurel apologised, as he began to measure her bedroom. She hastily scooped up most of the lingerie and nylons that were strewn on the bed, and tossed them into the bottom of the wardrobe. He aimed his camera.

"Like Tracey Emin on a bad hair day," she joked in an embarrassed voice, conscious that his gaze had followed the nylon, satin and lace.

"Don't worry about it. I'm sure you'd have it tidy for any viewings, which might happen as soon as the weekend. The market for this sort of property is pretty strong," he said cheerily.

His estimated selling price gave Laurel a fillip. In the time she had been living there, the value had almost doubled. Even after paying off her mortgage, she would have a clear £180,000 profit. That, added to the bank's offer, would make a viable amount of capital. *More positive, Laurel, but this is a huge step.*

She sat down with a mug of coffee, turned on the early evening news, and checked her phone. The Kik symbol indicated that a message was waiting.

Hi, Laurel. How r u? Dad's a bit weird. Like dead quiet & not happy. Maybe missing u?

For the first second or two, her heart seemed to fizz. Adrian was missing her. Maybe. But had she wanted to see that? Did it make her dilemma any easier? Her heart was saying one thing, 'Go! Do it!'; her rational head, the opposite. She liked this flat; she had made it home, her home. As she scanned her living room, her eyes lighted on a photo of her father. He would have known what to do; but he was three years beyond asking.

"Aarrrgh!" she screamed, stomping over to the booze cabinet, and pouring herself at least a triple Irish whiskey. She reached for her phone.

Missing you — both of you — too. Fingers crossed, though. Agent thinks I can sell my flat at a good price. Got to decide what to do.

Emily's reply was a heart emoji.

By Wednesday, the novelty of being back at work was wearing off. Laurel sat in her office, poring over some figures that needed to go to head office; but her mind was not fully engaged in the work, and her heart was definitely not in it.

Normally irritated by interruptions, she was relieved when her personal mobile bleeped. A message from Stella.

Hope you're OK, sweet. Any news?

Laurel threw the reports across her desk and dialled Stella's number. They had spent a wonderful weekend in the Lake District; and on the evening of their anniversary, Don had given her an eternity ring, the diamonds set in white gold.

"So, how about you?" Stella asked.

"Hmmm," Laurel said sighing. "Back at work for now, trying to decide what to do. I haven't heard much from Adrian; in fact, he was a bit odd, preoccupied, when I last saw him. Emily keeps in touch. Even she said Adrian was being a bit weird, not saying much."

"*Mela*, he doesn't show his feelings easily. He's a thinker, *ta'*. In his own way, he's probably coming to terms with everything that's happened."

"I keep wondering if it's worth taking such a big risk for," Laurel mused.

"It, or he?" Stella asked incisively. *Laurel, this woman can see right through you.*

Having said goodbye to Stella, Laurel got up and closed the door firmly. She rummaged through her bag for the estate agent's business card. "Is that Nigel? Hi, this is Laurel Ashworth. Let's go for it." A moment later, Laurel called Maddie into her office, again closing the door behind her.

"I've told the agent to go ahead and advertise the flat." Maddie grabbed her hand and squeezed tightly. She clearly felt the weight of this moment, for Laurel saw her friend's eyes watering.

"Why not?" said Maddie, bravely. "Even if it's on the market, you aren't committing yourself."

"Oh, Maddie, I don't know what to do, or what I'm feeling," Laurel said tremulously.

"What's your heart telling you to do?"

FIFTEEN

As Laurel studied Maddie's face, twenty years rolled away from the features. "Remember the first time you asked me that? In that wine bar?"

It had been 1999: eighteen months after Laurel had moved to London. The two had recently become good friends, having met on a training course. While comforting Maddie through her marriage break-up, Laurel — still Lawrie — had faced a momentous decision: whether, after years of secret cross-dressing and occasionally venturing to a tolerant bar, to begin transitioning and to start dressing as a woman for work. And whether to spend most of her savings on a breast implant op.

Maddie had supported Laurel's transition all the way, even through her own divorce. One day, soon after Laurel had started wearing a skirt and make-up for work, Maddie had taken an afternoon off to go around to the branch where her friend worked; she had spoken passionately, even angrily, to those colleagues who had been making Laurel's life hell.

By the time Maddie's second daughter was born, in the autumn of 2002, Laurel had returned to work after her gender reassignment surgery. They had traded stories of pain, both glad that they would never have to go through what the other had.

Maddie released Laurel's hand and hugged her, saying, "I know you'll do the right thing. And whatever you decide, I'll be here for you."

Wiping a tear from her friend's cheek, and feeling her own eyes filling, Laurel kissed Maddie's forehead. "You're the best friend ever," she whispered.

The estate agent sent some photos for Laurel's approval. Scrolling through them, she yelped, "Oh my God! Look!"

"What?" asked Maddie, peering at the screen.

"Look, on the bed!" In the foreground, on one corner of the bed, lay the olive-green French knickers, with the roses of lace.

"Makes the place look lived in," Maddie laughed. "And now I know what my boss wears in bed," she added, running out of the office before Laurel could retaliate. The estate agent offered to swap it, but Laurel agreed with Maddie.

She left the office early and signed the contract at the estate agency, her blushes somewhat spared by the fact that Nigel was elsewhere. She would stick with the sole agency for now. She wasn't desperate to sell: if it happened, it happened.

Hi, Adrian, how are you? Bank offer not hugely generous, but put flat on market today. At least I can see what the market's like, then make a decision.

The last sentence was an afterthought, fearing that Adrian might feel pressured by her sudden re-entry into his life. Then, she spent a few minutes deciding which of the agent's photos to put on her Facebook page. The kitchen was bright, clean and tidy. So was the bedroom, but... *Do you really want the world and his wife to see your knickers, Laurel? Who cares? It's a nice photo.* She tapped, and it uploaded.

Seventeen likes later, but with no reply from Adrian, Laurel drained her glass of wine. Then, snuffing the scented candle that she had lit at dusk, she went to bed.

Next morning, Laurel's cheerful mood was heightened when she realised she was being admired discreetly by a well-dressed man, evidently on his way into the City. Her mother would have called him 'dishy'. She made sure of his attention before smiling generously as she stepped off at South Ken. *Perhaps you ought to take the District Line more often, girl, even if it's a bit slower than the Piccadilly.*

"Morning, everyone," she called out to the three staff who had arrived before her. However, her mood quickly altered when she read the note that had been left on her desk.

Meeting 10.30 — Mr B. Schuster & Mr Silverman. Laurel's heart sank. Schuster and Shyster; another round of sparring. She went outside. While she was still smoking, Maddie appeared.

"Showing everyone your knickers now, you hussy!" her friend quipped.

"Don't!" Laurel laughed. "And who made that bloody appointment?"

"Oh," Maddie said, looking guilty. "I didn't want to spoil your evening. But he did pay in yesterday."

As things turned out, Laurel need not have worried. The men were most polite and business-like, her customer having closed two good deals that would bring his overdraft well in line. Moreover, with another lucrative contract in the pipeline, he was amenable to rescheduling his loan over two extra years.

"It will mean we have to raise the interest rate by one percent," Laurel stated. The lawyer, fairly quiet until then, sucked loudly through his teeth. His client grimaced.

"But, my dear Miss Ashworth," Silverman began.

"Okay. A half." Laurel smiled. So did the men.

As they were leaving, the lawyer turned back. "I'm pleased to finally meet you. I apologise if, on the phone the other week, I was a little, you know, testy. I trust that there are no hard feelings."

Laurel, shaking his hand a second time, replied, "No apology necessary. In fact, Mr Silverman, you don't know how much you helped me that day." The lawyer looked at her quizzically for a moment, then nodded and followed his client out. Watching him go, Laurel was unsure who was the more gob-smacked.

Even by the Friday morning, Laurel had not heard back from Adrian. Maybe Emily was right, and he was weird; maybe Stella was right, and he was finding the situation difficult. His silence, however, was not helping Laurel to assess whether she was risking all for nothing. The pressure only increased when the estate agent phoned to say that he already had two parties interested in seeing her flat.

"Would you be able to do a couple of viewings tomorrow morning? How about ten and eleven thirty? They both seem highly promising," he added, with the cock-sure confidence that such people naturally exude.

"Erm, yes. Fine. Great," Laurel answered, momentarily flabbergasted. By the time she left work for the long weekend, Laurel had a third appointment, late on Saturday afternoon.

Once back home, Laurel contacted Emily, who reported that her father was still in a strange mood.

He isn't eating much and he's had a bad row with Mum.

Be nice to him, and give him a hug from me. Say I'll message him later.

She nipped out and grabbed a pizza, not being bothered to cook, or to have to deal with dishes and stuff before the first viewing. Leave the kitchen looking nice. Suitably relaxed after two glasses of wine, and with a CD of Bach's Forty-eight playing, she decided to bite the bullet.

Adrian, are you OK? Concerned about you. Got three viewings tomorrow. Agent hopeful of quick sale. Love u.

A strident foreign tone broke in upon the G minor prelude. Her phone was ringing. She was surprised to see that the caller was Adrian!

"Hello, long lost friend," Laurel said, turning down the music.

"Sorry, I've been a bit under the weather, and busy."

"Yeah, Emily said you weren't quite yourself. So, what do you think of my news? Exciting, isn't it?"

"Yes, I suppose so. I'm pleased you've got interest in your flat. But, have you thought this through properly? If you just quit the bank, what'll you do for an income? It isn't London, but you'll still need a living up here."

"I should have plenty to rent a flat and start a business," she replied, disappointed that he was thinking only of the potential negatives.

"What business? A bit risky at the moment, with Brexit and everything. Things are hardly booming up here."

"I thought you'd be happy…" *Laurel, that sounded lame and pathetic.*

"All I'm saying is think of the dangers. Look before you leap. You've got a home in London; a good job, which should give you a decent pension…"

"Oh, bugger, Adrian! Do you always have to talk like a bloody accountant?" Silence. A sigh.

"Why don't you request a transfer to this region? Lancashire, Manchester…" he suggested.

"The traffic crawling into Manchester is worse than London; and I'm not commuting on those rickety old trains they've had since I was a kid. They're ridiculously overcrowded; there are laws against doing that to animals."

"Okay, okay. It's your neck. Just weigh everything up before you commit yourself."

"Sure," she said, calming down. "I'll see what happens tomorrow." Maybe Adrian was right, too.

Gustav Leonhardt had just launched into the A minor fugue when Laurel received a message from Stella.

Guess who just called! He's worried that you're making a mistake. I asked why worry - it's your risk. Told him you're intelligent, you'd only risk everything for something vitally important. Invited him for Sunday lunch.

Stella, you're amazing! Thank you. I'll call you Monday.

'What a great friend,' Laurel thought as she lounged back on her sofa. She deeply appreciated how lucky she had been to meet Stella, and to have had Maddie as a friend for the last twenty years.

Fidgety, fiddling with cushions, Laurel spent more than an hour early Saturday morning, making her flat as perfect as possible. Then, she decided it looked too perfect, like a show house, so she fiddled some more. Nervous, never having done this before, she was conscious that there were not just bricks and mortar, functionality and décor on show: it was her home — herself — being examined. She checked several times that no lingerie was on display; she opened every window to let in fresh air, which created an unpleasant through-draught, so she closed most of them; she re-adjusted the cushions. Finally, she went for a walk to calm herself.

The first potential buyer arrived promptly at ten o'clock, accompanied by Nigel, who explained that the man had already made an offer on another property. *Don't pin your hopes on this one, Laurel.* The next visitor came alone, a stocky young woman in a black leather jacket and ripped denim jeans. She seemed much more interested, even excited; and she asked several questions about the area and the occupants of the other apartments.

"Would you like a cup of coffee?" Laurel asked, feeling comfortable with the viewer, though unsure whether it was the done thing or not.

"No, thanks, I've got lots to do. I'm getting married next week," the woman said smiling.

"Congratulations."

"But can I take a couple of photos?" the woman asked. "I'll send them to my other half. She's away in Berlin, doing a shoot. She moved in with me three months ago, but my place is just too small: the bedroom is about the size of your bathroom!"

"Could we come and have another look, maybe next week, when my partner gets back?" the woman asked, as she was leaving. It was only after saying goodbye that Laurel noticed Mrs H's door was ajar. Interrogation in three, two, one...

"Ooh, it is you," the owner of flat 2 bleated. "I heard voices, but I wasn't sure." Laurel smiled weakly. "You aren't selling, are you?"

"Maybe. They haven't had time to put up a sign outside yet," Laurel explained.

"Have you got a promotion in the bank? Are they moving you somewhere nice?"

"I might be moving back up north. We'll see." Not wanting to feed the Acton Argus with further titbits, Laurel smiled and closed her door.

Laurel knew all about counting chickens before they hatch, but she went through to her kitchen and prepared a salad, feeling pretty buoyant. While she was eating, Nigel called to advise her that the next appointment was a French girl, who was starting a Master's course after the summer.

When Laurel opened the front door, she found herself face to face with a middle-aged couple. The man was tall, silver-haired, and smartly dressed; his wife, considerably shorter, despite her two-inch heels, had copper-coloured hair, cut in a 1960s style. Neither looked like a student.

"Can I help you?" Laurel asked, but her question was drowned by the woman's shout of something in French, directed along the street. Laurel peered to her right and saw a pasty-faced girl, with glasses and a spiky punkish hairstyle; obviously the student.

"Good afternoon," the man said; and, with a slight bow, introduced himself and his family. "My wife does not much speak the English," he continued. Laurel assumed that his daughter did, and probably better, though she said almost nothing throughout. In fact, she looked totally uninterested, as if she wanted to be anywhere but there. Whenever Laurel tried to make eye contact, the girl turned away. The family chatted together in French, the parents sounding reasonably upbeat; Laurel did not need a translator to glean that they were more enthusiastic than their daughter.

"Do you need to know anything about the area?" Laurel asked the girl.

"Not really," the punk mumbled. Her father asked a few details, making notes in a small leather-bound

241

book, before divulging that he considered an apartment in London as an investment, as well as a temporary home for Little Miss Glum.

"One bloke who's already buying somewhere else, a keenish gay woman who's marrying a model, and a miserable French punk. Honestly, Maddie, a face like a smacked arse," Laurel told her later. "But there's obviously money in the background."

"Maybe she's just spoilt," her colleague suggested. "Still, one buyer is all you need. And you might get some more round next week."

"Hmm," replied Laurel, unsure whether she wanted to repeat the experience. "Are you still free on Monday?"

"Yeah. Trefor's playing golf somewhere. We're going out tomorrow, though. Not till the afternoon, I told him. I'll need to get over tonight's gig in Brighton. What do you want to do?"

"Let's have lunch. I'll come over to you. I need an escape after today."

The whirlpool of unknowing was still swirling in Laurel's head when she awoke on Sunday morning. She was in a state of flux, the pros and cons ebbing and flowing constantly. It was as bad as when she had pondered the massive life-changing decisions during her transitioning. Risk and reward? Worth the agony? Outcomes obscure? And time was closing in fast: she had to respond to the bank's offer in just forty-eight hours.

She took out the stress and frustration on her trainers, all the way to, and twice around, Gunnersbury Park. Once home, she relaxed in her bathtub with a rose and gold bath bomb by Fifi & Kiki, a Christmas present from Maddie; it felt and looked luxurious, and its scent was heavenly. Well worth having prune fingers for! She spent the rest of the day in silky knickers and her kimono, clearing out her wardrobe and drawers. Getting rid of stuff was a must if she was going to move. IF!

It was dusk when she tied up the second charity sack. A good job done, she grabbed some deli cheese from her fridge, posh crackers and grapes that needed eating; then, she settled on the sofa with a bottle of Shiraz Cabernet. Between checks of her social media, she sipped her way through the wine. All of it. There was no news from anyone. It was just after midnight when a Kik contact appeared. Emily had sent a picture of Stella, Adrian and her in Lytham.

Lovely photo! But you're up late!

No school next week! Love u.

Love u too.

At ten the following morning, with no further contact from the estate agent, Laurel put on her new burgundy lace dress, checking in the mirror. *Good choice, Laurel.* She applied matching lippy, slipped a long black cardie on, and walked to the Underground. Once she was on the Hayes train from Cannon Street, she messaged Maddie, who was waiting at Ladywell.

They walked through the fields, pausing by the curly modern bridge that spans the stream. "You can walk all the way to Deptford Creek now," Maddie said.

"Sounds delightful!" Laurel sneered jokingly.

"Or we could just have lunch. There's a café here in the park; but a nicer one just around the corner. Yummy cakes and desserts." That would negate yesterday's extra-long jog, but this was Maddie, her best friend.

"Trefor?" Laurel asked, once they were seated in La Delice.

"Yes." Maddie grinned, before devouring another forkful of tart.

"What does that mean?"

"You know," Maddie said, nodding. "We're getting along really well. Steady at first…"

"And?"

"And," said Maddie, surrendering. "He kissed me properly yesterday, under a tree in Richmond Park. We sat down to talk and…" The glint in Maddie's eye told Laurel all she needed to know.

"I'm so happy for you both," Laurel said smiling.

"What about you?" returned Maddie, forking more tart. "Any progress?"

Laurel shrugged, then showed her the Kik photo, explaining that Stella had invited Adrian. "It's like

244

having two secret agents working for me." Laurel laughed, a sparkle now in her eye, but Maddie became serious.

"Are you sure about what you're giving up?" Maddie asked, fixing her gaze.

"No, I'm not, but …"

"It's usually me that does the mad thing isn't it? But, tell me straight, Laurel. What do you really feel about him? In love? And he with you?"

"I honestly don't know, honey. I think I am. And I want to believe he is with me, or at least getting there. Otherwise, why am I doing this?" *Hang on, Laurel, you'd made up your mind about the bank before you even got back in touch.* Maddie had got there already.

"So, there's more to all this than him, isn't there?" Laurel nodded slowly and sadly. "I'll miss you if you go," Maddie cooed. Laurel was about to quip about her now having Trefor, but held back.

They each had two glasses of wine in the pub along the main road, where Maddie's current jazz band had played one of their first gigs. That prompted a lazily pleasant two hours of reminiscing about the last twenty years.

"We had a long heart-to-heart," Stella related that evening, getting straight to the point. "Don took Emily to play crazy golf. Adrian is very deep — it took a while to get him talking, like most men. Don would be just the same. They don't give much away, *ta'*. Apart from the surprise — and he's glad that you contacted him — he said you're quite a different person from the one he knew." Laurel's mouth went dry: how much had Adrian said?

"I think he just needs more time. But there's something there; he needs someone, *ḥanina*. And he's open to believing it could be you. And Emily, well, you don't need me to tell you… Don't pressure him; give him some space and time; but don't give up, Laurel. It will happen."

D Day: Laurel was acutely aware of that as she boarded at Acton Town. How long could she delay making the call to Alison? The severance offer; the flat; Adrian; London or Lancashire; her future. *What a situation you've got yourself into, Laurel!* Should she stick with what she knew, plodding on in relative security; or should she leap into something risky and, as yet, hidden from her? *Remain, or Leave? Bugger Brexit!*

She had only been in the office a few minutes, pondering her dilemma, when her mobile rang. Surely Alison didn't need to know first thing! It was Nigel, the estate agent; she guessed that the lesbian couple wanted to arrange a visit.

"I've got some good news for you," the cheery realtor began. "We've had an offer."

"Really?" she gasped, unable to disguise her astonishment.

"A little under the asking price, but it's a cash purchase, so there's no chain."

"I'm surprised. The woman said she wanted to look again, when her partner returned," Laurel explained.

"No, this is the Frenchman. He thinks your property has better investment potential than the one his daughter preferred. He's offered nine thousand below, so not a huge gap." Laurel gulped, speechless.

"If you want a couple of hours to think about it…" Nigel went on, though she wasn't really listening. *Snatch his arm off, Laurel. But wait: what if Adrian…? Don't refuse, you can pull out later.* The argument raged in her head. She closed her eyes.

"Yes. Yes, that's fine. I'll accept his offer."

Shaking, Laurel dropped her mobile, grabbed her bag, and went out for a cigarette. Afterwards, she occupied herself with paperwork until her appointment arrived. When he left, shortly after eleven, she checked her phone. Was there a confirmatory sign from Adrian? Nothing. Another cigarette, her third that morning. The weeds in the yard were lush; so was the trash from the tenant above. Something had to be done.

Laurel strode into her office, seized the phone and dialled.

"Alison? It's Laurel Ashworth. I've thought this through, and …" She paused to collect herself. "Although it isn't as much as I'd hoped, I'm going to take the offer you made last week." There was disappointment in Alison's voice, as well as in her words. Laurel even detected a note of bitterness.

"Notice? Yes, I guess I am."

"Could you confirm that by email today, then?" the HR manager asked officiously.

"Erm, sure." There was a momentary silence. "What… what happens now?"

"So, Laurel, it's time to weed the vegetable patch and tend the roses."

"Sorry?"

"Gardening leave."

"Uh?"

"It's the best way; the usual way now. Several hacked off managers have screwed the bank over while working out their time. Falsifying returns; loans to non-existent customers; you name it, they've done it."

"When from, then?"

"Tomorrow."

That was it. Just that. Twenty-seven years, and that was that. Talk about an unceremonious exit! Laurel was unsure whether to laugh or cry; to scream with rage or cheer from the rooftop. Having replaced the handset, she inhaled deeply, then she called out, "Maddie, have you got a minute?"

"Shall I tell the rest of the staff?" Maddie asked, not altogether surprised by Laurel's news, but shocked, as people are when bereaved. It had actually happened.

"No, I'll do it once we've shut the doors at the end of the day."

In the late afternoon, Maddie returned to Laurel's office with a sheaf of papers and some folders. She spent a long time, asking questions about specific accounts, going into what seemed unnecessary detail, until almost ten past five. *Maybe she's clinging on, just can't let go, Laurel.* Then, Maddie's phone bleeped; and the fussy questions ceased.

Moments later, it was Laurel who could not let go. Grasping Maddie's hand tightly as they emerged into the banking hall, Laurel gasped. A few coloured balloons had been hastily stuck to the walls and the woodwork. All her staff were there, and Trefor! There were hugs and handshakes and a few tears. Then, young Steve stepped forward, clutching a large paper carrier. He looked around nervously, but nobody else volunteered to do it.

"Erm, we wanted to… I mean, we didn't want you to leave… not without a present," he stuttered.

One of the older staff came to his rescue. "So, only hearing about it today, somebody nipped out and… Well, please accept this with our best wishes; and we're all very sorry that you're leaving."

As Steve handed over the bag, there was a general round of applause. A bottle of champagne, that was obvious; and something soft, wrapped separately. Carefully, she placed the bottle on the counter and opened the item. It was a silk scarf, printed with purple and gold butterflies.

"Thank you, ever so much," Laurel uttered, forcing the words past the lump in her throat. They hardly seemed enough. "I… Oh God, I hadn't planned for this to happen so suddenly," Laurel apologised. "Look, everyone. I know you all have trains to catch, so just let me say that you've all worked tremendously hard to make this branch successful. Thank you for supporting me in that; and I'm sure that whoever takes over will feel lucky to have such a great team."

There were 'Ahs' and expressions of agreement; then, after more hugs and tears, the colleagues drifted out, leaving Laurel, Maddie and Trefor together. "You'd better take my keys," Laurel said, handing them to her friend.

"Do you fancy a quick drink?" Trefor asked.

"Normally, Tref, I wouldn't say no, as you know; but there's something I need to do. We'll make a date soon and have a proper drink-up," Laurel replied. Kissing both of them, she gathered her presents and her bag. Then, she stepped out, onto the busy South Kensington street; out into the big, new world.

A few weeks earlier, she had marched to the Underground, defiantly determined. Now, having quit in such blistering order, she was practically shell-shocked. She had sworn she would not be back; okay, she had done another week. However, when she had left her flat that morning, had she really expected to arrive home no longer a bank manager?

There was something else that she had to resolve. And there was one way to do it.

PART THREE

It is a myth that a butterfly will die if you touch it.

SIXTEEN

Adrian, can you call me urgently?

Laurel sent it as an SMS and on Messenger. An hour later, with no reply, she opened Kik. Cowardly? Maybe, but shrewd.

Emily, I'm coming up by coach overnight. Can I sleep on your sofa tomorrow night? Will explain when I see u.

She showered and changed into a T-shirt and a brushed cotton tracksuit for the journey. Spring and summer clothes were packed into a large suitcase, together with the lingerie she had folded and put away only two days earlier. Her make-up went into her tote bag, along with the scarf she had been given that afternoon.

Dad says OK and are you OK?

Thanks, honey. You're GOAT. See you tmrw.

Trundling noisily to the Underground, Laurel stopped to drop her spare keys and a note to the estate agency. She had not told Mrs H, but that was unnecessary; she would have heard the case bouncing down the front steps and watched her until out of sight. There was more trundling than she had bargained for: Victoria coach station was further from the Tube than she had imagined.

By the time the coach reversed out of its bay, almost full of a diverse ethnic mix of travellers, the evening had become night. She nodded off from time to time, apologising when her head lolled onto the shoulder of the Indian man next to her. Milton Keynes, Coventry, Birmingham punctuated Laurel's rest; and by the time they reached Manchester Airport, it was fully daylight.

Beyond the central Manchester station, the coach was fairly empty; the Indian man had left, so Laurel was able to spread herself out more. It was only during the long descent from the moors into Darwen that she thought, 'Nearly seven o'clock, I would have been getting up for work. What on earth have I done? And what the hell am I going to do for the next ten hours? Is anything open here at this time?'

The coach pulled up at Darwen Circus. Yawning, Laurel staggered to the front and down the steps. The driver lifted her case from the storage space and placed it on the pavement. She muttered her thanks and, zipping up her top completely, scanned the near-deserted streetscape. A car horn sounded.

"Here! Get in!" Laurel's heart jumped. She knew the voice. The coach drove away, revealing Adrian's car. "When Emily told me, we checked what time the coach from London came through. So, I got up a bit earlier. I'll drop you at home, and then I'll go off to work. You can have a rest."

"Thanks, Adrian," Laurel said, still in a semi-stupor.

"Emily won't be around very early. We stayed up talking till late. No netball this week, it's half term. I would have suggested you rest on my bed this morning; but Martin's at home. That might draw comment."

Laurel nodded, asking, "So, if Martin's there, what about dinner?"

He laughed. "Are you volunteering to cook again?"

"If it will help. I ought to do something…" She yawned again.

"So, what happened with the bank?" Adrian asked, after a polite pause.

"Gardening leave. Bloody cheek!"

"What? Why?"

"I'll tell you later," Laurel promised. "Thanks again," she said, kissing him lightly on the cheek. *Near enough, Laurel: overnight mouth, not nice.*

Adrian let Laurel into the house, which was otherwise silent. She brushed her teeth, poured a glass of orange juice, and lay down on the sofa. Within a minute or so, she was fast asleep. When she awoke, the sun was shining brightly through the living room window.

"Hi," said a little voice; and Laurel felt a kiss on her forehead.

"Emily! Hi, darling. Oh, God, what time is it?"

"Eleven thirty," the girl replied. "I tried not to wake you while I was having breakfast and emptying the washing machine. And Martin's wearing his headphones, so you can't hear his horrible music."

"That's very kind of you both," Laurel said, stretching her arms.

"Do you want some coffee?" asked Emily, gliding into the kitchen.

"I'd love some."

A few moments later, Martin lurched through the room. "Hi, Martin," Laurel said cheerfully. Grunting an acknowledgement, he passed into the kitchen, grabbed a handful of biscuits, and returned upstairs. Emily made a face as she handed Laurel a mug.

After finishing some school work, Emily made a salad, which they shared. Laurel thought about going for a walk, or even a run afterwards, but the sky had turned grey and threatening. The doorbell rang. Emily let in her friend, the slightly goofy kid who Laurel had seen in Sunnyhurst. The two exchanged glances of recognition. Alexandra was introduced to 'Laurel, Dad's girlfriend.'

While Laurel was washing the lunch plates, big rain splatters began to scar the kitchen window. All three rushed outside to rescue the clothes from another soaking. Emily scurried to where her underwear was hanging, including the black lacy bra, which she smuggled into the basket, hiding it beneath the shirts that Alexandra threw in. Laurel smiled at the girl's coyness. Emily saw the smile and blushed.

On the way in, Laurel whispered, "Don't be embarrassed. I brought it in the other week. I love wearing lacy, feminine things like that. And silky stuff. I'll show you something I got yesterday."

Emily looked startled for a moment, fearing that Laurel was about to lift her T-shirt. Reaching into her bag, Laurel pulled out the silk scarf. "One of my leaving presents," she said, handing it to the girls.

"Nice," said Alexandra, holding out the scarf to admire the butterflies. Emily drew it through her friend's hand and put it around her own neck, posing in the mirror. They chatted all afternoon about clothes, Laurel's wardrobe and London shops, locating them on her laptop.

"Shepherd's pie okay for you?" Laurel asked Martin, during his next sortie to the kitchen.

"Yeah, cool," he replied, munching a Cadbury's Boost. "Have you got that chocolate fudge cheesecake again? That was wicked."

Laurel shook her head apologetically. *And I'm not traipsing through the rain to get one.*

"Can Alexandra stay?" Emily asked.

"If that's okay with her mother and your dad. Not my house, not my rules." While the girls were dutifully texting their respective parents, Laurel sorted through her bag.

259

"Michael Kors, that's cool," Alexandra said.

"And you've got some lovely make-up," Emily added, eyeing the items on the coffee table. "I wish I had. Dad won't give me any money for it; he says I'm too young. I have to get it from the pound shop, and it's rubbish."

By now, Alexandra had pulled the cap off a No7 'plum beautiful' lipstick. "Nice colour, Laurel," she cooed, as she held it inches away from her face.

"Go on, try it." Laurel smiled, reading the girl's thoughts.

Emily grabbed an eyeliner pencil and went to the mirror. "Lit!" she exclaimed, turning round.

"Come here," Laurel said, sitting the girl down and finishing the job neatly. Then she applied some dark bronze shadow to Emily's smooth young eyelids, complementing the eyes with her favourite shade of lippy. The girl looked several years older and amazing.

"Wow!" she squealed, still wearing the scarf, as she glimpsed her reflection.

Having repacked her bag, Laurel went to prepare the meal, leaving the girls to talk about how others dressed and made themselves up. That was something she had missed out on; at that age, Lawrie had been expected to turn up at the cricket nets and to shave once a week.

The vegetables had just started to cook when Laurel heard Adrian come in. Only he and Alexandra were in the living room. Emily hurried downstairs and into the room a moment later, her face cleared of cosmetics. *Maybe you need a quiet word with him, Laurel.*

After Alexandra had gone, Emily went up to her room. Laurel, relaxing, rested her head on Adrian's shoulder. He listened as she recounted the events of the past few days, only observing that he was not overly surprised by the bank's attitude, as it had, in his words, been getting shitty when he left to join Atkinson's.

From an oak cabinet, he produced a bottle of whisky and two tumblers. Laurel could not recall ever seeing him drink spirits before. He poured generous measures and sat down again. "Everything gets shitty in the end," he sighed.

"Tell me," Laurel said gently, but looking at him searchingly. "Your marriage?"

"It all started... I don't know when, really, thinking back. We'd probably lost interest in each other even before it went wrong in the bedroom. It became stale, uninteresting. She would just lie there and expect me to do it. And that became more difficult as she was getting fatter and less attractive."

"Just Pauline?" Laurel ribbed him, stroking his belly.

"Most of that is recent," he replied. "Less exercise, more work, and more ready meals." He drank. "So, the duller it grew, the less I felt like taking the lead, a kind of vicious circle. We just watched TV in the evenings, did our own things, went to bed, got up. Routine. It needed something to spice it up, to make me want her, you know. I tried hinting: wear something tempting, do something different, but she used to say she was too shy. Too shy after fifteen years!

"Then, one day, I decided to paint the bedroom; and I found an Ann Summers bag stuffed behind the wardrobe. It hadn't been there long — I'd done the skirting boards a couple of weeks earlier. I thought my luck had changed."

"And?"

"Nothing. Not for me, anyhow. It was Emily who found the photos on her phone: Pauline posing in a red and black… thingy, you know. Well, half in it, half out of it, if you can imagine. Someone else had obviously taken the pictures. He's moved on since." Adrian laughed ironically and took another sip.

"Oh, Adrian. So, what did you do? Turn to porn and give your wrist a good workout?" Laurel joked.

"Occasionally," he mumbled, embarrassed by the suggestion. "But I don't really like much of that stuff…"

"Except?" Laurel quizzed, for valuable future information.

"Except what?"

"So, what kind of stuff does tickle your fancy?" she teased, rubbing her finger over and around his shirt-covered left nipple.

"Actually, some femdom stuff, where the woman's in charge." He reached for his glass, but didn't make it.

"Really?" Laurel remarked, pushing him back into the sofa. She climbed over and straddled his face, though he was relatively safe as she was still in her tracksuit pants. The more he squirmed, the more she giggled, riding on his face. A door shut loudly somewhere in the house.

"Stop it!" He yelled, half muffled by the brushed cotton. She released him, dismounting just in time, as Martin bumbled through to make hot chocolate.

"Adrian, it's your home," she chided, when the teenager had lolloped back to his lair. "You're entitled to some private space and time. No doubt he's up there, every night, jerking himself off; and Emily is probably experimenting too. At least, she ought to be. She'd really like to experiment a bit with make-up as well."

He opened his mouth to speak, but she went on, "If you want to be dominated, you should be surrendering to me, not to them!" *Whoa, Laurel! That was a bit strong!* "Sorry, Adrian, that was out of place. They're your kids, after all."

He was staring at her. Was he hurt? Even angry? He raised his hand from his lap; surely, he wouldn't! She prepared herself for the worst. His hand settled on her jaw, pulling her face towards his. Their lips, then their tongues met. It was almost brutal. After an eternity in fathoms of passion, they came up for air. They were both trembling.

"I'm sorry," he began.

"I'm not," she replied. "I've been wanting you to do that since…"

"The Handel's Arms car park?" She nodded and kissed him tenderly. "I'll fetch the light duvet. Probably best if you sleep here."

"Probably," she murmured. She wasn't disappointed; how could she be?

After using the bathroom, Laurel slipped into a strappy mid-thigh-length burgundy satin and lace negligee. Snug in her chrysalis duvet, she typed a quick message to Maddie.

Just had a real pash. And he the aggressor! But sleeping on sofa. I AM in love.

"It's not a fucking Airbnb," growled Martin the next morning, stumbling over Laurel's bag on his way to the kitchen. Adrian had already left.

"Good morning to you, too," Laurel replied sarcastically, brushing her sleep-tousled hair back with her hand. She glared at him through disappointed, drowsy eyes.

"What?" he barked. *Teach him about behaviour towards a house guest, Laurel.*

"And I'm not a fucking stranger who paid thirty quid to doss here. I am your father's invited friend." *Only just true, Laurel.* She was displeased with herself for batting his f-word back at him, but he got the point.

"Sorry," the lad muttered, returning with his breakfast.

"Okay. Don't you use coffee? I need one," said Laurel, forgetting how she was dressed. Martin's eyes nearly popped out as she swung her bare legs, most of their length visible, out from the cover. She made a feint of tugging the lace hem downwards; but she knew that she looked good.

"No, thanks. I'll get it later," he said, scurrying to the safety of his hideout so quickly that he missed the flirtatious smile she gave him.

Bad girl, Laurel; but one—nil to you. And Mr Attitude needs sorting out. Having filled the kettle, she smoothed the satin over the curves of her bum. *Bloody hell, Laurel, you're not even wearing knickers!*

During the morning, perhaps unsurprisingly, the boy's mood mellowed. He even asked if Laurel needed anything from the supermarket in town. Emily had already gone out to her friend's house, having 'borrowed' Laurel's eyeliner, mascara and a deep red lip gloss. "Little rebel," Laurel whispered, as the girl handed back the tube.

Alone, Laurel sorted through her clothes, hanging the dresses and skirts in Adrian's room, where she plugged in her laptop to charge. Eating her lunch on the patio, she recalled Martin's startled expression. *Actually, Laurel, that is what he needs: someone to sort him out.* Inspired, she phoned Adrian.

"Can you give me Martin's mobile number?"

"Martin's! Why?"

"I've had an idea. I'll tell you later."

The lad was playing pool in a pub in the centre of Blackburn when Laurel got through. "Meet me outside Lloyds Bank at three thirty."

"Why?"

"Just be there."

Doubting whether Martin would show up, Laurel took the train from Darwen. Well, at the worst, she could browse in The Mall. While walking through the cathedral grounds, however, she spotted him leaning against the stone wall of the Old Bank.

"I'm taking you shopping," she announced. He pulled a face. "It's not going to be like shopping with your mum. Think of me as a cool aunty or something. But first," she said, as they headed through the market, "Sit down in there." She pointed to a barber's shop, where the proprietor was idle. The teenager demurred for a moment, but he surrendered to Laurel's determined look. Twenty minutes later, his hair washed and cut in a trendy style, Martin nodded his appreciation.

"Right, what about clothes?" The boy looked quizzically at her. "It's okay. I'm being paid full salary for three months of not going to work." Martin instinctively headed towards Primark. She grabbed his hand, almost pulling him off balance. "Let's look around first," she suggested firmly, hooking her arm through his. An unlikely couple, but Martin suddenly felt cool, having a good-looking older woman on his arm, wishing his mate would walk by. She hauled him into New Look, where they chose two smart casual shirts and some cotton trousers.

"Try them on, silly. Take the next size up as well; see which fit better," she insisted. "There's no rush. And when you're done, you can help me look for something." Meekly, but secretly proud, he obeyed.

While he was away, Laurel's eyes roamed across the women's section. There was a rail of black blouses, almost see-through; the kind girls wore over... Of course! She knew Emily's size. Pushing her hand inside the shirt to test how transparent the fabric was, she debated for a moment; but, seeing Martin re-emerging from the fitting room, she grabbed a size ten.

"Nice," Laurel said, running her fingers over a minidress. "Hold that and stop here while I try it on." He looked around, uncomfortable at being surrounded by lingerie and short skirts while holding a girl's blouse. "Well, stand over there, then, near the till."

Laurel changed as quickly as she could. It was short, slightly shorter than her night attire, but her legs were arguably her best features. She beckoned Martin over. He shuffled warily; but his eyes were practically out on stalks.

"What do you think?" she said, trying not to be too flirty, but knowing that she was.

"You look... I dunno... hot," he gasped.

"Second time today?" she winked. *Shameless, Laurel; he's not quite seventeen.* His cheeks turned the colour of a radish.

As they left the checkout counter, Laurel said, "You know, you aren't so bad-looking yourself. If you cleared up those zits and looked after yourself a bit... Come on." She led him into Boots, where she threw some Clearasil, a No7 eyeliner and some healthy snack bars into a basket.

"Do you like those things?" asked Martin, grimacing.

"Not for me; for you. I've seen all the chocolate wrappers and crisp packets. And those Babybel thingies. Less fat, less spots. Just try them." She smiled. He acquiesced.

Of course, the end of the checkout queue just had to be at the Durex display. Laurel tried to look away, into mid-air; then she stared ahead at the backs of heads and bodies. She turned to whisper to him about the rather too-tight jeans the girl in front was wearing, but he was studying the assortment of condoms and lubricants. When he noticed she was watching him, he blushed again. Despite the gruffness, there was something sweetly disarming about him.

The afternoon was quite warm. They were both thirsty. "Is there a pub with outside seats?" she asked.

"The Wetherspoons one, opposite Radio Lancashire," he suggested.

Passing Debenhams, Laurel's thoughts turned to Adrian; could she find something to warm him up even more tonight? As they reached the foot of the escalator, however, she had second thoughts. *Can you really make*

a gauche boy stand there in the lingerie department?
Haven't you made him blush enough today?

"What do you drink, lager or bitter?" Laurel asked, as they plonked their bags on the only two vacant seats.

"But I'm only…" he began.

"Like you've never had a drink before, Martin." He grinned guiltily. "Sit there, and I'll get them." She returned with a large glass of wine and a pint of lager. Propping the shopping against the table leg, she pulled her cigarettes from her bag. She put one in her mouth, then offered the packet to him.

"How do you know?" he asked, abashed.

"I have two nostrils," she grinned. He took a ciggie and she handed him her lighter. "I know your dad doesn't like it. He never did, even when we were younger." She lit her own and relaxed into the seat.

"Laurel, erm…" He hesitated. "I'm sorry I was rude to you this morning. You're really lit. I mean, you're…"

"Wow, Martin!" she replied, looking into his tidied-up face. "That's the nicest thing anyone's said to me all day. You're pretty lit yourself underneath that grumpy teenager front and those spots that we're going to clear up…" She thought for a moment and added, "And I haven't had a run for a few days. Fancy getting up early tomorrow and coming with me?"

"Running? Me?"

"Yeah, you know. Like walking, only quicker. And a bit sweatier." They both laughed. "Are you man enough to take me on?"

He thought before replying. Challenged by a woman, testosterone forbade him to duck it. They both drew on their cigarettes. "When I've finished with you, you'll be so handsome and fit that you'll have girls fighting over you." He started to redden. *In for the kill, Laurel.* She leant across the small table, adding in a stage whisper, "And then you'll soon be needing those things near the checkout in Boots." Crimson.

"Can I ask you something… about you and Dad?" Martin tentatively began, as they were riding back to Darwen. The long silence was almost as awkward as his facial expression. "Are you…?" Laurel sensed he was searching for an acceptable phrase.

"Sleeping together?" Laurel helped.

"You don't have to tell me if…"

"Well, we're clearly not sleeping together because you practically fell over me this morning," she said smiling. "But, okay, Martin, I'll be totally honest. No, we aren't having sex." She wanted to add 'not yet', but stopped herself. "It's a bit early for that."

Nodding, he turned his gaze towards the hills. She gently nudged him. "But it was okay for you to ask."

Martin had barely disappeared after dinner, and Laurel was washing up, when Adrian came into the kitchen. She went to kiss him, but he held her at arm's length. His face looked tense.

"I didn't expect you to cook for us again, but thanks. And Martin's hair, I expect you paid for that. You didn't need to…"

"No problem. And I know I didn't need to. It was quite fun in the end, after I'd embarrassed him a couple of times." Silence. "Adrian, is something wrong?"

"No, not really…" The tension was palpable. Something was eating at him. "I'm just saying he isn't your responsibility." Adrian returned to the living room and turned on the television. Laurel fetched the coffee, and there they sat for several minutes.

"What are your plans?" *Strange question; but, after all, Laurel, you had only asked to stay one night. That must be it.*

"Plans?" she asked, dumbly.

"Tomorrow, and the weekend, and next week, and… the future?"

"My most important plan is you," she cooed. "And number two is looking for a business to buy into," she added, trying to snuggle closer. He edged away.

"But what is this business? Where? You'd be best to start looking now, especially at the coast. It's practically June already."

She gazed at him, unsure. He became silent and deep again. "Look, Adrian. If having me here is a problem, just say so." *Tetchy, Laurel, but where do you stand?*

"It's not that, but it's difficult…" He tailed off, turning back to the TV.

271

When Emily arrived home, after nine o'clock, all traces of make-up had gone. Laurel handed her the New Look bag containing the eyeliner and the blouse. She peeped in, grinning naughtily when she saw the pencil; but her eyes opened wide when she examined the blouse. She glanced nervously at her father, who was half asleep, lulled by the business news. Laurel ushered her out of the room.

"It'll be perfect over that pretty black bra. Aren't you going to a birthday party at the weekend?"

"But it's see-through!"

"Exactly. Your bra isn't, though. Not where it matters. You'll look amazing," Laurel assured her.

"Thank you," Emily said, kissing Laurel's cheek.

"Look what I bought!"

"That's really nice."

Holding the dress against Laurel's body, Emily giggled. "It's very short. I wish I could wear things like that. You know, a bit… sexy."

"You can," said Laurel, gently tugging the blouse in the girl's hand.

Laurel hung the new dress behind her other clothes. She would wear it the next evening; she would take Adrian out for dinner and explore his feelings about the future. She might even manage to charm her way into his bed. To spare his son any further blushes in the morning, however, she donned the green French knickers.

SEVENTEEN

"Steady on, soldier! Pace yourself!" Laurel called to Martin, who had set off like Usain Bolt. "It's a long run, not a sprint; and I'm forty-eight, not eighteen." She had already pulled him back in the driveway, reminding him that he needed to warm up before pounding the roads. His lack of stamina began to tell, however, and they rested for a minute before turning for home. He was panting harder than her when they arrived.

"Oh, your dad's car is still here!" Laurel remarked.

"Yeah… I think he's… he's starting at ten today. He sometimes does on Fridays," the boy puffed, bending over. "I'm knackered." He laughed. "You're fitter than me, even in pink trainers!"

"You need to do it regularly; then, you'll get the benefit. We'll soon work you into shape, don't worry. Then, the girls will be chasing you, not you chasing a girl in pink pumps." She laughed as they bundled into the house.

Assuming that Martin was headed for his bedroom, Laurel followed him upstairs, intending to jump straight under the shower. Suddenly, as she reached for the bathroom door handle, he stopped and turned. They collided in the doorway. "Oh," he said diffidently, unnerved at such close contact with a sweating Lycra-clad woman.

"So, who's going first?" she asked. He hesitated, still flustered. "Well, I'm not offering to have a shower *with* you!" Laurel realised that she had embarrassed him again. "You can find your own girlfriend to share that experience." She tapped his bum. "Go on, I'll wait."

Laurel skipped downstairs to make some coffee, and found Adrian in the kitchen. Delighted with her progress on the Martin front, she bounced in and kissed his cheek. "Sorry I'm sweaty, but I've been giving your boy a good workout. He's in the shower. Proud of me?" She kissed his lips.

"Well done," Adrian replied, leaning in to return the kiss. He stopped, however, and pulled away; Emily was approaching through the living room. She filled a glass with orange juice, gave Laurel a 'good morning' kiss, and left.

"What's the matter?" Laurel asked.

"Nothing."

"Nothing, he says."

"What?"

"For goodness' sake, Adrian, we weren't even snogging. Every time we're close, you push me away. It's your house! They're your kids, living under the roof that you provide for them! Are you never going to be able to make love to me because Emily might hear from along the landing?"

"It's not that. I'm just finding it difficult…"

"You keep saying that. You've been saying it since we first went out. What's so bloody difficult?" *Steady, Laurel, the temperature's rising; and you're tired and pumped up from the run.*

"You, and the past; and you staying here like this. Look, can we talk about this later? I need to go to work."

"Work?"

"Yes, the thing that pays the bills."

She had rarely heard him be sarcastic. "Oh, well, I'm sorry. If it's rent you want from me..."

"Don't be silly."

"I mean, Adrian, I know it isn't paying the gas bill, but I spent a lot of money on your son yesterday..."

"That's not what I meant," he protested, trying to reduce the heat.

"Okay, okay. But I don't see why you... why we can't enjoy each other and being with each other." A pause. Calm restored?

"You seem to get plenty of fun from being with Martin," he said, picking up his car key. Laurel's mouth dropped open.

"Oh, so that's it. You resent me helping him because he resents you and prefers his mother. You're jealous of your own teenage son!" Outrage and disbelief registered on her face.

"This isn't helping. Let's talk this afternoon."

"Email me, then. I won't be here. I don't want to be under your feet," she snapped.

Letting out an exasperated sigh, Adrian shook his head and closed the door behind him. Her fists clenched in fury, Laurel stood motionless, listening to the car engine as Adrian reversed down the drive. She slammed her hands on the kitchen worktop.

"What's wrong, Laurel?" Emily was staring at her, wide-eyed.

"Nothing," she said, shaking her head. *Liar, Laurel; even the kid can see that.* "Your dad and I don't seem to be on the same planet," Laurel sighed, giving the girl a squeeze. *The jealousy jibe was a bit cruel, Laurel.*

"Shall I make you some breakfast while you're in the shower?" the girl asked. "I think you probably need one."

In the shower, Laurel began singing a song she had loved when she was younger than Emily. '*I've got pieces of April, and it's a morning in May.*' It was sung by Twiggy, on an album that had been one of her — Lawrie's — favourites. As a thirteen-year-old, Lawrie had stared at the photo on the album cover, dreaming of being her, walking through fields, her hair flowing behind, free and gorgeously feminine.

Smelling sweeter after breakfast, Laurel hugged Emily, promising to see her soon, but saying that Adrian had been right: she should not waste the summer running down her gardening leave. She needed to shape her future.

"For tonight?" Doug, at the Cumbria Hotel, checked. "Yes, we can. And for how long? Yes, I remember you extended last time. We're not too busy over the next week or two. Okay, I'll see you this afternoon."

On the train to St Anne's, after hurriedly packing for the second time that week, Laurel found herself humming the hit song from the Twiggy album — *Here I go again*. How many times, over the years, had she ended up singing that to herself, regretting another failed relationship? She stabbed a message into her phone.

I love you, Adrian. But I need to know that I am loved too. I need to know where I stand. Call me later.

Her phone remained silent. No calls, no messages. She didn't call Maddie. *Why ruin her weekend with your angst, Laurel?*

Laurel spent much of Saturday trailing around Lytham St Anne's, assessing different locations and pondering various options. Her heart, however, was not really in it, not even after learning that twelve-bedroom hotels in the side streets of Blackpool were selling for a song.

Seven o'clock. Still no message from Adrian. Emily, however, getting ready for her team mate's sixteenth birthday bash, sent a photo. Beaming in her new blouse, Emily's pale skin highlighted the black lacy bra, which accentuated her curves. Her eyes were alluring, though she had used the eyeliner subtly. The text was short.

You left your lipstick here.

I left it for you. Use it. I've got plenty. You look stunning, sweetheart. Enjoy!

Thanks. I will.

As Laurel lay down, glad that Emily had found the lippy before her father had, she recalled her first time out dressed as a girl: New Year's Eve, 1998, after spending hours, perhaps days, plucking up the courage, planning and self-daring. Lawrie had arrived at the pub in a fairly sheer black top, with a silver stripe, a black mini skirt, patterned black tights, three-inch heels and a wig.

"Gosh! Are you wearing a bra?" a female bank colleague had exclaimed.

"Course, aren't you?"

The woman's perturbed husband had kept his distance all night. The problem was that Lawrie had looked so convincing that when he went for a pee in the Gents, a guy at the urinals, hearing the clatter of heels, turned around, startled. Lawrie, equally embarrassed, had squeaked an apology, rushed out, and used the Ladies.

Drizzle was falling on St Anne's, so Laurel watched old sitcoms on the TV, chomping her way through a supermarket salad and sipping wine from a teacup. It was after nine thirty when another message hit her phone.

I hear you're back in St Anne's. Meet me at Caffe Nero before church tomorrow.

Stella's message was more like an order than an invitation. Although Laurel had not yet decided to go to church, she felt called to obey.

Laurel, who had made sure to arrive before ten, noticed immediately that Stella's normal radiant smile was absent. She kissed Laurel, but there was a lack of warmth. Stella paid for the coffee, which Laurel carried to a table. They sat in tense silence for a minute or so.

"Laurel, why didn't you tell me?"

"Tell you? That I left Adrian's?" Silence.

"About you. Lawrence to Laurel." The Maltese woman's voice was calm, yet firm.

"Oh God, Stella. You probably hate me for keeping a secret like that. I didn't think… I don't know. I met you at the church and…" Laurel grabbed her powder compact from her bag, hastily checking in its mirror. Stella observed the reaction silently, smiling wryly. She waited several seconds before speaking again.

"You thought I would push you away because of that, *aw?* I was a nurse, *ħanina.* I've seen everything, heard everything and, believe me, I've had to touch everything. And I mean everything." She smiled. "I haven't told Don. Not because he'll react badly, but because that's for you to do when you're ready. And no, Laurel, I don't hate you for not telling me; and I love you even more now that I know. God knows how brave you must have been and what you went through."

Laurel felt tears forming. Having feared she was to be reprimanded for something, she had been affirmed and supported. They hugged tightly. "Oh, Stella," Laurel sobbed. Stella handed her a tissue that she had kept ready.

"That's why I needed to speak to you before Mass. I wasn't at peace knowing something like that, when you weren't aware that I knew."

"You've spoken to Adrian, I guess."

"Spoken to him, darling? I've given him a bloody good talking to." Laurel giggled at hearing this devout Catholic lady swearing.

"When?"

"Yesterday evening. We were on the phone for an hour. And he told me what you did for Martin. And I spoke to Emily."

"Oh no! Emily was there when he told you?" Laurel asked, horrified that Emily now knew her secret. She made another grab for her compact, this time applying some powder.

"Don't worry about your make-up, which is fine, or about Emily. She had to go out, so she didn't hear that part. That was totally private. I'd spoken to her earlier because I knew that you and Emily had kept in touch while you were in London."

"You know what Emily would say about you, Stella? You're GOAT."

"What's that?"

"Teenage slang. Greatest of all time. You're fantastic, awesome."

"No, my dear," Stella laughed modestly. "She's upset that it isn't working out between you. Drink up, *ħanina*. Don will be waiting for us."

"Effectively having three months holiday on full pay, I've got some breathing space," Laurel told Stella, as they walked along Clifton Street. "I need to complete the sale of my flat, find one to rent up here, and to start looking seriously for business opportunities. People say avoid Blackpool, and there's limited scope here."

"Try Preston — and speak to Don over lunch. You are coming to lunch, *mela?*" It was uttered as a question, but like her text message, it was a nuanced instruction.

Don was already in their usual pew, smiling broadly as they approached.

"I keep worrying that I've done the wrong thing — again. I always seem to get bounced into making the wrong choice," Laurel said, genuflecting and crossing herself.

"Always?" Stella asked, fixing a penetrating look on her. Laurel cast her eyes downwards, not exactly caught in a lie, but an exaggeration. "I need to patch things up with Adrian," she said, meekly.

"Look at her," Stella whispered, pointing to the fresco of Mary above the chancel arch. "The artist who painted it was an Italian, I believe, well into his seventies. He stood on planks of wood to sketch it out, then to paint it; all within a week. He trusted. She trusted, even when faced with disgrace; and look at her, rising serenely to heaven, totally at peace with her destiny."

It was not until the Peace, enfolding one another's hands, that Laurel noticed Stella's new ring. Pristine and sparkling, it was beautiful. She gave Don an approving nod. "He wasn't a bad choice, *mela*," Stella smiled beatifically.

"No, you lucky thing, he was a bloody good one." *Honestly, remember where you are, Laurel!* Imploring the ascending Virgin's pardon, Laurel crossed herself; Stella smiled.

Over lunch, Laurel fascinated Don with the story of her French buyer and her discharge from the bank. All the time, she felt a nagging doubt about revealing her personal history. She trusted Stella's tact; but was it fair to burden her with keeping a secret?

Don chatted away helpfully concerning Laurel's quest, recommending websites like Daltons and an agent in Preston. He agreed that keeping her eyes and ears open around the Fylde, and chatting with people, was as good a strategy as any. "Of course, having a specific sector in mind might help to focus your search," he added. *Yes, Laurel, apart from coveting Patrick's café in St Anne's, you really haven't given this much thought.*

"Have you considered counselling?" Stella asked, returning from the kitchen with a bowl of fresh strawberries and a tub of Bourbon vanilla ice-cream. "With some time on your hands, you could do a course. There must be people — *mela*, I know there are — in this area who are facing the things you went through. Your experiences could help them and loved ones who find it hard to understand. Like Adrian," she added, dividing the strawberries into three small dishes.

For a moment, Laurel tensed, transfixed, like a rabbit in the headlamps of a car. Unwittingly or not, while focused on serving up dessert, Stella had, more or less, forced Laurel's hand.

"Oh, a marriage counsellor, or whatever they call them now," Don said. "I didn't realise you'd been married." *You could side-step this, Laurel, by telling a fib.* However, feeling Stella's right hand caressing her left one, Laurel made a furtive glance at her hostess, who was smiling sweetly, gently nodding her head. *Lying is not an option. Just breathe deeply, and go for it, girl!*

"Good heavens, Laurel! I'd really no idea. I mean… Nobody would ever… When?" Don was reacting like most men had over the last twenty years or so, struggling to find the right words, while trying to avoid giving offence.

The decision to go ahead with the surgery had been sudden. Laurel had been in two minds for years, weighing up the effects of changing body chemistry, the pain, the stigma, and discussions with several surgeons. Finally, it had come down to one evening, nearly two years into dressing *en femme* for work, even longer since starting hormone treatment. Lounging in a clingy dress, proud of her pert new boobs, she had glanced further south. Okay, being alone, she had been careless with underwear; but the dress only accentuated the bulge. She had phoned the surgeon the very next morning.

"If the funds are in place, I have a slot early next month," he had said breezily. 'Slot' had seemed a cuttingly inappropriate lexical choice. Her father's reaction had been unexpected. Only a couple of years beforehand, he had tried to talk her out of it; but on the second occasion, he had simply said, 'I think you're doing the right thing.' He had never explained why he had changed his view; and she had never asked.

As for outcomes, once the extraordinarily varied manifestations of physical pain had worn off, and the hassle of regular follow-up appointments had ended, she had felt able to join the sisterhood as an equal, rather than as a freak of nature who had inveigled her way in. Although she could never be a natural mother, she had periodically considered adoption.

"If anyone ever tells you that taking oestrogen and testosterone blockers in large doses is like eating Smarties, don't believe them. That was the worst period, really; not just seeing and feeling my body change, which was scary enough at times; but the things it does to your mind! You lose all control over your emotions. How many times did I run to the loo in tears at work, usually over nothing? Even something like that." She laughed, indicating her dish. She had been speaking so intently, and for so long, that her ice-cream had melted completely.

"*Hanina*, let me give you some more," Stella said, picking up the scoop. Laurel politely refused; the strawberries were just as delicious with a richly flavoured vanilla sauce.

"Don't you feel more vulnerable as a woman, though?" Don asked sensitively.

"Sometimes, but you learn to deal with it. I'm more careful where I go, especially alone. But the worst was when I was transitioning. I had this morbid fear of being arrested for something, then told to strip, only to reveal what was hidden in my knickers. Lurid tales circulated of abuse within the confines of a police cell. You could end up like many an adolescent, brutally sodomised by some desperate old lag, with the tacit blessing of the Metropolitan Police."

"Well, I think you've been terribly brave," Don said, after chuckling at Laurel's colourful language. "Even for talking about it to us."

"*Mela*, that's why I think you could help and inspire other people," Stella added. "Although I understand why Adrian, who knew you as a young man, might be finding it tough to deal with, *ta'*."

Back in her room at the B&B, Laurel called Adrian's mobile. It was switched off. She texted, deleted, and tried several alternative versions.

Adrian, I'm sorry I didn't understand. Can we talk?

EIGHTEEN

After breakfast on Monday morning, Laurel put on her light raincoat and, umbrella at the ready, walked to the station. So much for 'flaming June'; and her winter clothes were in London. The plan was to phone Don's friend while she was on the train, fix up a meeting with him, and to spend the afternoon investigating some of the businesses that had caught her eye.

She was under the canopy at St Anne's station, sheltering from a shower, when her phone rang. Smiling as she recognised her old office number, she answered.

"Laurel! I had to tell you first," Maddie squealed. "We're official! Trefor and me! I'm going to tell the others in the branch in a mo; but I wanted you to know first."

"Wow! That's wonderful, Maddie. So…"

"We decided yesterday that we'd make it clear to everyone, and then there would be no rumours and stuff. I'd got wind of comments circulating last week. He's going to tell his staff this morning, too."

Laurel felt elated for her friend, congratulating her several times. When asked about Adrian, she brushed it away, saying nothing had changed. Hearing Maddie's news and her voice had brightened a dull morning; and despite having no word from Adrian, Laurel was determined to stay positive.

Don's friend, a chartered accountant, had an office in Winckley Square. Watched over by graduation photos of his three children, they chatted for nearly an hour. While agreeing that the catering sector was a rational place to begin, not needing huge technical know-how, he cooled her enthusiasm for a sandwich shop in the heart of the university area: trade would be seasonal, and the clientele on tight budgets.

He suggested another, in a better residential area, close to a commuter station. It had a good reputation, with potential for developing the offering; yet even there, she would have to find over three hundred and fifty pounds a week for rent and business rates, before she bought any ingredients. More off-putting was the fact that it opened at eight every morning, including Sundays. *Donkey work for peanuts, Laurel.*

"You'll find several fish and chip shops on the market. Frankly, I wouldn't touch them with a barge pole. It's a dying trade, sadly."

"Yes, I saw one that had a little flat above. But imagine the smell! You'd never get away from it. Even on your clothes!" Laurel shuddered at the thought.

"Well, that should have given you food for thought," he said, proud of his pun. "I'm sure that, as a bank manager, you know the right questions to ask. You know, 'Why are you selling if it's such a great business?' Here's my card. If you need any advice, I'll

288

be happy to help a friend of Don's. We go back all the way to grammar school."

Thanking him, Laurel made for the commercial area, but another sharp shower caused her to hurry into a café. She dialled the number of a promising sarnie outlet. Nobody answered; perhaps, being late morning, they were rushed off their feet, bashing out butties. *Take a walk round there, Laurel; get a feel for how busy it is and the clientele.*

Five minutes later, her hopes were raised as she entered a street of varied businesses, with plenty of pedestrians. Reaching her destination, however, her heart sank. It was closed. Two or three weeks' mail, including junk mail, lay on the floor. Not just closed, but closed down. She glanced down at the screenshot: Turnover £150,000. *Actually, it's zero. Your trade and goodwill have baguetted off elsewhere.*

While clutching her phone, she checked for contact from Adrian. Email, Facebook, Voicemail. Nothing. Feeling that the day was becoming increasingly fruitless and depressing, the rain becoming persistent, Laurel bolted for the imposing Harris Museum. For a couple of hours, she lost herself in art and ceramics.

Just after four, she was heading towards the station when the heavens opened, so she ran for shelter in a pub doorway, being jostled by a few like-minded others.

"Sorry," a tall, balding man muttered. His companion was shaking herself dry.

"Oh, hi! Didn't realise it was you," the woman said, flashing a familiar dimply smile at Laurel.

"Claire!" Laurel exclaimed, before glancing at the man. Was he Dennis? Indeed, he was. Laurel was initially rather sheepish, for she had last seen him stomping off after catching the two women smooching. Finally making eye contact, Laurel was amazed to see him beaming from ear to ear.

"Fancy bumping into each other here," he said, adding, "Literally," with a dryness that must, Laurel thought, be the preserve of local government administrators. "It's slackening off. Shall we have a drink? Somewhere a bit nicer?" Laurel was stunned at his suggestion, and at his new-found urbanity. They ended up in the same wine bar where they had sat a month earlier.

"So, you two seem... fine," Laurel fished, while Dennis was at the bar.

"Fantastic," replied the cute woman. "I'm so glad we had that fun at my flat." Laurel gave her a 'tell me more' look. "The day after that, we had a long talk. Very frank, totally honest. I told him openly what we'd done and how you'd satisfied me. He sat there, looking half shocked, half amused. The next thing he said, bless him, was that he wanted to know how, so that he could make me as happy as that. And, my God, Laurel, he's certainly getting the hang of it! Last night, I was absolutely..."

Claire paused, seeing Dennis returning from the bar. "So, thank you. You've saved us — taken us to wonderful new places. What about you?"

Dennis settled on a stool while Laurel began to relate the saga of returning to London, the gardening leave and, of course, Adrian. "Oh my God! So, you're bi!" Claire squealed.

"Yeah. I guess I always have been," replied Laurel, pitching her voice at 'discreet'. Dennis and Claire could not hide their curiosity.

"Okay, I'll let you into a secret." As succinctly and as non-dramatically as she could, Laurel related the history of her gender change. Dennis roared with laughter, while Cutie looked a little guilty for a moment: was cheating with an ex-man worse than with another woman?

"What's so funny?" Laurel asked the bald administrator, who was struggling to control himself.

"Not your change, honest. But after your encounter, Claire got worried that she might be a lesbian; or, at least, turning into one. And, all the time, she was with someone who was really a feller!"

Laurel was genuinely shocked that someone of his background should make such a boorish comment.

"Sorry, Laurel," said Claire, apologising on her boyfriend's behalf, before glaring at him. Mortified at the inelegance of his statement, Dennis also apologised.

"Look, Dennis," Laurel said firmly, trying to keep her cool. "I really am a woman. And I'm not flashing it in here to prove it." Claire screamed with laughter, nearly falling off her stool. "Even in my teens, I was a young woman, but with the wrong equipment; even if it was rock hard whenever I was near anyone gorgeous." Leaning towards Dennis, she whispered, "And it would be now, being around such a hot girl as you've got." He nodded and grinned back.

Momentarily, Laurel had the wicked notion of proposing a threesome in Claire's flat, and giving Dennis further expert instruction. Yet, the couple seemed to be so happily in love, quite obviously satisfying each other, that she smiled and resisted.

They parted from her near the station, hugging and wishing each other happiness. Laurel watched them walk away, hand in hand. *Lucky Claire; lucky Dennis, even if you are a bit of an oaf. Will Adrian and I ever get there?*

There was a Kik message on her phone. She had missed it while they were talking and laughing in the wine bar. Emily's netball team had been thumped on Sunday, everyone being tired and some, the girl suspected, hung over from the party. One of the older girls had warned her not to drink the clear liquid from a litre bottle labelled 'Tonic Water'.

Did you have a good time, though?

Seriously lit. They loved my top. 3 girls asked where I got it. Coach said she'd never seen me like that, kept looking at me.

Hmm. What about your dad?

He didn't see. I wore a black jumper over until I got there! Then I put the lippy on. He was in bed when I got home.

That wasn't exactly what I meant, Emily.

Very sensible. Learning fast! Dad OK?

Guess so. U gonna see us this week? Missing u.

Miss u too, sweetheart. X

Laurel shed a couple of tears after putting down her phone. She really did miss Emily. All in all, it had been quite an emotional day, what with her own frustrations in Preston and over Adrian, the excitement of Maddie and Trefor, as well as Claire and Dennis.

The delight of Monday's news, however, was nothing compared with what Laurel heard the following morning.

"Hello, kiddo."

"Oh, Aunty Hilda! I'm so sorry. I meant to call you last week, but so much happened…"

"What did happen? When I called your work number, they said you'd left." Laurel retold the story, having to explain the term 'gardening leave'.

"The cheeky beggars! After all the years you've given them. Still, if they're paying you for doing nothing, enjoy it to the full."

"Now, tell me about you," Laurel said, laughing.

"Well, I hardly know where to begin, kiddo."

"The last time we spoke," Laurel prompted, "you were going to talk it out with your friend over lunch. Was that all right?"

"Yes, it was lovely. We went to a little French restaurant down in Mumbles, and… well, we decided not to worry and just see how things went, and how we felt. And that's why I rang, kiddo. Something else happened, and I think… Well, at my age!"

"Go on," Laurel urged, her mounting anticipation matching Hilda's crescendo.

"Well, a couple of days later, after choir practice, Rosemary drove me home. It was a nice evening, so we sat in the garden, and I opened a bottle of wine; but the only one handy was a big one, you know, double. She doesn't normally drink much, but we were talking about her marriage and things; just talking and filling up our glasses. And then, when it got a bit chilly, we came inside. And I played, and she sang *Some Enchanted Evening*, you know. Honestly, kiddo, it was beautiful.

And she put her hand on my shoulder; and we looked at one another. Well, with the wine and the song, I was all emotional; and we started kissing again. We were both in a state — I was trembling and she was giddy. Well, the bottle, kiddo, the double one, was empty. She said, 'I can't drive like this; I'd better sleep on the sofa.'

"And, Laurel, I just blurted out, 'You can if you wish; but the bed is big enough for two.' And then... Well, finally, we dropped off in each other's arms." Laurel was almost ecstatic, her imagination filling the gaps in Hilda's narrative.

"Oh, kiddo. I never thought I was, you know, that way. I don't know what to do."

"Surely, you don't need me to draw you a diagram." Laurel laughed.

"You daft thing! I didn't mean that," Hilda said sniggering. "I think we've found that part out for ourselves." That caused Laurel to squeal with delight.

"No, I mean... what to do from here," Hilda continued. "We'll have to leave the church, I suppose."

"Whatever for?"

"Well, two women... together."

"Aunty Hilda," Laurel began, with kind firmness, "What kind of God would stop two single mature people, who've found something really special, from loving each other? And what kind of Christians would they be that can't accept love?"

"But like that. You know, in bed. Not just friends, are we?"

"Nobody has the right to judge you, especially after you've played the organ for them, week after week, for nothing." Even as she spoke, Laurel felt a pang of hypocrisy. Had she always lived by her own advice? How often, in the past, had she held back through dread of other people's opprobrium?

"You know how people are, kiddo, you more than most. Some of them have such little minds. I'm not saying anything against that church as a whole; there are some lovely people there. And the vicar is a delightful young man; very well educated — Oxford." Laurel paused, thinking twice before she spoke.

"So, why don't you and Rosemary go and talk with him? Be honest, say how you feel, and sound him out. If he ties you to a stake and burns you, then you'll know he doesn't approve," she added in a joking tone.

"Ooh, if I get my hands on you," said Hilda chuckling.

"Save them for Rosemary!" Laurel giggled. "Honest, Hilda. Go and talk to him; then, you'll know where you stand. Don't worry. And I love you. And tell Rosemary I love her too for making you happy."

Unbelievable! The whole world was falling in love around her. Laurel could have drooped into one of her morose moods, wondering why she was the one left out again. She did not; how could she? Her favourite relative, the wonderfully eccentric Aunty Hilda, was rediscovering love — and sex — in her early seventies!

Laurel was still joyful when she met Stella for lunch in Lytham, on the fourth day without word from Adrian.

"You see, *ħanina*," the Maltese woman observed, after listening to Laurel's bulletin. "Everything comes in time, often when we aren't expecting it. And one day, it will be yours. I keep telling you, don't panic. Give it time; and trust. *Mela*, let's choose a dessert!"

Walking home, Laurel was conscious of Twiggy's voice in her head, echoing Stella: '*Everything comes in time, girl, don't be so impatient with the world. It may not be tomorrow or today...*'

Adrian's silence remained unbroken at bedtime. She had reached out to him. What more? If only she knew what he was thinking, or how he felt. Why did men find it so hard to communicate their feelings? *Laurel, you weren't so brilliant at it yourself — Handel's Arms?*

Waking to bright June sunshine, and conscious that she had been lax on the exercise front, Laurel pulled on her cropped Lycra leggings and matching bra top. She checked in the long mirror. *Not bad, girl; bum and legs good; a pound or two on the tummy over the last couple of weeks. Still, you couldn't have gone out in that outfit twenty years ago!* With her hair in a ponytail and gossamer-light in her pink trainers, she left the B&B.

After breakfast, she scrolled through Dalton's Lytham St. Anne's page, making notes and screenshots. There were two car mechanic businesses for sale, but she was more into camisoles than camshafts. Her interest was aroused by a B&B on a corner site. Although the investment was considerable, she would not be paying rent: what she earned would be hers; and she had always fancied the idea of running a guest house. Without borrowing, though, it would be a financial stretch unless she sold both Blackburn houses.

The property looked in good shape, but it was so far from the seafront, with no obvious attractions nearby, that she wondered how many people would want to stay there. In any case, the traditional B&B market had declined so much. *Doable, but doubtful; back burner, Laurel.*

Her planned return to the town centre took her past a café that was for sale. Double-fronted, with twin Georgian style bay windows, some of the panels decorated with roundels, it could be made nice. Laurel pictured it at Christmas, tastefully and traditionally adorned; charmingly Dickensian. The rent seemed standard for the area, substantially less than the one near Preston. It would swallow her severance payment; but, being near the main square and the station, it had possibilities.

Feeling positive, Laurel had just sat down in the Frenchman's café, when her phone rang. Quickly, she snatched it from her bag. Was it Adrian calling at last?

"Laurel, you'll never believe this," Maddie said, her voice almost trembling.

"What on earth's happened? Are you all right?"

"Yeah, yeah. I've just had that Alison from regional office here. When she arrived, she had Trefor with her. I thought, 'Gawd, don't tell me someone's objected to us having a relationship.'"

"Surely, they…" Laurel began, but Maddie bubbled on.

"Well, she'd been round to Knightsbridge first, swearing him to secrecy, you know, all confidential," Maddie continued.

"What about? Stop teasing, Maddie, I'm nearly wetting myself with excitement!" Laurel's voice had risen to a pitch that gained the attention of the couple at the next table.

"So, basically, they're going to downscale this branch; and Trefor is going to be the senior manager of both. There'll be a kind of manager-in-charge here — ME! I get an upgrade — another four thousand a year! Laurel, can you believe it? I was shaking when she finished. That's not like me, is it? Tref had to give me a squeeze after she'd gone, just to calm me down!"

It was wonderful news for Maddie; and Laurel said so, joking that she might come to see her about a loan. Although she had intended to speak discreetly with Patrick about his café, he had become busier; it could wait. It was only when she entered Ashton Gardens that Maddie's news really hit home. *You really have done it, Laurel; there's no way back now.*

There are few things as astonishingly beautiful, as ravishingly fragrant, as a mature English rose garden in the early summer. Laurel stood for a few moments, taking in the splendour of the scene, inhaling, almost imbibing the perfume. From pure white, through cream, lemon yellow, sunshine yellow, pink, lilac, orange, red and claret, some roses had already opened, petals engorged, nectared and prone, ready to receive their flitting lovers.

While she was walking towards a bench, the years swirled through her mind, the tides of their memories ebbing and flowing. Her phone bleeped; without looking, she fumbled in her bag and switched it off. Beauty, ordered beauty; she marvelled at the human capacity to take the best of nature and to work sensitively with her; to present her, as the danseur does the ballerina. In touch with beyond the here and now, with eternity, Laurel gently became aware of a special loving presence.

"Dad, I'm coming back home," Laurel whispered, "I'm going to be able to talk to you here every day. And I'm going to get a bench in memory of you and Mum." The rope that had bound her to London had been severed, redundant; she had reconnected with something more visceral via the tender cord of her childhood.

Having bought some food from Sainsbury's, Laurel took a second look at the Dickensian café. On the way home, something caught her eye: in the window of the salon she had visited a month earlier, a computer printed sign read: BUSINESS INVESTOR WANTED. She halted, curious, and peered through the glass. The hairdresser was finishing a customer whom Laurel recognised. Her first instinct was to turn away and continue home. *Don't be daft, Laurel; go and find out.* Her fingers fluttered nervously on the door handle. *Go on, Laurel.*

"That's probably my taxi," the mother of the gay solicitor said, hearing the bell tinkle. "I wouldn't have needed one if Bertram hadn't gone to Dubai with his boyfriend. Why on earth would anyone want to go there? Especially with the laws they have. If they're caught doing what they do here, they'll probably get them chopped off." The stylist, who had already acknowledged Laurel's arrival, screamed with laughter.

"Honestly, Mrs S, you get better every month," the girl said, helping the woman out of the chair.

"So do you, my darling," Mrs Simmonds replied, admiring her hair and sucking on her front teeth. "And no more talk of closing down, do you hear?" she continued, pressing money into the hairdresser's hand, squeezing softly, kindly.

"First Wednesday next month, then?" the girl asked, reaching for her diary.

"That's more like it," the older woman said, in an encouraging tone. "Nine thirty, mind, as normal. Bertram will be back by then..." She waved at a car that was pulling up. "If he isn't in jail for sodomy!"

"Hi, you've been before," the girl said to Laurel, who was holding open the door for Mrs Simmonds while stifling a giggle. "Do you need something now, or can it wait till tomorrow? I could do with getting away…"

"No, no. I'm fine. I happened to see your sign. Are you finishing?"

"Well, I don't want to, but," she sighed, "She was the second I've had today. And both of them old enough to be my granny. You see, the place needs a makeover; but my turnover's dropping, and…" She paused, recognising Laurel. "Oh! I remember you — you're the bank manager from London. Well, you'll understand," the tattooed stylist went on, tidying up her things. Laurel scanned the salon, nodding in agreement.

"You need some more capital, basically. Have you costed out a refurb?" *My God, Laurel, you've reverted to type!* "How much do you think it would need?"

"More than I can get my hands on," the hairdresser confessed, "Especially with my partner on reduced hours. If I can't get the place looking a bit more swish, you know, more appealing and classier, I might as well shut up and try and get a job at another salon. I had to finish the part-time girl because I'm only just covering the rent." Her voice quivered and she looked away sharply.

"Look, erm…" Laurel hesitated, then gave a nervous little laugh. "Sorry, I don't even know your name."

"Melissa."

"The thing is, Melissa, I'm in the process of leaving the bank and moving back up here. And I'm looking for a business to buy, or buy into, essentially to give me an occupation and a future income. This wasn't the kind of plan I had in mind, but…" Laurel glanced around the salon again. "But I might be able to help. And with my business experience…"

"Wow! Yeah, great," the stylist began, unable to conceal her surprised joy. "Wow, I don't know what to say…"

"Look, if you need to get away, why don't we talk again in a couple of days? You have a good think about your vision for this place, how you'd like to change it, and how much it would cost; and I'll give it some thought. Then, we can meet up, say Friday or Saturday morning." *Heavens, Laurel, you're taking the lead here; you aren't her bank manager.*

"Friday's better — I do have three booked in for Saturday. Here's my card, with my mobile and email on it," Melissa said, handing Laurel a nicely produced business card.

"Thanks, Melissa. I'll confirm tomorrow about Friday," smiled the ex-bank manager.

"Sure. Hope to see you then," the girl said, as Laurel turned to leave. "Oh, and thanks," she added sweetly.

Despite having so easily fallen back into her professional persona, Laurel was strangely excited, her stomach aflutter, as she strode along. *Not exactly on script, Laurel; fancy yourself as a business angel now?*

Instead of heading straight back, she walked to the promenade, where she lit a cigarette, staring out to sea near the boating lake. She keyed Melissa's number into her phone, in case she mislaid the card; she also checked for any missed calls or messages. Nothing.

Adrian, can we talk some time? Think we need to clear the air.

She stubbed out her cigarette on the top of a bin.

NINETEEN

'Come to think of it, being a business angel isn't such a bad idea,' Laurel thought at breakfast the next morning. 'Help someone like Melissa, add in some knowledgeable advice, then recoup the investment with a profit. But there would be an initial time-lag; and I'd still need somewhere to live!' Squally rain spattered the windows.

Having nipped out to buy a large exercise book, Laurel sat in the guest lounge all morning, mind-mapping and jotting the pros and cons, together with various possibilities that she saw for the salon. She only broke off when Doug entered, offering her a cup of coffee as he was making one for himself. There was still no response from Adrian. *What on earth is wrong with him, Laurel, and could you really live with this?* She thought deeply; then, she sent another message.

Maybe I expected too much too soon. I was probably wrong to rush up here and ask to stay last week, but I was so shocked that day.

She hit 'send', with the gloom of approaching finality darkening her mood, and not expecting her phone to buzz barely a minute later.

You didn't need to go like that. We could work something out. I'm sorry if I let you think the wrong thing when I kissed you.

Exasperating! Typical! The one moment when he let his passion take over, and now he regrets it! She tried to collect herself, then keyed the thoughts of her heart.

A week ago, I was certain I wanted to be with you. But if you don't feel the same way, it's better to be honest. I just need to know, Adrian.

"Busy, eh?" Doug said, handing her a mug. Laurel explained what she was working on. "Aye, well, it isn't easy to make money in this town nowadays. The ones that survive are usually offering something a bit different. Anyway, don't let me interrupt you." *Food for thought, Laurel.*

By three o'clock, several pages of her exercise book were covered with random brainwaves, arrows, asterisks, exclamation marks and deletions. There had been nothing more from Adrian, though she was not banking on a swift reply. She had put him on the spot.

Although the sky was still cloudy, the rain had cleared. A good walk would allow the haphazard germs of ideas to ferment in her brain. Pulling on a thicker jumper, Laurel glanced in the mirror: a few greying hairs at her temples, crow's feet more pronounced, as were other facial lines. Dusting powder directly onto her moisturised skin, she was struck by a new thought, which she added to her notes. As she was leaving, her phone rang.

"Hello there, kiddo."

"Oh, hi, Aunty Hilda. How are you?" Laurel asked cheerily.

"Are you sitting down?"

"Erm, no. Should I be?"

"Probably. Well, I took your advice. We — Rosemary and I — went to see our vicar yesterday evening. You can imagine how we were feeling. Honestly, she was shaking so much that she could hardly drive."

"And?" Laurel asked, urging some progress.

"Well, we sat in his study and he brought some tea and some really nice biscuits…"

"Go on, Aunty Hilda."

"He said, 'Now then, ladies, I can see you're both a little nervous. So, how can I help you?' And both of us started talking at the same moment; and we laughed. Well, you can imagine. And…"

"Hilda!" Laurel said, in a mildly reproachful tone. "Get to it! What actually happened?"

"Well, we're engaged!" Silence. "Laurel, are you there?" Stunned into the form of a gaping-mouthed statue, Laurel took several seconds to process the information.

"Oh my God!" she squealed. "That's… that's bloody fantastic! Oh, Aunty Hilda, I want to hug you!"

"I would have called earlier, kiddo, but we didn't get up until nearly twelve. On the way home, we stopped off and bought a bottle of champagne. Of course, I put it in the freezer to chill it, but we had to wait a bit. And we sat and made some plans. And we had a little cuddle. And then… Oh, she's here. Have a word with my Laurel, Rosemary."

It was a wonderful moment for Laurel to speak, for the first time, with the woman who had turned Hilda's world upside down. She heard the details of the conversation with the vicar, that he was delighted for them, promising to support them in any way that he could. A church wedding was not permissible, but he would be pleased to do a service of blessing; naturally, they would have to wait for the divorce to be finalised.

"So, he can have his divorce. I was going to fight it, Laurel, but I've found new happiness. Good riddance."

"I'm delighted for you," Laurel began.

"And, kiddo," Hilda took over, "That's where you come in. We want you to be a witness at the registry office, and a bridesmaid at the church."

Laurel took an audible and involuntary gulp of air. Tears flooded her eyes. She gasped, almost dizzy. "Oh, Aunty Hilda! I…" Words failed her for a moment. Aged ten, she had been to a wedding, enviously eyeing a little cousin beautiful and princess-like in her bridesmaid dress. She had longed to fulfil that role ever since.

"You've just made a very old dream come true," Laurel said, regaining some composure.

"Never mind your old dream," said Hilda, laughing. "I'm going to be the oldest bride in Wales."

"Just one thing, though. I'll do it so long as I don't have to wear red," Laurel declared.

"Red! It's in a church, kiddo, not a ruddy brothel!"

She had to retouch her make-up before heading out. Overjoyed for Hilda, elated for Maddie, delighted for Claire in Preston, positive and optimistic for pierced Melissa, Laurel just needed some of that luck to rub off on her. More in celebration than frustration, she downed two large glasses of Shiraz at the bar of Salter's Wharf.

"Want a brew?" Melissa asked, when Laurel arrived at the salon on Friday morning. A week into June, the weather felt like November. They spent a while sharing their histories before Laurel, sensing that the girl was reaching out for some counsel and guidance, turned to business.

"So, what would you really like to do with this salon?"

"I think I need to offer more than just hair-dos. And I need to get younger people through here. I'd thought of having a tattooist in here as well."

"Your friend's boyfriend?" Laurel asked, recalling their first conversation.

"No, he's got a place in Blackpool."

"I'm not sure," Laurel began carefully, "Tattoos might not give the stylishness you're looking for. And they turn quite a lot of people off."

"Yeah, I know," Melissa admitted.

"Start by building on your own skills. Mrs Simmonds, the solicitor's mum, clearly thinks you're great. And she tries to look a little younger than her age." The girl nodded. "So, think one generation younger. Teens have no money; many people in their thirties are stretched, raising kids and paying mortgages. But women like me, late forties, fifties, early sixties — that's not old these days. Their kids get jobs, leave home; they have more spending power. They want to look good; and they aren't ready for a blue rinse and Damart passion killers." Melissa, attentive and scribbling notes, chuckled.

"And yesterday afternoon, when I looked in the mirror, I noticed the dreaded lines of doom!" The hairdresser scrunched up her face into a cute smile. "Why not work with a beautician? There's enough empty space in here. You could either employ someone and pay her a wage; or, you work it so that she keeps her money and pays you for her trading space, covering light, heat, and so on."

"Erm, yeah. I don't know which would be better," Melissa mused.

"Okay, we can think about that later. And if we act quickly," Laurel continued, but checked herself. *Steady, Laurel, you're taking over.* "Sorry, I mean you. If you act quickly, this could be the ideal time. Women will want to look their best and have a makeover before going on holiday, or out to social events. Imagine: one customer has a nice new hairstyle, plus manicure and a Polyfilla job, so her spend trebles. And you're not working your knickers off trying to get new clients."

"I like you. You're not like a bank manager. You're so funny," the girl said giggling.

"And," Laurel paused for effect, "there must be people graduating as beauticians from colleges around now. You could probably find someone who'd be grateful for a start."

"You're right. And I *have* thought about doing that; but look at this place." Melissa sighed.

"That's where my capital comes in! How much do you think you'd need?"

"I've made a quick list," the girl replied, flicking through some papers. "Probably at least fifteen thousand."

"Hmm." Laurel nodded, then glanced around. "Nearer twenty-five. Don't forget, you'll need to stock up with product, get extra furniture — and do some promotion." The girl, clearly not stupid, was quickly persuaded by Laurel's preparedness and reasoning.

"And one more thing that might set you apart from the others," Laurel ventured, recalling her chat with Doug. "If you're going to expand into beauty services, why stop with women?" Melissa looked quizzical, even half stunned. "Why not offer help to men who identify, or want to appear, as women?"

"What? You mean… trannies?"

"If you like." Laurel smiled kindly. "Being near Blackpool, there must be cross-dressers and trans women around who would love help with make-up, waxing. We could offer tutorials and advice; you know, friendly, welcoming and non-judgemental support."

"Whoa! This is a bit… radical, even for me!"

Laurel took stock, breathing slowly. "You see, Melissa," she said, in a calm and confidential tone. "I do have some personal knowledge and experience."

The hairdresser froze, her eyes almost the size of rugby balls. "You?" she gulped. "Seriously? No! But you look… Oh, I'm sorry! When I said 'trannies', I didn't…"

"Don't worry. I've been called far worse," Laurel said laughing. "It's nearly eighteen years since I had the final surgery. Look!" Laurel pulled out her driving licence and a photo taken on the last day she had gone to work as Lawrence. The hairdresser's eyes flicked between the snap and Laurel's face.

"Obviously, Melissa, we'd need to talk more about financial arrangements. It would be an investment, not a gift; but I feel there's opportunity here." A brief silence. "I've given you a lot to take in, haven't I? So, let's think about it for a few days. See if you can get some quotes for the redecoration. You've got my contact now; just call me any time if you want to ask something."

"Gosh!" Melissa exclaimed, standing slowly, like a boxer floored by several meaty blows. "Thank you, Laurel. Thank you so much." They stood motionless for a moment, both in recovery mode. Simultaneously, they smiled. Then, on impulse, the hairdresser flung her arms around Laurel's neck, hugging her tightly. There was no need for words.

"See you sometime next week, Melissa," Laurel said, opening the door.

"Liss — call me Liss. That's what my friends call me." The heavily pierced and tattooed stylist smiled innocently.

"Okay, Liss. Keep in touch."

After closing the door, Melissa allowed several large tears to roll down her cheeks. Her salon suddenly felt less like a dungeon.

Rain was rolling in, so Laurel jogged back to the Cumbria, where she remained all afternoon. No incoming messages. She scrolled through some more businesses for sale; then, feeling a little tired, she lay down and closed her eyes.

"Laurel!" Knocking at her door. She came to and leapt from the bed. "Laurel," Doug said, "There's someone at the front door asking for you: a man and a girl." Roused from sleep, and still a little disoriented, Laurel checked her appearance in the mirror and followed the hotelier downstairs. She almost dared not hope; but the outlines of Adrian and Emily were unmistakeable.

Emily, in a jumper, a summer-weight skirt, which finished above the knee, and black tights, hugged her; Adrian smiled weakly. Laurel kissed them both on the cheek, then led them into the lounge. The teenager handed her a bag containing some clothes, washed and folded. On top of the bundle lay the olive-green French knickers, with their roses of lace. Laurel smiled coyly, recalling that she had changed quickly before running with Martin; they had got rolled up in the duvet.

"Sorry," Emily said. "I was supposed to bring your laptop as well; but I was in a hurry and forgot it."

"No problem. I haven't really needed it. But I might do soon. I'll pop over one day next week to get it." The girl nodded, smiling. Her father continued to stare through the bay window, into the middle distance.

"So, you drove all the way over here in the rain to see me," Laurel said pleasantly, attempting to break the silence. "It's a nice little hotel... very comfortable."

"We don't want you to be sad, alone over here," Emily said, nervously glancing for her father's approval.

"And... and it's stopped raining," Adrian added, almost childlike. A fellow guest nodded to Laurel as he came in through the vestibule.

"Well, why don't we go into town and stroll around the gardens? Then we can talk more easily," Laurel suggested.

They wandered through Ashton Gardens, where Laurel was keen to point out the roses and their deep significance for her. Adrian, who had been quiet and ill at ease during Laurel's reminiscences, suggested they find somewhere to eat. He had picked Emily up from home, without stopping off for dinner.

"What's that?" the girl asked, indicating the tall art deco monument ahead.

"Go and take a look," Laurel replied, willing Emily to allow the adults some space for a meaningful conversation. He remained withdrawn, though, as they neared the war memorial. Emily was captivated by the figures on the far side: a mother and her small child, naked and about to climb onto the woman's lap.

"Look at her expression. It's heart-breaking, desolate," Emily said. Adrian reacted oddly to her artistic sensibility, shrugging his shoulders. "She doesn't even notice her child; she's staring into space," Emily observed.

"Good, Emily. Yes, she's contemplating the awfulness of facing the rest of her life without the man she loves." Whether prompted by Laurel's summary, or by her compliment to his daughter, Adrian acknowledged Emily's interpretation.

Meanwhile, Laurel's mind had wandered back forty years, but only a few yards, inside the pavilion theatre. Billy Bigelow and Julie, thrown together, were sitting on a bench, under the blossom and the stars. *'Say, you're different all right. I don't ever remember meeting*

315

a girl like you… Are you trying to get me to marry you?
I don't know what it'd be like… If I loved you.' 'But you
don't.' 'No, I don't…'

The evening had brightened, if half-heartedly. In
the gaps between the Victorian villas, the sky revealed
a pale golden glow. There was stillness, except for the
light traffic that passed along Clifton Drive. Walking
towards the road, Laurel leant on Adrian's arm, their
first moment of tenderness for more than a week.

The picnic benches outside the Lord Derby were
still very damp; so, they found a table in a quiet corner
of the lounge. While Adrian was getting the drinks,
Emily and Laurel talked about him.

"Martin says he's guilty over Mum, but I don't
know," the girl confided. "I don't think he knows what
he wants. He didn't even kiss you when we got here. He
says he likes you, but then he goes all quiet. And he
won't talk about the time when you two were working
together in the bank."

"Like Stella says, he probably just needs time. And
that's something I can give him now. I've been looking
at business possibilities; and from tomorrow, I'm going
to start looking for a small flat. I can't stay in a B&B for
ever."

The next hour passed off civilly, albeit tentatively.
Adrian listened and commented positively while Laurel
was describing the progress she had made and the
options she was considering. When she started

enthusing about Melissa's salon, however, he made a sour accountant-style dubious face.

"Why can't she get a bank loan, or ask her family? And when would you get your money back? You're not a charity. Nor does it give you the job and income you're looking for," he averred.

"Her trading account can't be wonderful; so, would I have lent to her two weeks ago? Possibly not. But she has ability, and she's a nice girl underneath all the ironmongery; she needs a leg-up and some guidance."

"It's your funeral," Adrian replied.

When Emily went to the bathroom, Laurel broached the subject that needed to be aired. "So, Adrian," she began, making certain of eye contact. "I care for you. I want to be with you. I'm in love with you again. But I need to know your feelings. Have you thought about us, our future?"

"I meant it — you didn't need to go," he began diffidently, even evasively.

"But sleeping on your sofa was cheeky, if something of an emergency. I just couldn't stay in London. But that's not the point, is it?" She looked hard at him; he shifted awkwardly.

"Do we have a future, Adrian?"

"It's not easy. I still can't reconcile… you and the change."

"Isn't it easier, now that I'm a woman?" She gently stroked his hand, Billy Bigelow's lines iterating in her mind.

"And you're an attractive woman, no doubt. But you're also Lawrie, the guy I used to drink beer with."

"Sorry, Adrian." Laurel hurriedly left the table. Adrian looked confused, especially when Laurel shepherded Emily back towards the toilets.

"What's wrong?" the girl asked, as the door closed behind them.

"This," Laurel said, tugging Emily's skirt out of her pink underwear.

"Oh no!" the girl yelped.

"I noticed as soon as you came out. I don't think anyone else would have seen. Don't panic! It happened to me, in the middle of London! I'd walked a hundred yards down Oxford Street, on a Saturday morning, before a woman kindly stopped to tell me. Luckily, I had some really nice undies on."

"You've got lots of nice undies." Emily smiled.

"Did you find them, or your Dad?"

"Neither. Martin did, when he was moving the duvet." Laurel was momentarily mortified.

"We put them in the wash before Dad came home. Don't panic," she echoed Laurel's advice cheekily. "Martin thinks you're really lit. Well, he said something else."

"Oh yes?"

Emily whispered one word into Laurel's ear. They were still giggling when they reached the table.

"You're in a jolly mood," said Adrian, perusing the dessert menu.

"Why not? Everyone around me is finding love and happiness. My two friends in London have got together; and you won't believe what my Aunty Hilda told me yesterday. She and her female friend, whose husband walked out on her, have got engaged. They want me to be their bridesmaid, or whatever. I'm so excited."

"For God's sake!" exclaimed Adrian, "Don't you know anyone who's normal?" Laurel flinched. It stung. But only for a moment. She was too happy to be cross.

"I used to know you," she said, smiling quizzically and teasingly. Touché. Pause.

"What? I don't understand. Used to?" Adrian questioned. Had he misread the signal?

"You've got me all wrong, Adrian. It was just…"

"I've got it wrong? Two women of that age — getting married! It's… it's just sick!"

"Dad!" Emily protested anxiously.

"Why can't you be pleased that someone very dear to me has found some happiness? What's wrong with you, Adrian?"

Laurel stomped outside, shaking so much that she struggled to light a cigarette. *Did you do the right thing in walking out like that, Laurel? It didn't look good in front of Emily, but you need some time to get back in control.* Having been drawn on so furiously, the cigarette had almost burned down when Adrian appeared.

"I… I realise that I said something I shouldn't have… about your aunt."

"Stuff Aunty Hilda, Adrian. This is about us!" She stubbed the glowing tip. "Do you want this to be over?"

"No, NO. Of course not," he insisted. "Do you?" Pause. *You're the one who just walked out, Laurel. Think: think before you speak.*

"Would it be easier for you if we didn't see each other?" Laurel ploughed on, stressed, her anger rising.

"Well, erm…"

"Easier for you just to sit at work with your figures, then sit at home feeling sorry for yourself over your failed marriage." The red mist was now obscuring the red light. She drove on recklessly. "Is it easier for you not to deal with the questions your kids are asking about us — about me? Did you bring Emily with you for protection, so it was easier to deal with me? Isn't it easier for you not to have to say my name? Because you can hardly ever bring yourself to do it, can you? 'Laurel' sticks in your throat, doesn't it?"

There is a reason why we have made laws against reckless driving. The sad thing is that when we are pumped up, we only stop to consider those laws after the inevitable accident. They are primarily intended to protect us from ourselves.

"It would be far easier for you and your little life if I just got the hell out of it. You've got a beautiful daughter, who notices that you're cold around me. You're weak, Adrian! No wonder your son doesn't want to spend any time with you!" Silence. *That was harsh, Laurel; better cool it.*

"And I'd prefer it if you didn't encourage Emily to dress like a tart."

Outraged, Laurel's mouth fell agape. "I beg your pardon?" Her fury baited, she hammered out the words.

"I saw photos of her at that birthday party."

"And she looked bloody gorgeous."

"She's a child…"

"She's fourteen and a half, Adrian, not nine! And she was only with other girls. I suppose all the others there were dressed like nuns," Laurel added sarcastically. A beat later, she stamped her foot on the top concrete step. "It isn't Emily who needs to grow up, Adrian; it's you!" *Brace for impact, Laurel.*

"Perhaps we'd better call…"

"Call it a day, is that it? Don't worry, Adrian, it's done. For good." Laurel turned away and took two steps down.

Emily, who had been peering through the window, rushed out onto the pub steps. "Laurel, what's wrong?"

Wrestling with rage, hurt and disillusionment, Laurel tried to smile bravely. "It's just… I have to go, honey. See you soon." She turned again and descended the last two steps.

"Laurel!" the girl called, her feet clattering on the concrete. Laurel did not stop to reply. So much did she want to hug the girl, and to say sorry, that it was for the best; but her heart was ripped apart already. To linger would destroy her, possibly both of them. She bit her bottom lip, steeled herself, and walked into the street.

That was that. Over. Good.

There is something about the wiring of the human mind which, at times of difficulty with a loved one, drives us into the arms of a monster. Whether that be fury, alcohol, depression, cheap sex, or a more destructive relationship, it is, inevitably, a monster.

Half an hour after arriving back in her room, Laurel was showered and naked, rummaging for her sexiest lingerie. After redoing her make-up in more sultry colours, she reached for her phone. She sprawled across her bed, taking selfies in different outfits, from several angles, checking they were alluring, not obscene. For the final one, she kept on the sheer lace-topped black stockings, changed into her green French knickers and stayed topless, her left forearm covering her nipples. *Inviting, Laurel.* She clicked.

Within fifteen minutes, aroused by her own sexuality and her incandescent anger, she had selected a dating site, paid a subscription, and completed a basic profile. Scrolling through the photos she had taken, she uploaded those she thought would titillate the discerning viewer. Compared with many profiles, hers was classy; tempting, not vulgar; seductive, not slutty. Many women gauged their seduction of men by intuition and experience; having been a young man, Laurel possessed an extra fund of knowledge. *Bugger Adrian, let's have some fun!*

TWENTY

"Knob head!" Laurel moaned the next morning, trawling through the contacts that her profile had attracted. The illiterate and the desperate had been well occupied in the preceding hours, boasting of their size, prowess, or level of deviance. One Asian man desired her so hotly that he had sent no fewer than eight messages, offering to drive over to Lytham St Anne's a little after three a.m. *You'll end up turning the Cumbria into a brothel, Laurel!*

Most of the replies were from punters looking for a quickie or a new piece of meat. One or two were less cringe-making, however; and she returned flirty messages, having studied their profiles. Only after breakfast did she receive the most interesting contact. He was a barrister, in the middle of separating from his wife, and currently involved in a major trial at Preston Crown Court.

Can't make it today or tomorrow — wife coming up for the weekend. Hardly good form! We could meet Wednesday, there'll be a break in proceedings. My hotel?

OK. Let's meet Wednesday. Eleven o'clock. What briefs does a brief wear?

Legal ones, my dear, though not as enticing as yours! And please wear those stockings.

He was three years older than Laurel, with distinguished greying hair. Of his three photos, one had been taken on a beach. His smile was relaxed and genuine. He had a manly, slightly hairy chest and, he claimed, a penchant for slow, lingering sex. Laurel read and reread his profile, enlarging the photos in turn; and slowly, her fingers slipped inside the waistband of her panties.

Her phone was lively that morning, particularly with calls from Adrian; and she was not in the mood for him. Maybe later. One message from the hook-up site was an invitation to a Sunday dogging meet, somewhere near Lancaster. *What the hell have you got yourself into, Laurel?* She switched off her phone, left it on the bedside shelf and caught the bus to Blackpool.

In fact, Laurel did not switch on again until Sunday morning, when she was on the bus to Lytham. She had not spoken to Stella for a few days, and the reason soon became clear.

We won't be at church. Don's brother was taken seriously ill on Thursday, so we rushed over to Yorkshire. Had a call from Adrian this morning. What is the matter with you two? Don't give up on it, Laurel. God is testing you, testing how strongly you love him. Just don't close your heart and mind to him.

Laurel was unsure whether Stella's 'him' was Adrian or God; but her throat was lumpy and her eyes were watering. She got off the bus in Lytham, but could not face church. Instead, she walked over the railway to Park View. With coffee in a paper cup, she sat at the same table where she had sobbed the day after her father's funeral.

"I don't know what to do, Daddy. I don't know if he loves me; I don't know if I really love him now. I wish you were here to help me," she murmured. Unnoticed by Laurel, the uppermost branches of the tall trees stirred. Her phone showed an unanswered call from Adrian; she switched it off. Two missed connections.

Later that afternoon, after more rain, Laurel strolled along the near-deserted promenade. Walking through the ornamental gardens, she climbed the little hump-backed bridge. Had her feeling of freedom, standing here a few weeks ago, been illusory? There were more messages from Adrian. She was sorely tempted to chuck her phone into the water below; but her phone was essential. Finally, still on the bridge, she resolved to chuck the relationship with Adrian.

Once back in her room, Laurel opened two messages. Emily was asking why Laurel had walked away without saying 'goodbye', and why she was not replying to her father. Emily had cried all Friday and Saturday night. That tore at Laurel's soul.

Honey, I'm sorry. I thought if I'd stayed to hug you, it would have made things worse. Didn't want to upset you because I love you. But I got it wrong again. Your dad and I have to decide if we want this. XXX

There was also a text from Stella.

If you want to talk, I'll be in Nero at ten Tuesday morning.

Laurel smiled at the nuance. A week or so earlier, it had practically been an order. This time, it was an offer; one that she would find difficult to accept, but impossible to decline.

In between showers and cups of coffee, Laurel spent Monday morning combing the estate agents' windows and gathering details of flats for rent or sale: her mind was still open to both options. She carefully avoided walking past Melissa's salon, not wanting the girl to think she was being spied upon. In the middle of the afternoon, however, Laurel received a message.

What colours do you think for salon? Pink, yellow? Got a guy coming to quote soon. Meeting a beautician tmrw. Liss.

Great progress, Liss. Well done. Maybe more sophisticated colours — gold or bronze, dark green — relaxing. Even purple? Think pampering, make a woman feel a million dollars. Ask the decorator for his thoughts, too. And get another quote to compare. X

The butterfly — Madam Butterfly, she laughed to herself — was taking a cadet under her wing.

"How is Don's brother?" Laurel asked, sitting down opposite Stella the next morning.

"Comfortable, in hospital. He'll live," she said, almost dismissively.

"It's you I'm concerned about."

Fixing an X-ray gaze, the retired nurse listened patiently as Laurel, striving for words initially, opened up her deepest feelings, her fears and frustrations. When Laurel had let fly for a good ten minutes, Stella paused thoughtfully.

"*Mela*, what were the first words I ever said to you?" Laurel was dumbstruck. What a question! She racked her brain. "It was in the church, before I even knew your name." Still no light shone in the darkness. "The first words I spoke to you were, 'Peace be with you'." Laurel shrugged, not grasping the significance.

327

"Stop being anxious, Laurel. Do you think you can find happiness by worrying? Torturing yourself like this is not going to change anything — except your blood pressure, *ta'*."

Laurel opened her mouth to respond, but stopped herself. *How can you argue a point like that with a devout Catholic, Laurel; especially one who has been uncannily correct about you several times before?*

Stella took Laurel's hand softly in her own. "You have enough love inside you to deal with this." Stella paused and inhaled deeply. Laurel felt her friend's hand stiffen. "Maybe you need to start loving yourself more. Then, you might find the ability to love him as he needs." Heavens, this was a bit strong.

"On account of your past, and all the things you went through, you never stop judging, assessing yourself. And you're stifling the flow of love. Love isn't a mill stream that you can direct and control, whose power you can harness. It's a broad river that is fed by other streams — your experiences — with the latitude to make mistakes, to do slightly crazy things; to slow down, or to speed up; to float with others, or to swim alone for a while. And there may be rocks or small islands in the way, but it finds its path around them.

"You have a beautiful soul, Laurel. Don't uglify it." A flicker of doubt flashed across the Maltese woman's face. Did that word exist? "Remember the fresco in the church? Our Lady rising serenely towards heaven? From the moment that Gabriel visits her to the moment of her assumption, she surrenders herself. Why? Because she knows, in her heart, that however difficult the path may be, it is the good and the right one. It is where she should be.

"Many a time I've sat there, giving my anxieties to her, imagining them floating, drifting up and away, in the cloud at her feet, vanishing into the invisible..."

"But you have faith."

"Don't you?" Stella's look was piercing. "Then, why did you turn up at St Peter's that Sunday morning when we first met?"

Laurel, unable to explain, thrashed out: "But I can't believe in this God that makes things happen because you ask for them." A pause.

"I'll let you into a secret, *hanina*. Neither can I. I don't believe in a God with a fluffy white beard, hiding out there in space, at the end of a magic telephone line, who'll say 'Abracadabra', and make everything as I want it. No, when I pray, I awaken that part inside me which is God; and I find within myself the strength, or the courage, or the hope. And, Laurel, the love."

Laurel sniffed back a tear. "Oh, Stella. I've been an idiot, a bloody idiot." Her lips stiffened; her fingers tightened as she gripped the steering wheel of her emotions.

"No, you've been hurt; and you've reacted by closing your heart," Stella said kindly. "Emily likes you. No, Laurel, she loves you. And I think you're very fond of her. She can see that you and her father should be together. Children often see the truth more clearly than we do."

Trembling now, Laurel gasped, her composure clinging by a thread. Why did she have to bring up Emily? Emily, whom she had recently hurt? Laurel had been driving through her frustration with Adrian; she could burn off her negativity on the road called Adrian. But Emily?

Like a car hitting a patch of ice, control was ceded to the laws of emotional physics. She crashed into Stella's slight shoulder, tears bursting from her with the force of an inflating airbag. Naturally, the former nurse was well prepared with paper tissues.

That evening, Laurel updated Maddie on the Adrian saga; she also told her about the dating site and attached the profile photo. Minutes later, her phone rang. Maddie sympathised with her over Adrian, adding that it was no wonder Laurel had moved to London if people 'up there' had such a small-town mentality. Then she changed her tone.

"But those websites, Laurel, they're used by hookers and scammers. And you never know who's looking at it — maybe some of our clients! What would they think — she's quit the bank to do that? Remember that customer we had? Scamming men by leading them on with a few saucy photos and asking them what they'd like her to do with them, then pretending she was coming into a fortune…"

"Oh yeah — then emailing them, supposedly from Nigeria, saying she'd been robbed and was being held prisoner by the hotel manager until she'd paid the bill. Always the same amount," Laurel recalled. "Eight hundred and forty quid. Doing about two suckers a week, remember, when we checked the account."

They laughed for a moment. "Come on, Laurel, you're better than that. If you're doing this to get back at Adrian, it won't work. I know you, don't I? You'll only beat yourself up with the guilt stick. Adrian won't even know about it."

"Forget Adrian, Mad. I'm going to try to," Laurel sighed bitterly. "This guy is obviously educated; he's nearly single — and a barrister."

"How do you know, lovey? He's in a hotel. He'll probably turn out to be a barista who can't spell." Laurel laughed. "That's better. I wish I could give you a cuddle."

"Me too," Laurel sniffed. "I miss you." A momentary pause.

"Have you spoken to Adrian since Friday?"

"No, I can't. I really think it's over, Mad."

"Has he not called you?"

"Yeah, about thirty times, either calls or texts. I've ignored all of them."

"Laurel! You're crazy! You went all the way up there to be near him. You can't quit now; not yet, anyway."

After a thoughtful smoke in the rainy hotel car park, Laurel went back to her room, made a cup of coffee, and played what she had decided would be her final hand in the Adrian game.

Adrian, being with you is still my dream, my heart's desire. Wish I could change the past, so that Lawrie had never existed. But whatever Lawrie was, inside — all the time — was me.

The night we talked about buying that small house together, I didn't tell you the whole truth. I said I was fed up living with parents. But I wanted to live WITH YOU, just couldn't say it there and then, in a pub. Everything changed, but nothing's changed.

She sent the message. She finished her coffee. She waited. She had another cigarette out in the drizzle. There was no reply. She went to bed.

Having clipped the lace-topped stockings to her suspender belt, Laurel pulled up the green French knickers. She would normally have gone for black, but if Queen's Counsel had been attracted by her photo, who was she to contest his judgment? Despite Maddie's misgivings, she ought to be safe in a city-centre hotel. *Just have a bloody good time, Laurel, and get Adrian out of your system.*

She made herself up a little more heavily than usual, but not tarty; then, she pushed her black high-heels into her tote bag. A few squirts of Coco Mademoiselle, and she was heading to catch the Preston bus.

Although she knew that her skirt, short as it was, amply concealed her stocking tops, Laurel felt occasional pangs of self-consciousness. She opted for the one vacant seat downstairs, wary of giving an upskirt treat to some fellow passenger. What would Queen's Counsel be like? Suave and gentle, or a rampant beast? The bus seemed to be stopped in Lytham Square for ages. Would he have champagne on ice in his room? Would he be waiting in a plush dressing gown, or...

They had scarcely been moving for a minute when the bus slowed to a crawl. Laurel glanced out of the window; they were opposite St Peter's Church, with its tower built by one of the Cliftons as an act of penance. Inching forwards, she could practically count the bricks. Then, as the bus began to accelerate, something caught her eye; something she had never noticed before. In the garden, against the northern wall of the apse, stood a white statue of Mary, suppliant hands raised, gazing heavenward. *What the hell are you doing, Laurel?*

A lump in her throat, a dizziness in her head, and Laurel slammed the 'Stop' button. She got to her feet, teetered as the bus negotiated the mini roundabout, and lurched forward when the driver braked at the stop. Beep! She nearly stepped right in front of a speeding van.

Somehow making it across the road, she stood, seduced and transfixed by the image. Control was relinquished once more. Words formed subconsciously on her lips, ones she had learned in childhood.

"Holy Mary, Mother of God, pray for us sinners now and at the hour of our death."

Tears were trickling down her face as she repeated the prayer, the words birthed not in the rational brain, but flowing from her heart. Broken, she leant forward into the brick wall for support. There, from the shattered rock of her heart, a spring gushed.

Partly recovered, she walked towards the green, barely able to see for tears. Although struggling at times to breathe properly, she mouthed the prayer over and over, dragging her hand through her hair. Beside the estuary, a sobering breeze blew into Laurel's face; above her hung a remarkable cloud formation, like wings. Her hair was tousled and disturbed. *Welcome the wind, Laurel; it will blow the crap out of your life.*

An hour later, after gathering herself together, Laurel was walking back along the coast road when her phone started ringing. Without looking at the screen, she answered it.

"Look, we need to talk and sort this out."

"Whoa! Good afternoon to you, Adrian," she replied, with more than a hint of sarcasm.

"I'm sorry, but I have to leave for a meeting shortly. Look, I need stability; so do my kids. Emily, in particular… I can't have her turned upside down and seeing what she did last Friday."

"You wish I'd never come back into your life. I get it, Adrian. It all came like a whirlwind and I've wreaked devastation across your lives."

"Don't be like that."

"Well, that's what you're saying. I'm disruptive."

"They've been through the break-up and the divorce — I can't…"

"I know, I know." Laurel took a deep breath and let out a long sigh. "Look, I get what you're saying. And I don't want to make your family life worse, or to upset your kids, especially Emily."

"Yes, it's a pity. She's grown fond of you, but she can't understand why we… why it's difficult."

"To be honest, Adrian, neither can I." There was a long silence.

You were foolish, Laurel, to think you could just pick up again, trying to reconnect what had never truly been connected. Had your imagination made a quantum leap from 'I'm falling in love with this boy' to 'we had something special between us'?

"Are you still there?" he asked.

"Yes. You?"

"Obviously."

Laurel sighed. He was in sullen mode. It was clear where Martin inherited it from. There had been days, when they were much younger, when breaking through was impossible.

"Lawrie… Laurel, I just don't think this is going to work."

"That's it, then?"

"I guess so, sorry. If you want to collect your things…"

"Things?" Laurel felt the numbness of expected shock. Although she had told Maddie it was over, she was reeling.

"Well, your laptop is here, and…"

"Okay, I'll come over tomorrow."

"Tonight, would be better." A pause. "Problem?"

"Tonight? For a start, Adrian, I'm in St Anne's; and…"

"I'll be in Blackburn this afternoon. Meet me early evening in McDonalds." *This boy has style, Laurel.*

"You don't want me at your house?"

"I don't want Emily to get upset if we start… if it gets difficult."

"Okay, fine. Fine. I can get the twenty past five train. I'll be there by six thirty, or just after."

Dropping her phone back into her bag, she glanced across the road. A blue plaque commemorated the house where George Formby had lived. At that moment, she could have suggested one good place to shove his Little Stick of Blackpool Rock.

In her room, she emptied her bag and refilled it with a change of clothes, in case she did not make the last train back. She changed into the grey dress that she had bought in St Anne's a few weeks earlier, when she had fled north. On the way out, she slipped a note under the breakfast room door, saying that she might not be in overnight.

It's a mess, Laurel. But at least, by the time darkness falls this evening, you'll be rid of one headache. Painful though the next few hours and days might be, there'll be no more guessing, wishing, wondering, dreaming and planning a rosy future with him. It'll be over.

The train rattled past the fairways and greens of Pleasington golf course, towards Blackburn, where she had grown up, where it had all begun. Prompted by the rhythm of the train, she started to sing to herself: *"Here I go again, off down the road again, thinking thoughts of things gone by..."*

On the slow approach to Mill Hill, Laurel's phone rang. "Hi, it's... it's me."

"Hello, me," she said flatly.

"Sorry, change of plan. I'll have to postpone till tomorrow evening."

"I'm almost there. I thought you couldn't do tomorrow," Laurel replied impatiently. "For heaven's sake, Adrian, get your bloody life sorted out. No wonder she walked out on you." *Not nice, Laurel.* "Sorry, that wasn't fair." He had been hurt, and no matter how frustrated she had become, he was still too good a person to hurt again.

"Sorry. I love you, believe me." *Now you sound desperate and pathetic, Laurel.* "Okay, tomorrow it is.

Look, instead of McDonalds, let's have a last drink. Meet me in the Drummer's Arms, opposite the Town Hall."

She could have dashed through the tunnel at Blackburn station and caught the next train back to St Anne's, but that would have meant faffing around, changing platforms at Preston. She was tired; physically and emotionally drained. She phoned the guest house where she had stayed when her father was in care, at the end of his life. It had always been clean and comfortable; and the couple who ran it were nice.

Chimneys was a ten-minute walk from the town centre; but she took a taxi, mainly to avoid the dodgy area under the car park ramp, where people drank, urinated and slept, not necessarily in that order. And anyway, she had medium heels on.

Before she settled in, Laurel nipped up the road for a takeaway and a bottle of wine. Having taken off her skirt, she switched on the TV and flopped onto the bed. Without much food since breakfast, she was ravenous, which made the pizza especially tasty. Between slices, she poured a mug of wine.

Suddenly, perhaps because she was dropping off, Laurel felt the pizza box sliding from her lap. She made a grab for it, but her reaction jolted the mug in her other hand, spilling the Shiraz Cabernet blend onto her midriff and the green knickers. "Bugger!" She wriggled off the bed as smoothly as possible, laid the mug on the bedside table and the box on the floor; then, she pulled off the pants and rinsed them in the washbasin.

Laurel looked around for a means of drying them. It was June; the heating was switched off. Her only option was to hang them out of the window. Carefully, she flopped the knickers through the gap, clamping them tightly in the window. They would blow dry in the breeze overnight.

Resuming her pizza, she muttered, "Can anything else go wrong?"

TWENTY-ONE

Relaxed by the wine, Laurel slept soundly for a few hours. At some stage, however, she was disturbed by the wind, which was flinging the branches of a nearby tree against her window. She rolled over, unable to settle, her brain churning over the events of the last week, and rehearsing what she would say to Adrian.

"Why don't you keep the room for tonight as well?" the lady owner suggested at breakfast, after listening sympathetically to Laurel's story. "You might not feel like travelling back to St Anne's after you've said your farewells. And if you want to chat, we'll be in the lounge until nine thirty. Anyway, the best of luck with it."

Laurel took a long calming shower and dried her hair. Only while fastening her bra did she remember hanging the green knickers out of the window. Pulling back the curtain, she was horrified to see the window slightly ajar, but no lingerie. *You must have brought them in during the night, Laurel.* Increasingly frantic, she fruitlessly turned the room upside down and inside out.

From the window, Laurel scanned the road: nothing but traffic and drizzle. There was a melancholy familiarity about grey skies and wet slates; she had grown up with them. She could kill time in the library and the shopping mall, but the wait until evening would be like the hours before dental treatment that you know will hurt.

With the drizzle petering out, she set off on foot, keeping her eyes peeled for her pants. She had covered about eighty yards when she noticed a grey-bearded, Moslem man stretching over the bonnet of his car. He pulled some olive-green material from his windscreen. She gulped as he began to unfold the fabric. Realising what was in his hands, he quickly glanced around; then, he scrunched up the pants and stuffed them into his pocket.

What could she do? She could hardly march into his driveway and say, 'Excuse me, I think you've just trousered my knickers!' She would spare both of them considerable embarrassment. Nevertheless, she was fond of them; they had caressed her most intimate parts at some very memorable moments.

Laurel spent some time browsing the lingerie department of Debenhams before selecting two pairs of lacy boy-shorts. At least, she would have clean underwear tomorrow, when she travelled back to St Anne's to begin her new life, single again. *Who knows, Laurel? You might meet another Cutie on the train.*

While she was in the market, Laurel received a call from Maddie, ecstatic that Trefor had invited her for a weekend at a romantic country hotel in the Cotswolds.

"You've certainly worked your magic there, honey. A few weeks ago, he was still finding it difficult to cope after Carolyn."

"You know me, Laurel. I'm a quick worker."

"Well, you deserve it, Maddie. Have a wonderful time!" Glowing with fulfilment, Laurel scrolled down to Trefor's number.

Just spoke to Maddie. Have a great weekend, you two. You're the GOAT, Tref.

As soon as she had hit 'send', a panicky regret seized her. *You idiot, Laurel: he'll think you're commenting on the weekend away, and calling him lecherous. He won't know teen talk.*

Sorry, Tref. Don't take that the wrong way. It means Greatest of All Time!!

A moment later, she received a reply that was typical of Trefor's humour.

WTF — which may mean Why That Frase? or We're Travelling Friday!

Laurel was halfway through a glass of wine when Adrian walked into The Drummer's Arms, carrying her laptop. Life had been surprisingly doable without it. She bought him a drink, and asked about Emily and Martin.

Naturally, the conversation flowed like frozen treacle, both of them struggling to give their thoughts utterance.

"Don't take this badly, but what do you actually want? Do you know?" he eventually asked. His question sounded harsh, but his eyes were kind, as kind as they had always been. If anything, that made it worse.

"No, no. I don't know," Laurel stuttered. "Last month, when I contacted you, and we met, I knew I wanted you. It was an audacious dream come true. Then, we started circling each other like boxers; and suddenly, since I came back from London, we've been trading punches. I do love you; I know I do; but perhaps this is for the best."

There was a long silence, during which he glanced around and beyond her. "Say something, Adrian." Her voice was not tetchy, but pleading; not abrasive, but coaxing.

They stared at one another, entwined in time. His eyes appeared exactly as they had on that precious, awful Friday night in the pub car park. They were partly steely, unyielding, unfathomable; and yet, they evinced that kindness she had long cherished. She knew his sweetness and his latent capacity to love.

She shrugged; there were no words for this. Gesture would have to speak, to release him from this torture. Then, the butterfly would flit away, looking for other flowers, just as before; just as so many times over so long.

Without any detectable flicker of an eyelid, tensing of muscle or sinew; without any discernible signal or warning, the net swooped through the pregnant air.

"So, marry me," he said, still staring. There was neither a twitch, nor a breaking of the stare.

"Wh… What?" she stammered.

"Marry me," he repeated, his eyes boring into her anima; no longer just staring, but lasering into her soul.

"Seriously?" she asked, half gasping, half laughing.

"Very." His expression eased, moulding itself into a smile.

Laurel's mind, teetering and giddy, flashed back to the desperate loneliness by the Thames, twenty years earlier. Why had they not had this conversation all those years ago? Why had neither dared to step over the edge? She had advanced, then withdrawn, ashamed. He?

"But what happened between yesterday and now?" she asked in bewilderment.

"I needed to be absolutely certain; certain that I could trust you and myself. I fibbed: I didn't have anything to do yesterday; I needed time to consider what to do and what I wanted. It really wasn't easy."

"I know." She nodded.

"Well?" He took Laurel's hand, holding it tenderly, more tenderly than she had ever imagined possible.

"What about Martin and Emily?" she asked. *Oh, for heaven's sake, Laurel!*

"What about them? They're old enough to deal with… And Emily likes you a lot. She looked

344

devastated when I told her why we were meeting, and that we'd probably not be seeing one another again."

"Oh, Adrian!" Laurel grabbed at her glass. Her head was spinning, freefalling through cloud and sunshine, disbelief and delight.

"I've still got that Valentine's card," he added, almost nonchalantly.

"You what?"

"You said you were embarrassed; you thought it was trite and obvious. Actually, it took me ages to work it out. I'm not a crossword buff like you... and Don," he added, sniggering. "He kicked my arse on the phone last night. Apparently, he saw you yesterday morning, holding up a church wall, or something. It's his fault I'm here at all." Laurel beamed. What a wonderful couple she had met!

"You never answered that Valentine, though," she moaned.

"I didn't know what to do. I couldn't get my head around it. And I..." He shook his head. "The next day, I nearly phoned you at the branch where you were working, just to check. Then I couldn't figure out how to ask you. I'd have been mortified if I'd got it wrong. I put the receiver down and went on counting cash."

"You should've..." She stopped. *You were equally guilty, Laurel.*

"I did, just now." He pressed her hand between both of his. 'Twenty bloody years late,' she thought, but stayed silent. They studied one another, in still life.

345

"And now you owe me an answer. Just don't make me wait twenty years," he smiled kindly.

Laurel opened her mouth to speak, then closed it, swallowing hard. "I don't," she began, her eyes full of tears. "I don't need twenty seconds." Her lips, taut and tense from fighting back the emotion, widened into a soft, generous smile; but as her mouth relaxed, so did everything. The tears burst from her; the pent-up frustration, bitterness and disillusionment flooded from her. "Yes, yes. Yes, yes, yes," she blubbed. "Of course, I'll marry you."

He moved round to sit alongside her. She kissed him gently, eternally; for it reached back across twenty-odd years, and forwards into however long they would have. She nestled her head against his chest, entwining her fingers around his. Her heart was working out furiously; but it was healed and whole.

"Can you drop me at Chimneys in Preston New Road?" she asked, when they had drunk up. "I don't want to walk along with the laptop; and my legs are all wobbly."

"Erm, not possible, I'm afraid." Laurel was taken aback for a moment.

"You're coming home with me. Home. And we're going to spend the night together. And the next night. And…"

The switch was flicked. Something stirred. Before he could utter any more words, the butterfly — now magnificent, with her Eden spread before her — dived deeply between the silenced petals of his mouth, lapping hungrily around the stamen that was his tongue.

"But I need to get my overnight stuff," she gasped, coming up for air.

"Get it tomorrow," he ordered in a whisper, hands cradling her head, steering until their mouths docked again.

As they drove towards Darwen, he explained that Martin was away, but Emily would be at home. They hatched a plan to surprise her. Opening the car door, Laurel kicked off her heels, so as not to give the game away. The concrete was cold and rough on her feet.

Adrian opened the front door and walked into the living room while Laurel waited, with childlike excitement, in the hallway. He manufactured a grim expression, which was met by Emily's glance. She shook her head, asking, "Dad, why?"

"When you're older, you might realise that sometimes things just don't work between people. And that…"

"But she's nice and lovely. She's good-looking. She wears nice clothes; she's intelligent…"

"I know," Adrian admitted, struggling to keep himself from smiling.

"You're crazy!" Emily scolded, pushing herself off the sofa. "I'm going to bed."

Grabbing his daughter's hand before she could reach the door, Adrian said solemnly, "You really like her, don't you?"

"You know I do. And I thought you did," Emily protested, trying to wriggle away.

"And that's why Laurel is going to be your Mum — step mum, I mean — my wife."

"WHAT?" *Time for your entrance, Laurel.*

Emily's face was a picture, which Laurel, opening the door, glimpsed very briefly. On seeing Laurel, Emily clasped her hand to her mouth; but her eyes were visible, sparkling with delight. Released by her father, she threw her arms around Laurel. For the second time that evening, Laurel had tears rolling down her cheeks. They embraced, all three of them, for a few seconds; and when they separated, Laurel noticed droplets trickling down Emily's face. She kissed them, savouring their sweet salinity.

"Have we got any champagne, Dad?" the teenager asked.

"No, and it's too late. The off-licence will be shut. We'll all go out for dinner tomorrow. I'll phone Martin to tell him." Then he paused, looking at Emily. "Oh, you can't — Friday — you've got netball practice."

"Stuff netball, Dad."

"But the county…"

"Stuff the county." Emily laughed. "This is more important."

Laurel laughed too. She admired this cute kid, with eyes just like her father's. She was spunky enough to hold her own, without being insolent.

"I'm so excited that I won't be able to sleep," Emily protested mildly, when Adrian mentioned bedtime.

"You will, honey," Laurel said, stroking the girl's head. "We're together now."

"Are you going to wear that minidress tomorrow evening?" the girl asked. "The one you bought and left in Dad's room."

"What...? I wondered where that had gone."

"When we drove over, last Friday, Dad told me to bring it; and I said, 'No, because I want her — you — to come back'."

"Oh, Emily, I love you," Laurel said, so touched that she nearly cried again. "Yes, I'll wear it just for you." A male throat was cleared theatrically. "And you," she added, kissing him.

By the time Adrian and Laurel made their way upstairs, she had already teased and tantalised him into a state of expectancy. *Lucky afterthought that you chucked the lube into your bag, Laurel. Pity you have no lingerie. Or is it?* Wrapped in a large towel, she returned from the bathroom to find him in bed, bare chested and waiting for her.

Recalling his femdom interest, Laurel took the lead, approaching the bed with her eyes fixed on his chest. As she climbed onto his body, she loosened the towel, revealing her smooth contours.

"God, Laurel, you're beautiful! Incredible!" he exclaimed, clutching at her breasts.

"Bet you never imagined I'd look like this when I was checking your till difference twenty-odd years ago," she purred. By turns aggressive and gentle, she assumed and ceded control until he reached his peak, groaning until he was drained; slowly, he wilted beneath the majestic newly-sated butterfly.

Gently, she rolled herself off to lie alongside him, their lightly sweating bodies fused. "Well?" she asked, stroking his cheek.

"Wow! Just like…" He hesitated. Her arm moved down his body.

"Don't you dare say, 'Just like the real thing', or I'll twist them hard," she teased, his scrotum and its contents enclosed tenderly, as yet, within her hand.

Adrian's alarm clock woke both of them. When he tried to slide out of bed, Laurel's arm flopped across his chest, pinning him down. She kissed him repeatedly, twisting the dark hairs on his chest, and occasionally pinching one of his brown nipples. "Hmm, so good," she cooed. It was. Never mind the thrusting and grinding, it was exhilarating to be waking up in the arms of someone she really loved. Home, he had said.

"Remember that night in the pub car park?" she murmured. "Let's go back one evening and you can do that to me there."

"It's a private house now," he replied.

"We'll shag in their garden, then." Laurel laughed. "Imagine the headlines: Late forties couple caught copulating in the cucumbers!"

"Late forties! I'm only forty-six," he said chuckling.

"And you're going to remind me of that every day, I bet." She playfully bit his lower lip.

"Last night," he began, a little coyly.

"Last night," she aped, tweaking his nipple harder.

"That was amazing, the best I've ever … Promise me it'll be that good next time."

"Better," she whispered, nuzzling into him. "If you're up to it at forty-six."

As she rolled away, laughing, he slapped one of her bare buttocks, saying, "I'd be up to it now if I didn't have a meeting at nine." She stood up and wiggled her bum at him. He lunged across the bed and kissed her smooth rounded flesh. "Beautiful," he cooed.

"You'd be amazed how many squats it's taken to get it like that." She winked.

Wrapping his dressing gown around her, Laurel offered to make coffee while he was shaving and showering. She had a quick smoke outside the back door. When she returned, Emily was in the kitchen.

"I'm surprised you're up so early." She smirked.

Laurel cocked her head, inviting clarification of the comment. "Well, you seemed to be having a pretty good time last night." Laurel covered part of her face with her hand. Perky little Emily stood there grinning. *Why the hell be embarrassed, Laurel?*

"Oh, God! Were we noisy?"

"You were," the girl replied, coyly looking away.

"Yes," said Laurel, recovering herself. She pulled herself up straight, meeting the girl's eyes directly. If she was to become part of this family, she would have to get used to dealing with teenage curiosity. "Yes, we did, Emily Williams. It was lit. Abso-bloody-lutely lit."

The teenager giggled at the language, leaned forward and kissed Laurel's cheek. "Good."

"And you," said Laurel, smiling and embracing the girl, "You've got it all to look forward to. Just don't take me as your model for how-to-do relationships."

"Huh?"

"When the time comes, and you find someone who makes you ache whenever you're apart from them, tell them. Don't hold back, hinting, dithering, worrying, before you do." Laurel kissed Emily's forehead. The girl turned and gathered her school stuff.

As Laurel watched, she mused, 'Okay, those twenty-two years were lost to us; but, my sweet Emily, if your dad and I had got together back then, you would never have been born.' That thought could not be voiced, so she simply said, "Have a good day. See you later."

"Sure," Emily said, opening the front door. Then, glancing up the stairs, grinning cheekily, she added, "Enjoy!"

Laurel screamed with laughter. "The chance would be a fine thing; he's got a meeting in Bolton at nine." The two girls giggled, and Emily closed the front door.

Laurel returned to the sunlit garden. A Small Copper, startled, fluttered away; she traced its flight until it was invisible.

Cute, sassy, nicely developing figure; athletic and feminine; rising gorgeous. But, Laurel, if you're going to be Emily's stepmother, you'll have to learn to be good; very good.

And she would, wouldn't she?